LITTLE CHILDREN

BOOKS BY ANGELA MARSONS

OTHER BOOKS

Dear Mother

The Forgotten Woman

If Only

LITTLE CHILDREN

Angela MARSONS

bookouture

Published by Bookouture in 2025

An imprint of Storyfire Ltd.
Carmelite House
50 Victoria Embankment
London EC4Y 0DZ

www.bookouture.com

The authorised representative in the EEA is Hachette Ireland
8 Castlecourt Centre
Dublin 15 D15 XTP3
Ireland
(email: info@hbgi.ie)

ISBN: 978-1-83618-655-7
eBook ISBN: 978-1-83618-654-0

This book is dedicated to Francesca Withnell (Bailey's best friend) and all the team at Bromyard Vets who do a wonderful job of taking care of our furry family.

PROLOGUE

Kim tapped her phone screen as the minute hand of the clock took another step towards 6 a.m.

Four minutes until Steve Ashworth's segment aired on Sunrise News.

After harassing her for weeks, the man had offered her the courtesy of letting her know when he was going live with his big story. She'd headed into the office early this morning to be sure not to miss it – she'd had to worry about this man trying to destroy her career for too long.

Three minutes to go.

'Hey, guv,' Bryant said, entering the squad room.

'You shit the bed?' she asked, taking a sip of her coffee. Briefing was always at seven.

He glanced at the time as he removed his overcoat. 'Oh, you know, got a bit bored at home. Fancied an early one.'

Her colleague and friend obviously shared her anxiety about what they were about to hear.

Two minutes to go.

'Hey, boss,' Stacey said, breezing through the door.

Kim raised an eyebrow. 'Another early bird after the worm?'

'Filing,' Stacey explained. 'Urgent filing that I didn't get to yesterday.'

'And I suppose…'

'Morning, folks,' Penn said, sliding into his seat.

'Did you fancy an early one or was it urgent filing for you too?' Kim asked, hiding her smile.

No one on her team, including herself, had a clue what was about to come out of Steve Ashworth's mouth or how it would affect them afterwards.

'Nah, I just want to hear what that git has got to say about us,' Penn said, making no effort to lie.

Kim felt a small knot in her stomach. She knew for a fact that Woody would also be watching, and she expected a summons to his office once the report had aired.

One minute to go.

Her whole team, including her boss, were aware that she'd encountered the reporter on their last major case and that he had become obsessed with exposing her as a corrupt copper.

They knew that he'd uncovered an old case of which she was less than proud.

But they also knew that a lot had happened in the last month.

The clock hit six, and she clicked on the link she'd been sent.

Kim took a deep breath as the face of Steve Ashworth filled the screen.

ONE

One Month Earlier

'You asked to see me, sir?' Kim said, taking a seat opposite her boss.

The chair she always tried to avoid had been pulled away from his desk by a metre or so – it was going to be *that* kind of meeting.

Over her years working for DCI Woodward, she had learned that meetings where she was required to take a seat rarely worked out well. They could be one out of two categories.

First and most frequent were those instances where she was being questioned about her behaviour, attitude or actions following a complaint. In those meetings, Woody was irate and she calmly answered for her crimes.

Second, and less frequent, were those times when Woody was giving her an instruction that he knew she wasn't going to like. Flip side. Then he was calm and she was irate.

What was worrying her at the moment was that he looked totally calm, a signal that he was minutes away from some kind of explosion.

He sat back in his chair and steepled his fingers over his stomach. Not a movement she was familiar with and therefore difficult to read.

'Not been a bad couple of weeks, eh, Stone?'

'No, sir,' she said somewhat dubiously, as though they'd done very little since their last major case; in fact they'd been chasing clues around the Black Country for thirty-six hours straight. She was guessing that he meant more recently, since they'd had a two-week period without a body.

'I suppose a bit of a holiday,' he added.

She fought the urge to show outrage. He didn't really think they'd been sitting on their hands doing nothing all day. He was leading her somewhere, and she wasn't sure she wanted to follow.

'Anything major at the moment?' he asked, despite already knowing the answer. If they had anything major, she'd be briefing him about it.

'Got an armed robbery in Gornal,' she said.

'That can go to Dudley,' he answered.

'A serious assault in Lye.'

'Brierley Hill can take that.'

'And the usual Monday morning reports to go through.'

It was barely nine o'clock and she'd been summoned to his office straight away, so she wasn't sure what else might warrant their attention.

'Which can all be passed to other teams,' he answered.

'Sir, do you want to just tell me the correct response here and save us both some time?' she asked.

'What I'd like to hear is that there's nothing you can't disperse amongst other teams.'

'Okay,' she said, wondering what exactly he was freeing her up to do. 'There's nothing I can't disperse amongst...'

'Hilarious,' he said without any hint of humour. When his face was this set, she truly worried what was coming next. 'I've had a call from an old friend of mine,' he continued. 'Her team could do with some help on a case they're working.'

She tipped her head. 'Sir, you were present in my last appraisal when you said I don't play well with others.'

'I like to think that was in the past, Stone.'

'It was two months ago.'

'I think you've come a long way in recent weeks.'

'You mean Bryant is coming with me?' she asked, referring to her long-time colleague, the man who was her conscience... and responsible for her manners.

He nodded. 'As is the rest of your team.'

'Sir?' she questioned as the wariness in her stomach grew. What could be serious enough for him to want to transplant her entire team? What the hell was he getting them into?

'Did you hear about the boy who went missing up in Lancashire?'

'Blackpool, wasn't it?' She'd seen it on the news.

Woody nodded.

'Wasn't that a week ago?' If he wasn't back by now, it was looking like a totally different kind of investigation. 'They need help on a case for a missing boy?' she went on, confused. Even if this did turn into a murder enquiry, she was sure the local CID teams could deal with it.

'There's another. It hasn't hit the wires yet, but a second boy went missing late last night.'

Okay, that shed some light on the reason for the secondment. Two boys in the same week.

'Ages?' she asked.

'Twelve and eleven.'

'And they don't have other local teams they can draft in?'

'You know anything about Blackpool, Stone?'

'There are lights?' she asked, remembering a trip there with Keith and Erica, her foster parents, when she was ten years old. It had been within the first few months of living with them, and she'd barely uttered a word to either one of them.

She recalled that the day had been grey and dismal, the arcades crowded and noisy. The chips had tasted of sand, and the heavens had opened once they'd set off for a drive through the two miles of illuminations. Her main recollection was of bright lights being distorted by the hammering rain pounding off the windows.

The day hadn't ended a moment too soon.

'They're about to start their busiest week of the year. It's half term. They're about to be overrun with unrelated offences. The figures Miranda quoted are horrendous.'

'Miranda?' she asked.

'Detective Chief Inspector Miranda Walker. We trained together back in the day.'

Okay, Kim kind of got it. They'd worked with other forces on joint investigations, but normally with a neighbouring force like West Mercia or Staffordshire. Surely Lancashire police could call upon help closer to home? Why involve a force from over a hundred miles away?

'What aren't you telling me, sir?' Kim asked.

Woody took a breath. 'There are whisperings.'

She waited.

'You're aware of the new reporting line?'

'Of course.'

Kim knew that Crimestoppers had teamed up with forces across the country to launch a new Police Anti-Corruption and Abuse Reporting Service, available to all communities across the UK.

The line could be used to report any police misconduct with total anonymity. The information was then passed to the relevant force's professional standards unit or specialised detectives.

'They've had an anonymous tip about a member of Blackpool CID?' she asked.

'Two,' he clarified. 'No details, no names.'

'What's the nature of the complaints?'

'No specific incidents or victims or even timelines, but both calls were about a specific team under Miranda's supervision. Apparently the complaints include inappropriate police conduct, officer violence and potential corruption within the team.'

His hands were still knitted together.

'What else?'

'Miranda thinks the complaints may have come from within. So you can understand why she wants to find the source.'

'Jeeesus,' Kim said, getting a clearer picture.

DCI Miranda Walker was in an impossible position. The minute she started asking any questions, she was potentially putting team members at risk. No matter how far the police had come, snitching on your own could get you killed.

'Sir, is there anything else?'

He shook his head and unlaced his fingers.

'So, what's our primary role, helping to find these two boys or trying to weed out bad coppers?'

'Pretty much both,' he answered.

'To summarise, we're off to Blackpool immediately to help a team that doesn't want us there, to solve a case, as well as to ask questions about inappropriate police behaviour but not any that will blow our cover.'

'Yes, that just about sums it up.'

'Cool. Sounds like just my kind of case,' she said before heading off to break the news to her team.

TWO

It was almost eleven by the time Kim placed her overnight bag in the back of Bryant's car.

Since her meeting with Woody, she'd given her team the briefest of briefings before sending them on their way to sort out their lives for a couple of nights away.

Bryant had dropped her off at home, where she had spent more time packing Barney's overnight bag than her own.

With lots of hugs and kisses, she had dropped him off with his favourite dog sitter, Charlie, who was more than happy for the company and the reason to leave the house for a walk.

Penn had been good enough to collect Stacey. Although they could all have fitted in Bryant's Astra Estate, she didn't want them stranded over a hundred miles away with only one car.

'Going somewhere nice?' she heard from behind.

Kim froze.

It was a voice she recognised but hadn't heard in a couple of weeks.

She turned to face Steve Ashworth, Sunrise News reporter, and someone who had become a nuisance during their last major case. She shook her head at Bryant, who was already getting out of the car. She wasn't going to give the man the attention he craved.

'Not bored yet?' she asked, folding her arms.

'Not even close. You're quite the character.'

Kim's heart sank. It wasn't that she hadn't taken his threat seriously; she'd just hoped his absence over the last couple of weeks meant that he'd found someone else to harass. For some reason, he had become fascinated with her while covering the Jester case and had decided to make his next big story about her.

'Must be a slow news month,' she said, heading to the passenger-side door. 'But hey ho, happy digging,' she finished, maintaining her show of bravado.

'You're almost convincing, Inspector Stone,' he said, moving away but not far enough. 'But I'm very good at what I do.'

'Splendid,' she said, opening the car door.

'Remember the name Amber Rose?'

Kim slammed the door shut, but not before she saw the smirk plastered across his face.

'Run him over and make it look like an accident,' she said as Bryant fixed his seat belt.

Her colleague wasn't so easily fooled by the forced joviality in her tone.

'You okay?' he asked, pulling away from the kerb.

'I'm fine. He's a dick,' she said, taking out her phone.

The best way of distracting her colleague was to show him she was busy doing something else.

He took the hint and focussed on driving them towards the motorway.

She stared at her phone without really seeing it while she composed herself. The damn reporter had just thrown a name at her that she'd hoped never to hear again. She just hoped he was going to break his shovel while digging for that one.

Her gaze focussed as her screen lit up with a text message.

She couldn't stop the groan that was in her head from coming out of her mouth as she read it.

Wanna grab a coffee after work?

'What?' Bryant asked.

'Nothing,' she answered, clicking out of the message.

Bryant glanced her way as he took the slip road onto the motorway. 'More mysterious text messages you're not gonna tell me about?'

'Correct,' she said, putting away her phone.

'And Amber Rose?'

'Never heard of her,' she said before turning away.

THREE

As arranged, Bryant pulled off the motorway at Charnock Richard services to meet up with the others. She wanted to do a quick briefing before they got to the station in Blackpool, where she intended to give them more information about the tasks at hand.

Since Bryant had made good time, she was surprised to see Penn's car already there. Once they were inside the café, he waved them over to a window seat as Stacey placed four drinks on the table.

Kim waited for her to get rid of the tray and sit down before she started.

'Okay, I gave you the bare bones back at the station. Two boys missing. One last weekend and one last night. We've been asked, unofficially, to assist with the cases as they're a bit thin on the ground.'

'No one closer?' Penn asked.

'Apparently they're a bit busy dealing with the busiest week of the year.'

'Still a few forces between us and them,' he pushed.

And now for the bit she hadn't told them, and the reason for this briefing.

'The DCI there is an old friend of Woody's. There have been murmurings of bad behaviour.'

'What kind?' Stacey asked. 'Corruption, brutality, racism?'

Kim shrugged. 'No specific details but possibly violence and corruption.'

'So, we're looking for bent coppers as well?' Stacey asked with a worried frown, which Kim could understand.

Although the Blackpool team didn't know all the reasons they would be there, poking your nose into the business of other forces was never going to make you popular. And it didn't particularly warm the cockles of the heart having to check on the behaviour of your own.

'We're looking for any indication that the anonymous complaints have substance.'

'More than one?' Bryant asked.

Kim nodded and took a sip of her drink before answering. 'It's unclear if the calls were external or internal.'

'Ooh, dodgy,' Stacey said, making a face.

'Exactly. It's delicate, which is why the DCI can't start asking questions and why she's asked for the help of a force a safe distance away.'

'So, we go straight to the DCI with any suspicions?' Bryant asked.

'Yep – and leave it to her to sort out.'

'What about the IOPC?' Penn asked.

The Independent Office for Police Conduct was a body separate from the police which investigated the most serious complaints and conduct matters. Police forces were required to refer the most serious cases their way even if there was no complainant. Normally such cases were incidents where any police action resulted in members of the public being badly injured or even dying in custody. Police could also choose to refer cases themselves, and in the last year, seven thousand cases had been sent to the IOPC.

'We don't have a case yet. The chief has only anonymous tips. She needs more before referring it across,' Kim answered.

'Did Woody give no idea what we might be looking for?' Stacey asked. 'There's a good distance to travel between one and three.'

Stacey was referring to the three distinct categories of allegations: police complaints made by the public; conduct matters raised internally; and ones where police actions appeared to have resulted in death or serious injury, assaults, sex offences or corruption.

'There were over fifty thousand public complaints against the police last year,' Penn offered.

'Given there's one hundred and seventy-one thousand police officers in the UK, that number ain't so great,' Bryant observed, adding a sachet of sugar to his cuppa.

Kim moved the container out of his reach.

'So, almost a third of all police had a complaint made against them?' Stacey asked, wide-eyed.

'Or some officers had two,' Bryant said.

'Over a hundred cops were found guilty of criminal offences last year,' Penn added.

'Okay, guys, enough,' Kim said, holding up her hand.

Unfortunately, police misconduct was a hot topic at the minute. The public would never forget how police officer Wayne Couzens had kidnapped Sarah Everard and murdered her. They were also unlikely to forget the damning report stating the Metropolitan Police Force was 'institutionally racist, sexist and homophobic'. Whether it was only the Met or not, most people tarred all police forces with the same brush, and much as it pained her to admit it, her profession did harbour its fair share of bad apples.

But were any of them working out of Blackpool station? And what was the best way of finding that out? she wondered.

'We need a strategy,' Kim said, finishing her coffee. 'We're gonna need to be approachable and non-threatening. We've got more chance of seeing something if we act it up a bit.' She turned to Bryant. 'You don't like me very much.'

'And here was me thinking I covered it up well,' he quipped.

'You're a bit disillusioned, craving retirement and you don't much like taking instruction from a woman. If there are any Neanderthals on the team, they'll gravitate towards you.'

'I'm basically a stereotype.'

'Yes.'

'Okay.'

She turned to the constable. 'Stace, I want you to be naïve and a bit overwhelmed. I want your innocence and vulnerability to elicit trust. People will assume you're too scared to be any danger.'

'Got it, boss,' she said with a smile.

'Penn, you're the hardest, cos...'

'Jeez, thanks, guv,' Bryant interrupted.

She ignored him. 'I need you to be a bit ruthless and pretty ambitious. Make people think you'll do anything to climb that ladder. I know I'm asking you to play completely against type.'

He was smiling as though relishing the challenge. A previous team member could have pulled off that one with very little effort. Unfortunately, Kevin Dawson was no longer with them, but she still thought about him often.

'Okay, new team dynamics sorted. We need—'

Bryant sighed heavily and rolled his eyes.

'Excuse me?' Kim snapped.

'Just practising, guv,' he said with a smirk.

Penn and Stacey tried to hide their amusement and failed.

'Right, about the case,' Kim said, shaking her head.

'The second disappearance has hit the wires,' Stacey said. 'And they're already getting some heat from the press.'

'Luckily not our problem,' Kim said. She'd had enough press attention on the last case and was of course still getting it from one reporter in particular. She shook away all thoughts of him and the name he'd mentioned.

'First boy is a local lad named Lewis Stevens, twelve years old. Last seen on Friday the eighteenth in Coral Island,' Stacey said, reading from her phone.

'Where?' Kim asked. She was dismayed to see all three of her colleagues show surprise.

'You don't know?' Penn asked.

'Let's assume that if it doesn't sell dog food or motorcycle parts, I'm unlikely to know.'

'It's a massive arcade on the front on the Golden Mile.'

Kim waited. She had, at least, heard of that.

'It's more than an arcade though,' Stacey offered. 'Last time I went, there were two restaurants, a café, a chip shop, a train ride, games for kids, fruit machines and I think a casino.'

'Kids can easily get lost round there, guv. I think it has four or five entrances,' Bryant added.

'Was he with parents?' Kim asked.

'They're not mentioned in any of the news reports,' Stacey said.

'And yesterday?' Kim asked.

'Eleven-year-old Noah Reid went missing from South Pier, opposite the Pleasure Beach. Got nothing else yet other than description and clothing.'

'Is he local too?' Kim asked.

Stacey nodded.

'Okay,' she said, pushing back her chair. 'Let's get to it. Over to the station and we'll do hotel check-in later.'

'Just one question, boss,' Stacey said, reaching for her satchel.

'Yep.'

'Are they gonna be pleased to see us?'

Kim gave thought to the question for a few seconds. She put herself in their position and wondered how she'd feel having a team of strangers foisted upon them while trying to navigate a major investigation. She was pretty sure it would prompt a heated debate in Woody's office, but not every senior investigating officer reacted like her, and she didn't want to put her team on the defensive before they'd even met the new squad.

'Not sure, Stace, but I guess we're about to find out.'

FOUR

It was almost three when they pulled onto the car park of Blackpool Police Headquarters.

The building was located close to the South Shore, and you couldn't miss it as you entered the town. It was a three-storey glass building beneath a white frame that clamped over it like some kind of transformer part that had been clicked into place. A couple of raised planter beds attempted to soften the area on approach.

They stepped through the door, and Kim noted the glass theme continued throughout. If the architect had been hoping to convey transparency, it was both clunky and obvious.

Bryant approached the front desk. The guy behind it made a quick call, smiled at something said on the other end and then hung up. He said something to Bryant before nodding towards a set of doors.

'Our contact will be with us shortly,' Bryant said, returning to where they stood. He gave no indication of who was coming to meet them.

They waited silently until the doors opened to reveal a man just short of six feet dressed in a charcoal suit. Kim immediately got the impression that he would have attended work dressed this way whatever his career had been, as though he'd been waiting his whole life to look this smart. He headed straight for her and held out his hand.

'Red Butler, Detective Inspector.'

Kim offered the briefest of handshakes while raising an eyebrow. Was he really named after a character from *Gone with the Wind*?

'Sorry, my real name is Mike, nicknamed Rhett, which somehow became Red. That's what everyone calls me.'

'Good to know, Red,' she said, finding it odd calling him a colour.

She turned towards her colleagues to introduce them, but he held up his hand. 'Save it for upstairs. The whole team is in, so we'll address the formalities in one go. Come with me.'

Kim remained silent as she followed him up two flights of stairs.

The man smiled, waved or nodded at just about everyone he met en route. Not all of them acknowledged him. Why was he trying to make it seem that he was so likeable? Likeable people didn't need to appear to be likeable.

Finally, they stepped through more glass doors into what she assumed to be the CID office.

There were more sheets of paper on desks in this one office than she'd seen during their entire journey through the building.

'Clear desk policy, but you know, sometimes you just need a hard copy,' he said as the heads in the room turned to face them.

'Oh, thank fuck, the cavalry's here,' said a man in his early fifties.

While Red gave the man a warning glance, Kim did a quick survey of the space and the people within it.

A team of five: four men, one woman.

'That mouthy git is Detective Sergeant Roy Moss. He's my number two.'

'Yeah, I'm his piece of shit,' Roy said with a smirk.

'DS Carly Walsh,' Butler said, pointing to the woman with red curly hair and freckles.

'DC James Dickinson,' he said, pointing to the fair-haired guy who looked to be late twenties, early thirties.

'And last but by no means least, we have Gonk in the corner.'

The Asian man raised his hand.

There was something unsettling about the only member of the team from a minority background being introduced by nickname rather than rank or real name.

Kim had no choice but to let it pass for now, but she had no intention of addressing the officer as Gonk.

'So, the top knobs decided we needed some help?' Roy asked, sitting back in his chair.

There was something instantly unlikeable about the man whose waistband rested below his ample stomach and whose buttons strained against the fabric of a shirt that had probably been white in its previous life.

She decided it wasn't a good idea to stand down wind of Roy Moss, cos if one of those buttons came flying off, it could take out an eye.

'We've been asked to assist,' Kim said, keeping her tone even.

Every member of both teams was paying attention.

'We've heard your colleagues are all busy on other business.'

She really didn't want to make enemies during her first half hour.

'Yeah, but I don't think any of them are chasing clues around the seafront on the bidding of a bloody jester,' Roy said.

Kim saw Bryant hide a smile behind scratching his nose.

Nice move. If she'd seen it, then members of the other team had seen it too.

From the lack of surprise on any of their faces, Kim realised that they all knew this ambush was coming from the team's mouthpiece. More concerning was that the man in charge was openly waiting for her response. If one of her team members had been so rude, they'd have been hearing about it directly from her. But every DI managed their team differently.

'If you're talking about the case where we successfully located a world class surgeon and returned her to the hospital to save a little girl's life, then yes, that was our case. Maybe if you weren't paying so much attention to cases outside your remit you'd have a better chance of solving your own.' She paused. 'Now, would someone like to show us where we're going to be working?'

So much for not making enemies straight away.

Red hesitated as though he wanted the show to continue. Eventually, he headed towards a room off the main squad room. He opened the door to reveal one large round table holding a laptop and a pile of access cards on lanyards.

The room was half the size of their own squad room back home.

'One person will be given access to our system, and the protocols will need to be signed.'

Kim pointed to Stacey to indicate that she was their designated person.

'Okay, I'll leave you to get settled, and I'll let the boss know you're here.'

Kim nodded as he closed the door.

She turned to Stacey. 'To answer your earlier question, I think they're overjoyed that we've come to help.'

FIVE

The first thing Kim noticed when she entered DCI Miranda Walker's office was that the woman looked tired.

Kim wasn't surprised. Policing in Blackpool wasn't a walk in the park. They faced their own problems back in the Black Country, but Blackpool now ranked as one of the most deprived areas in the UK. Despite the 20 million visitors a year, it was mostly a seasonal town with a high transient population.

Like mining towns, it had grown around an industry that was in decline. Back in its heyday, people had travelled there for a week's holiday. The appearance of the cheap foreign holiday had impacted the place considerably, relegating it to a venue that serviced the stag and hen crowd and the day-trippers.

In addition to the problems Kim faced back home, this team had the added headache of thousands of tourists rocking up every weekend.

'Take a seat, Inspector,' Walker said, pointing to one of the easy chairs.

The chief left her place behind the desk and came to join her. Kim guessed her to be mid-fifties; she had short salt-and-pepper hair, stylishly cut. Although a little drawn, her face was lightly tanned and attractive. She wore a pair of stud earrings – sapphires that matched the colour of her trouser suit.

'Thank you for coming. DCI Woodward is an old friend.'

'From training days, he said.'

The chief nodded. 'He has my absolute trust, and I'm hoping I can extend that to you.'

'Of course,' Kim said. Respect wasn't won automatically from her, but the seedlings were there for this woman. She was a northern success story, according to the reports she'd read during the journey north. Born to a drug-addicted mother, both she and her younger sister had been drug dependent on arrival.

Despite trying to keep the family together, Child Services had removed both children from the home when Miranda was eight and her sister was five. Thereafter followed a series of foster homes for both, until Miranda reached maturity and took control of her own life.

Kim suspected the woman's childhood hadn't been too far removed from her own.

She'd always felt that somehow she'd avoided the person she was supposed to be, that fate had set her up to be an aggressive, hateful, drug-fuelled person who'd die by overdose. Fate had decreed that, but she had dodged it, and she felt this woman had too. From the early cards they'd been dealt, they could both have been living very different lives.

'Had your work cut out on that last case, eh?' the chief asked.

Was there anyone who hadn't watched their wild goose chase around the country? Kim wondered.

The chief held up her hand. 'I don't expect an answer. It was an impossible situation. You had no choice but to follow his instructions.'

Kim nodded her agreement.

A smile tugged at the woman's mouth. 'Although my favourite part, by far, was the press conference you gave. I'm guessing very little of what you said came from the press liaison office.'

'I like to improvise.'

'Good. You may need to be adaptable.'

'Does anyone on the team know the second reason we're here?' Kim asked.

The chief shook her head. 'And it needs to stay that way. I need to know where the calls have come from.'

'And whether or not they're valid?' Kim asked.

'Of course, but the source is the priority. If it's a member or members of that team, I can't risk their safety. I know that you know what I mean.'

Kim completely understood. It wasn't beyond the realms of possibility for someone uncovered as a snitch to meet an untimely accident while out at a routine call.

'And the investigation?' Kim asked, wondering where her team fitted into that.

'It's been explained to you that manpower wise we're at breaking point. Every member of CID is working flat out. Unfortunately, we can't afford to ignore every other serious incident because we have two missing boys. Especially not this week.'

Kim waited.

'I want Red and the team focussing on Noah, the boy who went missing last night. They already have the knowledge of the first boy, Lewis, and will be able to ascertain quicker if the two incidents are linked.'

'Your suspicion?'

The chief opened her hands. 'My hope that they're not is dwindling by the minute, but there's still a chance Noah is going to turn up somewhere safe and sound.'

Kim noted that she didn't hold out the same hope for Lewis, who had now been missing for ten days.

'In which case, wouldn't we be expected to pack up our things and leave you to it?' she asked.

'I'd have to be creative in finding a reason for you to stay to dig into the complaints. Although, no offence, I'd rather we had Noah back and be sending you on your way.'

'No offence taken.'

'What I need from your team is to retrace everything on Lewis's disappearance. It's what my team would be doing if Noah hadn't vanished too. You'll have fresh eyes. Maybe there's something we missed or where we should have gone deeper. I want these boys found.'

'Of course. We'll do everything we can to make that happen.'

The chief smiled. 'I'm sure you're keen to get started. Let me know if there's anything you need. And if you have any problems with any members of my team be sure to—'

'Sort it out myself, marm, but thank you for the support,' she said, heading towards the door.

Good of the DCI to offer, but Kim had never needed anyone to fight her battles.

SIX

'Feel for you, mate,' Roy Moss said, standing in the doorway behind him.

Bryant had spotted the small kitchen on his way through and had taken the chance to make himself available while the guv was with the DCI.

He wasn't surprised that this guy was the one to take the bait. He'd hoped that would be the case.

'Feel what?' he asked, frowning.

'She's a bitch, eh?'

Bryant turned away. 'I shouldn't...'

'It's okay, pal, you're amongst friends here,' Roy said, moving further into the kitchen. 'I feel for you, that's all. You're not the only one having to take orders from a nipper. Fifteen years younger than me, my boss.'

'Twelve,' Bryant said, nodding towards the door.

'And a woman as well,' Roy said, moving closer.

Bryant found it ironic that this guy's boss's boss was also a woman. Since leaving the motorway services, Bryant had wondered how he was going to pull this off. He knew not to be too obvious about it to start, but he'd realised that all he had to do was act like everything he hated in the police.

'Yeah, it takes some work keeping my mouth shut sometimes,' he said, stirring his drink.

'Not like the good old days, eh, where they were seen and not heard while they were making the coffee?'

Bryant glanced down at his drink. 'Yeah, now I have to make my own. You miss the good old days, eh?'

'My predicament could only be worse if Red was black,' Roy said before laughing.

It took everything Bryant had not to show his disgust and shock. Rarely these days did such despicable thoughts get voiced. Most folks who still felt that way had learned to keep their mouths shut. A fact for which he was eternally grateful.

Oh, how the hell was he going to pretend to be anything like this guy? And regardless of whatever part he'd been instructed to play, never could he say anything like that.

'Just biding my time,' he said. 'Keeping my mouth shut and staying out of trouble.'

'Treading water until retirement?' Roy asked.

'Of course. You?'

'Hell, yeah, but doesn't mean you can't have a bit of fun along the way, eh?'

Bryant grinned. 'Oh yeah, anything to relieve the boredom.'

'Good to chat, Bry— Oh, gotta go, and you should too, cos the bitch is back.'

Roy left the room, and Bryant sighed heavily.

This was going to be much harder than he'd thought.

SEVEN

'Okay, first impressions?' Kim asked once she was back in the office they'd been assigned.

She'd grabbed a display board and pulled it in front of a couple of the glass wall panels to give them some measure of privacy, even though the squad room next door was now empty except for the officer they called Gonk.

'I've had first contact,' Bryant said. 'Tyrannosaurus Roy cornered me in the kitchen.'

'And?' Kim asked.

'He doesn't like you very much.'

'Gutted. Anything else?'

'He's a racist, misogynistic piece of shit.'

'Splendid,' Stacey muttered under her breath, echoing Kim's own thoughts.

She was pretty sure the constable had endured dinosaurs like Roy Moss before, but that didn't make it okay. Kim couldn't protect her from the man's thoughts, but his actions were another matter.

'Stace, you let me know if he...'

'Will do, boss.'

'Any other observations?'

'The others don't even want to look at us,' Penn offered. 'I've tried to catch their eyes, but they just look away.'

'No fraternising with the enemy,' Kim noted. 'Okay, on to priorities. The chief is equally keen to find out who reported the misconduct, so she can make sure they're not in any danger, and also to learn whether any of them is actually up to no good.' She turned to Bryant. 'I think you've got the best chance of finding out about anything shifty, so make Roy your new best friend.'

He grimaced and nodded at the same time.

'Penn, Stace, any opportunity you see to engage with any of the others, take it. But before anything else, we've got two missing boys, and our brief is to focus on the first case. The local team will continue to investigate the disappearance of Noah last night, and we'll be concentrating on twelve-year-old Lewis.'

She waited for the groans to pass. They all knew this entailed going over someone else's work, treading old ground and unlikely to find anything new.

'Bryant and I will be talking to family and friends.'

'Got all the addresses ready, boss,' Stacey said.

'Penn, I want you combing through statements. Is there anyone not spoken to that needs attention?'

'On it, boss.'

'Stace, you're on CCTV review.'

She nodded.

Both Kim and Bryant reached for their coats.

Kim's gaze rested on the officer in the corner of the squad room.

'And by the time I get back can someone find out that kid's name?'

EIGHT

NOAH

Noah felt the sickness in his stomach before he even opened his eyes. The second thing he felt was panic. He knew something was wrong immediately, but his head felt fuzzy and full of clouds.

He opened his eyes and his stomach turned in fear. The room was the size of the box room at home that his mum used for her crafts. But this one didn't have a desk or a sewing machine or baskets of wool. This one was dark, with a dirty window that let in a thin shaft of light that cut across his toes. There was a smell that reminded him of an underpass in town.

A bucket sat in the corner, and lying beside him was a packet of biscuits and a bottle of water. He searched his memory, trying to recall how he'd got here.

He remembered being out with his parents. It was his birthday. They went to the arcade. He had money to spend. His parents went across the road to get a table. He followed a few minutes behind. He frowned. The memory became harder to grasp. He remembered leaving South Pier. He recalled looking across the road to see if he could see them. He remembered crossing the tram line to get to the pavement.

His heart leaped in his chest as he remembered being grabbed from behind. He'd been too surprised to fight back. He hadn't known what was happening, then a door opened, nearly hitting him in the face. There was the sound of his shoes hitting metal as he was thrust into darkness. Someone grabbed him and covered his mouth. He tried to scream, but water was poured into his mouth. He had no choice but to swallow. The van started moving. He was forced to take another drink, and then he was held so he couldn't struggle.

After that, he vaguely remembered being carried and being given another drink... Was that when he'd arrived here?

The memory made him realise that he needed to pee, but there was no toilet. The urge had gone from non-existent to urgent in seconds. He felt like he was about to burst.

He pushed himself to a standing position, but his whole body felt weak. He swayed backwards against the wall as his head felt woozy. He swallowed a few times and then pushed himself towards the corner of the room, where he unzipped his trousers and relieved himself in the bucket. His mum would be so angry if she could see him now. She had once seen a boy having a wee behind a tree at the park and she hadn't liked it. He resolved that he'd never tell her.

The effort of standing suddenly overwhelmed him. He zipped up his trousers and staggered back to the corner. His body sighed with relief as he lowered himself down to the cold, hard ground.

The fog in his mind was starting to clear, allowing questions to make themselves known. Each question brought a fresh stab of fear, stronger than the last.

Why had he been taken?

What were they going to do to him?

Would he ever see his family again?

He choked back a sob as he realised that there were two possible answers to the last question, then pushed the thought away. They would find him. They would be out looking, and his dad would knock down anyone who got in his way.

He kept telling himself that over and over again until he heard a key turn in the lock.

His bravery departed, and he had the sudden need to pee again.

A man entered the room wearing a mask. He closed the door behind him and towered above Noah.

Noah pushed himself into a corner as the man spoke.

'Okay, young Noah, let's have a good hard look at you.'

NINE

After a couple of wrong turns, Bryant parked in front of Lewis Stevens's house on the Wickton Estate.

It was not unlike many of the housing estates back in the Black Country. Built in the sixties, it had welcomed young families who had since outgrown the area and moved on, each generation leaving the place a little shabbier than when they found it.

The boom of the seaside town in the seventies had brought the tourist area ever closer, so that the estate now sat just on the outskirts of the hustle and bustle of the town centre.

Kim already knew from Stacey's summary that the house was occupied by mum, stepdad and four other children.

The door was opened by, she suspected, the woman of the house.

'Mrs Stevens?' Kim asked as both she and Bryant held up their IDs.

The woman was stick thin with short, crudely cut brown hair. Despite the month and temperature, the woman was dressed in a vest top and leggings, accentuating her gaunt frame further.

She nodded, looking from one to the other.

'May we come in?' Kim asked as the aroma of something burning wafted past her nose.

'Who are ya?' she asked before moving.

'We're working with the local team to help find Lewis.'

'Oh, okay,' she said, stepping aside. 'Go back through to the kitchen. I'm cooking the tea.'

Kim did so as two children's heads popped out of the lounge. She could see there was another one sitting on the sofa watching the TV.

'Shirl, mek a cuppa, eh?' shouted a male voice from somewhere out of view.

'Mek it yourself. I'm cooking, putting the shopping away and I've got the coppers here.'

The owner of the voice suddenly appeared. He couldn't have been more different to his wife. He looked to be considerably older, with a messy beard that was compensating for the hair he'd lost from his head. He was a good foot shorter than his wife and a similar amount wider. He could only be the stepfather, Bobby Stevens.

'Who are yer?' he asked.

'They're helping Red and Roy,' Mrs Stevens said, taking frozen chips out of a Sainsbury's bag.

Kim was instantly struck by the use of the first name and nickname of the investigating officers.

'Bloody fuss about nothing,' Mr Stevens replied, filling the kettle.

'Out my way,' his wife said, starting to lay plates on the counter next to the oven. Although not particularly untidy, it was a kitchen where every space was being used to store something. Backpacks were stacked on top of the fridge. Umbrellas wedged between the fridge and the dishwasher. Every space was filled.

'You think there's no cause for concern?' Kim asked, turning her attention to Lewis's stepdad.

'He's run off again, hasn't he? It's not the first time. He'll be back when he's hungry enough.'

'He's done it before?' Kim asked.

'Yeah, came back when his mate's mum kicked him out. Just wait. He'll be back soon.'

'Has he ever been gone for ten days?' Kim pressed.

'No, but he's getting older, more resourceful. He's practically an adult.'

'He's twelve,' Kim said unnecessarily. She was sure he knew the child's age, but it was as though he needed reminding that Lewis was still a child.

'You seen twelve-year-olds these days?' he asked. 'Trust me, they can survive.'

Kim noticed that his wife was neither agreeing nor disagreeing with his conviction the boy was in no danger. Instead, she was focussed on portioning out chicken nuggets and oven chips onto four plates.

Mr Stevens followed her gaze. 'Food bill's gone down a bit since he went.'

'And you're his stepfather?'

'Yeah, known him since he was six, and he's always been a little shit,' Stevens said before heading back into the living room.

'You share your husband's opinion, Mrs Stevens?' Kim asked as the woman reached across her to put the plates on the table.

'I dunno. I don't know what to think.' She paused. 'Kids... tea's done,' she called out.

The three that Kim had already seen came careering into the kitchen.

They paid no mind to her and Bryant while seating themselves and reaching for the condiments in the middle of the table.

One plate with a larger portion remained unclaimed on the countertop.

'Come through,' the woman said, leading them into the lounge, where she immediately began collecting up toys and straightening cushions.

Mr Stevens shifted so he could see past her to the television screen.

Both Kim and Bryant took a seat on the freshly cleared sofa. She caught the flash of irritation on Mr Stevens's face. He'd clearly hoped they wouldn't be staying long or that they would be confined to the other room.

'Can you tell us what happened the last time you saw Lewis?' Kim asked as Shirley Stevens took a seat.

Mr Stevens rolled his eyes and lit a cigarette. 'We've been through this a hundred times.'

Mrs Stevens ignored him. 'It was just like any other day. It was mayhem. Everybody wanted something different for tea. I hadn't had a chance to do the shopping and—'

'Bloody hell, Shirl, tell the truth,' Mr Stevens said, shaking his head.

At that point, the last of the children appeared. Kim guessed him to be around fifteen. He carried in the last plate from the kitchen, took a seat and glanced at the smoke circulating around his stepfather.

'If you don't like it, stay in the bloody kitchen, Kevin.'

Kevin put the tray on his lap and started to eat, while Bobby Stevens extinguished the cigarette anyway.

'You're saying that's not how it was?' Kim asked the man now sitting forward in his chair.

'No. They were all being loud and annoying, and Lewis in particular was being a little shit.'

Shirley shot him a look. Kevin carried on eating his tea.

'I'm not gonna lie just cos the kid has gone off in some big sulk. He was acting up, hitting stuff, and it was only two days after he got suspended.'

'For what?' Bryant asked.

'Fighting,' Shirley answered. 'But he was only defending himself.'

Mr Stevens shook his head in despair. 'She'll have you believe he's a bloody angel. He's not. And the reason she didn't go shopping was cos we couldn't afford it. There, now you know,' he said, turning his attention back to the television.

'So, he went out?' Kim asked Mrs Stevens, unsure who was telling the truth. But she wasn't sure how much it mattered. Lewis was twelve years old, and he was missing.

'Yeah, I gave him a fiver and told him to go into town,' she said.

Kim hated the note of judgement that came into her head. Enough money for smokes and to get the kid out of their hair, but not enough to get food.

She pushed the thought out. They still had a son missing, whatever financial decisions they made.

'Did you know that's where he'd go?'

She nodded with certainty. 'Have you seen the place?'

Kim shook her head.

'You'll get what I mean.'

'Had he mentioned anything strange happening before then, like being approached or followed?'

Mrs Stevens shook her head.

'Any fights with friends?'

'Kid fights with everybody,' Mr Stevens offered without taking his eyes from the television.

Shirley Stevens nodded her agreement.

'Okay. Is there anything else you can think of that might help?' Kim asked, feeling they were not going to get a whole lot more, as the other three kids came bounding into the room.

Mrs Stevens shook her head as the smallest of the three bounced onto her lap.

'We'll show ourselves out,' Kim said before heading for the door.

She took her time. Something about the meeting had unsettled her.

Mr Stevens seemed to be convinced that Lewis was having them all on and would turn up safe and sound. Shirley Stevens didn't seem totally convinced, but her husband's conviction gave her something to hang on to. None of them seemed concerned that the boy had now been gone for ten whole days.

Also, Bobby Stevens didn't seem to like his stepson very much. Was Lewis really a little shit, or was Bobby's opinion biased because Lewis wasn't his son? Neither was the older boy, Kevin, but she hadn't sensed the same level of hostility between the two of them.

There was something else that occurred to her as she reached the car.

She took a good look around.

'Where is it all, Bryant?'

'All what, guv?'

'Family, friends, neighbours, posters, Facebook pages, GoFundMe campaigns. The works. Where's the community, the central point for sightings and searches? There's always someone ready to get it all going. Not one poster. Not one bit of evidence that a child has gone missing.'

She'd seen more activity for a missing dog.

'Dunno, guv. You think it's important?'

'Not sure,' she said, stepping away from the car. 'But I think we'd better try and find out.'

TEN

Stacey didn't disagree with the boss's logic. Review what had already been established and then look deeper and wider. Never the most satisfying task, unlike going on a voyage of discovery, unearthing facts for the first time. There was a despondency to going over someone else's work, as though your brain had already decided there was nothing new to find and so shut down part of its capabilities.

'Jesus, this is monotonous,' Penn said, turning another statement face down.

He was clearly feeling the same lack of motivation she was.

'How many you got?' she asked.

'Forty-seven.'

'Blimey,' she said, surprised. That was more than she'd been expecting. 'They've been thorough.'

'Hmm... I'll let you know. Only done five so far.'

Stacey remained silent to leave him to it. She had her own mind-numbing task to sink her teeth into. She had access to the footage that had been saved and a second file containing the footage deemed of no value. The contents of both surprised her, in the sense that there was not very much of it. She'd been known to amass dozens, sometimes hundreds of video files in her efforts to locate one useful image or clip.

In the saved file there were two clips.

One was three seconds long. It showed Lewis walking into Coral Island; the second clip showed him walking out again at 8.35 p.m., exactly thirty minutes later.

The clip ended when he went out of view of the camera.

She could see why they'd assumed that if he'd been taken, he'd have most likely been snatched between the amusement arcade and home, which was just under a mile away.

But she had a couple of questions. The cameras could see a bit further than the entrances, so why hadn't they got that footage? And what had he been doing in Coral Island for almost half an hour? According to the mother's statement, the kid only had a fiver, which Stacey was sure would have been gone in minutes.

She drummed her fingers on the desk and stole a glance over at the lone figure in the squad room. She was guessing the fact he'd been left behind meant he performed a similar role to her. If he was mainly deskbound, he might be starved of conversation, so who knew what he might reveal. She also wanted an idea of how deeply he'd gone on the CCTV.

She stared at his bowed head for a full minute, wondering how to make contact without it appearing obvious. She would bet her next pizza that he'd been instructed not to interact with them.

So, she had to give him no choice.

She spied something on the wall behind his head, and a slow smile began to lift her lips.

Something she'd done accidentally a week ago was now going to serve her well.

She took a fresh piece of crisp paper and slid it hard against the crease in her left forefinger closest to the nail.

Nothing.

She did it again.

Nothing.

She did it a third time and struck gold.

Penn raised his head. 'Stace, what the—?'

'It's okay,' she said, pushing back her chair.

She hadn't forgotten how sore it was, nor how much it bled.

She nudged the door handle open with her elbow while cupping her left hand. Perfect droplets of blood were landing in her palm.

'Hiya, you got a first aid kit?' she asked, heading towards the officer they called Gonk.

He froze for a second and then followed her gaze to the wall behind his head.

'Sure, sure,' he said, reaching behind. The only accent she heard in his voice was a northern twang.

'Here you go,' he said, passing her the box.

'Err...' she said, looking to her bloodied hand.

'Sorry, sorry, of course,' he said, opening it up and passing her a tissue. 'Here, press this onto the cut.'

She did as he said, holding her hands higher in the air.

He fiddled with different-sized plasters before asking to take a look.

'It was just paper,' she said. 'Bloody vicious stuff.'

He chuckled then stopped himself.

'It's okay, I won't tell anyone you spoke to me. It's a medical emergency.'

His lips twitched as he chose a plaster.

A quick glance to her left revealed Penn watching her with an amused expression.

'So, what's your real name? I don't really want to call you Gonk.'

'It's Adil.'

'So why the nickname?' she asked as he tore off the paper to reveal the sticky tape.

'It's Red's favourite insult for newbies. Apparently it'll be bestowed upon the next newcomer once I'm no longer the freshest member of the team.'

'Yeah, I had one of those,' Stacey lied. 'Boss called me Plank on my first day cos my last name's Wood.'

She hated lying about the boss, who had never done any such thing, but she wanted to try and build a rapport with the constable. 'I managed to throw it off after a week or so.'

'Did you mention it to her?' he asked.

'Goodness, no, I'm not that brave. I'd never do anything like that. I played dumb and stopped responding to it, and the boss got sick of saying everything twice.'

He laughed as she moved the tissue to reveal the cut was still bleeding. Maybe she should have pressed the tissue harder. She reapplied it.

'This is going to slow down my CCTV review.'

'You're going over my work?' he asked, frowning.

'Not just yours. Your chief wants us to focus on Lewis so you can focus on Noah.'

'Ah, makes sense.'

'Was it hard to get the footage from the arcade?' she asked. 'I've had some that make me wait for days.'

He shook his head. 'We gave them a description and a rough idea of the time. They narrowed it down and caught him going in and coming out.'

'Nothing during his time in there?' she asked.

'Struggled to locate him inside, so that's all we've got. It's all we need though, isn't it?' he asked. 'We know he left the premises.'

Yeah, but we don't know if he spoke to anyone in there, she thought. And because the footage they'd sent was so finely edited, she couldn't tell if anyone had followed him in or followed him out.

Stacey took away the tissue to reveal the cut had stopped bleeding.

Adil applied the plaster, and she thanked him before returning to her desk.

She'd thought reviewing the CCTV findings was a complete waste of her time.

Now she wasn't so sure.

ELEVEN

Unsurprisingly, the house next to the Stevenses' was the exact same layout. It was owned by a couple in their early sixties – Joyce and Dennis Smith.

Joyce had happily invited them in, and Dennis had put down his newspaper and turned off the television to accommodate them.

Although the house had the same bones of the property next door, that was where the similarity ended.

To Kim's eye, the walls had been freshly papered, and the paintwork was sharp and clean. The difference in the style of windows told her that this couple had bought their council house and a great deal of pride was taken in its upkeep. The same pride continued into the garden from what Kim could see.

Kim had seen places like this before. At a guess, she would say that the couple had moved in decades ago when the estate wasn't as rough. It had probably deteriorated around them, but they were happy in the home they'd made.

'How may we help?' Joyce asked once Kim and Bryant were sitting on the sofa.

'We're investigating the disappearance of the boy next door.'

The woman's lips pursed slightly, but she nodded, waiting for a question.

'Do you know Lewis well?'

They both shook their heads.

'I mean, we tried,' Dennis offered. 'When they first moved in, they only had the two boys. We invited them round, but they never came. Tried chatting to them out back, but they'd just go back in. You can only try so many times,' he finished.

Joyce looked like she wanted to say something. Kim waited.

'I'm not being mean, but I think they're just not very nice. We've not seen many friends dropping by over the years. Not for them or the children.'

Kim wasn't too fussed about that. Many families liked to keep themselves to themselves.

'Have they ever given you any trouble?' Kim asked.

They lived next door to a fifteen-year-old, a twelve-year-old and a bunch of toddlers.

They both shook their heads no, surprising her. At the very least, she'd have expected a bit of noise.

'And the parents?'

'Not directly,' Dennis answered. 'They're a bit loud sometimes, arguing and shouting. It's been worse since he lost his job. Money troubles, I should think. A lot of mouths to feed, so a lot of yelling and banging of doors. That last fight was awful.'

Joyce nodded. 'Funnily enough, it was the night the boy went missing. We saw him go out, then the older boy went out, and then the parents had a huge humdinger of a row, and then Bobby stormed out. There was no more noise, and we went to bed. First we knew that Lewis was missing was seeing the police car come to the house the next morning.'

'You didn't see any of them out searching, calling his name?' Bryant asked.

Often parents of missing children couldn't keep still. Even if it was a fruitless mission, they had to be out doing something:

knocking neighbours' doors, searching last-known places, talking to the child's friends.

Joyce shook her head. 'They called the police the last time he ran away, so we thought he might have done it again.'

Yeah, that seemed to be the general consensus from everyone, Kim thought.

'Are they close?' she asked. 'The parents and the kids, I mean. Did you see that?'

Joyce grimaced before shaking her head. 'No, I don't think so. They don't seem to spend any time with the older boys. I see Kevin with a couple of friends now and again, but Lewis is always on his own. Gets into trouble a bit for fighting I think.'

Yes, they'd already heard that as well.

'They had the police come and talk to him to straighten him out once. Scare some discipline into him. Same ones who came after the break-in.'

'They were burgled?' Kim asked, starting to wonder what else they didn't know.

'A couple of months back now. Never caught the robbers, but you don't really now, do you?'

Joyce's question wasn't at all malicious, and Kim understood why she'd said it. Burglaries were not easy to solve without some kind of hard evidence, and so many of them became embarrassing statistics.

'And they asked those officers to come talk to Lewis to straighten him out?' Kim clarified.

Joyce nodded.

If it was Red and Roy, she could now understand Mrs Stevens's use of their first names.

'Well, it's what I heard anyway,' Joyce said with a pensive expression.

'Joyce...' Dennis warned.

Again, Kim waited.

'I know, love, but he's been gone for days now,' Joyce said.

Kim sat up straighter.

Dennis sighed then looked at the two of them before continuing. 'There are things we know for sure which we've told you, and things we've only heard that we haven't mentioned to anyone,' he said. 'We don't want to send you looking in the wrong direction.'

'That's very considerate of you, but as police officers we have to consider every option. Please continue.'

Joyce hesitated again, but Dennis nodded for her to spill whatever beans were in her mouth.

'Well, when we first heard Lewis was missing, we thought it was some kind of punishment gone wrong.'

Kim felt the hairs on her neck prickle. 'Why would you think that?'

'We heard that once his brother was told to take him miles away to somewhere he didn't know and dump him there with no food and no money to teach him a lesson.'

'You really think he did that? Take his brother and put him in danger like that?' Kim asked.

Joyce shrugged. 'I don't know them well enough. It was something I heard at the hairdresser's. The mother of a friend of Kevin's said her son had been involved in the punishment.'

'Did anyone tell the police?' Bryant asked.

Joyce shrugged. 'By the time it came to me, it was third hand, so I didn't do anything.'

Kim wondered if there was any truth to the story, or if it was one of those myths that grew from nowhere when a child was missing.

'Have you heard about anything else like that?' she asked.

Joyce shook her head.

Kim stood to leave and then remembered the question she'd come here to ask in the first place.

'Just out of interest, do you know why there's been no

community involvement, posters, local searches, social media groups, that kind of thing?'

'They were asked,' Dennis told her. 'Sarah in the end house, who does a bit of cleaning for us, she offered to set stuff up. She asked for a recent photo to print some fliers, but they wouldn't give her one. They said they didn't want any fuss or attention cos they were just going to look stupid when he came waltzing back with his tail between his legs.'

'When was this?' Kim asked.

'The first full day he was missing. Trust me, if anyone could have mobilised the troops, it would have been Sarah.'

Maybe the Stevenses had thought that the first day, but they still seemed stuck on that belief ten days down the line.

Kim thanked the couple before heading back to the car.

Why was everyone so happy to believe the kid had just run away?

Her thoughts were stuck on a twelve-year-old boy who was clearly unhappy with something, and who seemed to find no joy either at home or school.

That was a situation she'd encountered many times during her career when dealing with missing children, but in Lewis's case, she was experiencing one new element. This twelve-year-old boy had vanished into thin air and not one person appeared to be bothered to look for him.

TWELVE

Penn glanced into the squad room next door and lowered his voice before he spoke.

'You know when you get a certain feeling starting to build inside, but you're really trying to fight it?'

'Penn, we've had this conversation. I'm married.'

'Yeah, tough for me. And stop picking at that plaster.'

'What's the feeling?' Stacey asked, finally leaving the Band-Aid alone.

'That so far this team seem to be doing a shit job.'

Stacey also glanced towards Adil before nodding.

To Penn, it was like speaking ill of the dead. You never wanted to think other officers were not up to doing the work.

'I mean, is it us?' he went on.

'Dunno,' Stacey answered. 'I've been wondering the same thing. All I know is that every day we're pushed by the boss to question everything. We're told once you think you can't go any further, dig deeper, go wider, think differently. I'm not seeing that here, at the minute.'

He appreciated the qualifier she put at the end of the sentence. It gave him hope that he might see flashes of brilliance, a measure of creativity, some passion to bring this boy home.

'How are the statements?' Stacey asked.

'As thin as my mum's pancakes,' he said honestly.

'But there are loads.'

'Oh yeah, but few that are useful. Wanna guess how many of his classmates were spoken to?'

'All of them?' Stacey asked.

'Three,' he answered.

Stacey's frown deepened, and he knew what she was thinking. You had to speak to them all. Some kids got scared and wouldn't volunteer information.

'And how many teachers, do you reckon?' he asked.

'Everyone who taught him, and the headteacher, and maybe even the dinner ladies, if they have them, cos they always know everything.'

'Two,' Penn answered. 'His form tutor and his English teacher. Definitely no dinner ladies.'

'Jeez,' Stacey said.

'Oh, it gets better. Seven of the statements mention a man called Roderick Skidmore, but guess who there isn't a statement from?'

'Roderick Skidmore,' Stacey answered.

'Correct.'

'Err... who is Roderick Skidmore?' Stacey asked.

'Glad you asked that. Roderick Skidmore is our local registered paedophile.'

THIRTEEN

Kim had felt it necessary to visit the last place Lewis Stevens had been seen before he disappeared.

From the second she'd walked in, her senses had been assaulted. Flashing lights blinked at her from every direction. Rows of fruit machines, grabbers, games and rides screamed different noises at her, vying for her attention. Horses raced across a track as people threw balls into holes to win giant cuddly toys.

Smells from the eateries wafted all around the huge space.

She tried to say something to Bryant, but he shook his head, pointing to his ear as a family shrieked in delight at a machine that was spitting out a stream of tickets.

From the kiosk she'd just passed, she guessed that tickets meant prizes.

The upper level was home to more of the same but with sectioned-off areas for adults only.

'It's a far cry from the arcades they had when I was a kid,' Bryant shouted in her ear as they found a quieter spot by one of the exits.

'Difficult to make all this back in the Stone Age,' she said, looking around.

'Harsh, guv, harsh.'

She could certainly see the appeal of the place. It was loud, it was busy; people were getting bumped and nudged all over the place. Hard-working folks were letting off steam with their kids for a few days. A short holiday before folks accepted the inevitability of winter and Christmas.

The shrieks and laughter were punctuated by the sound of coins dropping into trays.

The place was alive with fun and excitement.

She could understand why Stacey had reported that the security team had been unable to locate Lewis on the video footage inside. Trying to pick out the child amongst this lot would be a task and a half.

And yet it could be done, she thought, taking another look around. There seemed to be decent coverage from a CCTV point of view. If someone cared enough to go through the cameras, they'd find the boy somewhere.

'Come on – let's go,' she said to Bryant, heading for the exit. She'd seen all she needed to see. The kid had been given a fiver to go and amuse himself, and he'd come here.

Something she was sure he wouldn't have done if he'd been planning to run away.

FOURTEEN

It was almost nine when Bryant pulled into the car park of the station. When they approached the door, the entire Blackpool team was leaving.

'Was it something we said?' Kim joked as they passed.

Red smiled as Roy simply barged past.

'The on-call team and night shift have been briefed. Nothing more to be done tonight, and we gotta sleep sometime.'

She tried not to think critically of his team management. He was correct that personnel welfare was a priority. But when you had two missing boys, you could push the boundaries of clocking in and out and the tolerance of your team. She was further surprised to see that the hard day wasn't showing on his appearance. He looked as smart and presentable as he had when she'd first seen him hours ago.

The remaining three members of the team offered curt nods as they went by.

Jesus, the warning not to interact must have been a stern one. She had yet to hear any of them speak.

'And you'll get yourselves off pretty sharpish or suffer the wrath of Iris,' Red went on, offering a wave before leaving them to ponder what he'd said.

They made their way up to the squad room and his words made sense.

She guessed that the woman in her mid-fifties with the cleaning cart was Iris. Kim offered her a smile as she entered their war room, and then she nodded to Bryant to update Stacey and Penn on their progress so far.

Glancing out through the open door, Kim couldn't help but marvel at the woman in the squad room, who was attacking her job with vigour and efficiency. All the dusting had been done, and she was now dragging a Henry vacuum around at speed.

An occasional glance told Kim she was checking for signs of them leaving.

'And that's about it from us unless you have anything more to add,' Bryant said, raising an eyebrow at her.

'No, we're good. Stace, what's your view on the CCTV? Worth pursuing? Looks like the arcade has plenty of scope.'

Stacey considered before nodding. 'The parameters they used were too narrow. We know Lewis entered and then left almost half an hour later. Don't know what he did. Don't know who he spoke to. Don't even know if any of the cameras on the other entrances might have caught his direction of travel or any other interactions. I'd like to speak to the arcade tomorrow and see what I can find.'

Kim nodded her agreement, wondering why this hadn't been done already.

'Penn?' she said as Iris unplugged the vacuum and glanced their way again.

'Not happy with the statements, boss. Definitely not enough people spoken to at the school, either teachers or students.'

'Okay, I think—' Kim stopped speaking as her phone tinged receipt of a text message.

She glanced at it quickly and saw immediately it was a compilation of funny kitten videos with a row of laughing emojis underneath. She groaned as she put her phone back in her pocket but not before she caught Bryant's frown.

'I think we also need more canvassing at Coral Island. There are lots of staff. Someone might remember him.'

Kim glanced again at Iris, who was hovering close to the door. She strode over and stood in the doorway. 'Feel free to start.'

Iris shook her head. 'Not while you're still working.' She tapped her right ear. 'Might hear something I shouldn't.'

'Okay, two minutes,' Kim said, closing the door.

'Penn?' she asked.

'There's a local paedophile. Registered sex offender. His name has come up a couple of times in the statements. Obviously he's gonna be the first name on everyone's lips, but I can't see that he was even spoken to.'

Shouldn't that have been the first port of call?

'Okay, folks, best get moving or Iris is going to physically remove us, judging by the look on her face.'

They began to collect their things and headed for the door.

'It's all yours,' Kim said as they made their way through the squad room.

The woman was in there with her Henry before they were out of sight.

'Get some food, get some rest and meet downstairs at the hotel for breakfast at six thirty.'

They all nodded their understanding as Stacey got into Penn's car and she followed Bryant.

'Not impressed at the lack of thoroughness of the investigation so far,' Bryant said, driving away from the station. 'They've had ten bloody days.'

'Agreed. We're gonna be asking some uncomfortable questions at the group briefing tomorrow.'

'Talking of uncomfortable questions, are you ever gonna tell me who's blowing up your phone?'

'You do realise it might be private. Maybe I'm seeing someone.'

'End it,' Bryant said emphatically.

'Excuse me?'

'Given that your face shows extreme irritation every time you get a text, there ain't gonna be no happy ending.'

Kim sighed heavily. Maybe it would help to share the problem, and he was the closest thing she had to a friend.

He pulled up in the hotel car park and waited.

'Okay, I'll tell you who the messages are from.'

FIFTEEN

Ten minutes later, they were still sitting in Bryant's car outside the hotel. And still, her colleague couldn't control his laughter.

'Are you happy now?' she snapped.

'Not even close. Tell me again, and this time I want every detail.'

Jesus, where to even begin.

'Well, you remember I was there when Frost first opened her eyes after coming out of the coma?'

Who could forget that the reporter had been bullied into following the Jester's instructions just like the rest of them? It had been an email to Frost that had kickstarted the whole investigation. Her orders had been clear, and halfway through she had chosen to ignore them and walk out on the case. Less than six hours later, Kim and Bryant had found her at home lying in a pool of blood from a near-fatal blow to the back of the head. A coma had been induced following the surgery to help the swelling to her brain.

'Of course I remember. I also recall that you pretty much goaded Frost into waking up.'

'Yes, well, I stayed with her until the doctor came to make

sure she wasn't going to go under again. He examined her and declared himself happy, even though she answered a few questions wrong.'

'Like what?'

'The day of the week, the month she was born.'

'Really?'

'Yeah, I know, but I spoke to the doctor before I left. He assured me that some level of confusion was to be expected.

'She had no memory of what had happened. She remembered the case, in great detail, and storming out after Hiccup's death, but she didn't recall where she went afterwards or getting home.'

'Okay, so what happened next?'

'I went home happy I'd done my bit. She's in hospital – they'll take care of her head injury. I figured I'd next see Frost when she's back to harassing us on a future case. Job done. Hands washed. Conscience clear.'

'But?'

'A few hours later, I get a text message, asking if I can grab some clothes and take them to the hospital.'

'And you did it?' he groaned.

'How was I going to say no?'

As he had no answer, he continued to ask her questions. 'Next?'

'A couple of days later, she asked if I'd bring her a proper cup of coffee.'

Bryant's smile was tugging at his mouth again.

'Then she wanted some real sausage rolls from Greggs. And then three days ago, she was discharged from hospital, and guess who went to pick her up?'

'Bloody hell, Kim, and I'm calling you that cos it's a personal problem. I'm dying to know what she's texting you now.'

'Jokes, memes, funny things off the internet.'

'Things you'd send your best friend?' Bryant clarified.

Kim cringed.

'You're gonna have to tell her.'

'How, Bryant? If the woman thinks we're best mates, then she clearly is suffering some kind of brain damage. How the hell am I going to explain we don't even like each other?'

'Well, that's not strictly—'

'We're not bloody best mates. We've reached a mutual tolerance level over the years, which sure doesn't include clothes shopping or sharing bloody make-up tips.'

'As entertaining as this is for me, you're somehow gonna have to get the truth through to her. You're not being fair to her, and you're making a bigger problem for yourself down the line.'

'Maybe by the time we get back home, her memories will have returned, and she'll realise her mistake,' Kim said hopefully.

'And if she hasn't?'

'Shut up, Bryant,' she said, getting out of the car.

She stepped into the lobby and took her key from Stacey before making her way silently to her room to ponder the question that had been on her mind for days.

How did she tell a woman who had narrowly escaped death, and who seemed likely to have to learn to live with some level of brain damage, that she literally had no friends?

SIXTEEN

Kim got a sinking feeling as she entered the squad room. Not only was the Blackpool team already in full attendance, but also they looked like they'd been there for some time.

She pointedly looked at her watch as Red did the same.

'Good afternoon,' he said smugly.

'We're not late,' she snapped, realising she'd fallen for the oldest trick in the book. 'You said the briefing was at seven thirty.'

'You must have misheard. I said six thirty.'

'No. You definitely—'

'He said six thirty. I was right behind him,' Roy said, lounging back in his chair.

Kim knew this was an argument she wasn't going to win.

'Not our fault you Brummie lot can't get up and dressed on time,' Roy said, trying to soften his snide comment with a smirk.

'But at least when we do arrive, we're properly dressed,' she said, fixing her gaze on the unfastened button on his shirt and the tie knot hanging two inches away from his collar.

He tried to keep the false smile on his face as he fastened his button but failed.

'Well, we're here now. What did we miss?' she asked, taking a seat.

Her team followed suit behind her.

'We're all done now. No need to go through it all again. Definitely two separate cases, and—'

'You're sure about that?' Kim asked. 'Two boys of a similar age gone missing in ten days and they aren't linked?'

Red shook his head. 'We don't think so. All evidence indicates Lewis Stevens is a runaway, so there's no point muddying the waters with cross-briefings. The chief has given you instructions, so—'

'Yeah, but I'd really like a catch-up anyway,' Kim said, adopting her best insistent tone. From the corner of her eye she saw Bryant offer a small shake of the head at her actions. He was playing his part well, showing subtle frustration at her behaviour. 'You've got to stop assuming Lewis is a runaway,' she continued. 'If we share information—'

'Does look better for the figures if he ran away though, boss,' Penn interrupted. 'It's what I'd do to keep my incident rate down.'

Kim shot him daggers, as would be expected of her, but it was a nice move on his part. Presenting them with the illusion of a fractured team could only help make them more accessible.

Stacey bit her lip and stared at the ground.

'Why has no one spoken to Roderick Skidmore?' Kim asked pointedly.

'They're not his type,' Roy said quickly. 'He likes them a bit younger.'

'But you spoke to him and pinpointed his location just to rule him out, didn't you?' she pushed. Surely it was just the paper statement that was missing?

'Like Roy said, waste of time getting a formal statement,' Red offered testily. 'We know our own paedophiles, Inspector, and Skidmore has nothing to do with this.'

'Not sure your sex offenders differ greatly from our own, but I do know they're the first people we rule out.' She paused. 'We'll be following that up too.'

Red looked like he wanted to say something and then changed his mind.

Kim continued. 'Any reason why only a handful of teachers and students were interviewed at Lewis's school?'

'We were getting the same answers from all of them so it was a—'

'Waste of time,' she finished for him. 'Dying to know what you did with all that time you saved.'

Red's expression was darkening every time she opened her mouth. She hoped she was annoying him. She didn't like sneak attacks. If they were going to be enemies, she preferred open warfare and a combatant with big-enough balls to face her head-on. He was annoyed and she wasn't even finished.

'You interviewed Lewis's brother at length though, right?'

Red didn't answer.

'Seeing as we've been told he likes to take his younger brother a few miles away and dump him.'

'It was a prank,' Roy offered, indicating that they did know about it. 'He was just teaching the kid a lesson.'

'So you've asked him formally if he did it again and something went wrong this time?'

Red looked at his watch. 'We need to...'

So that was clearly a no as well, she realised.

'Okay, last question, why did you write him off as a runaway so quickly? I mean, I assume that's why it's barely been investigated. Is it because his parents said so?'

'He's got form for it,' Red answered. 'He's run away three times before. He had a few quid in his pocket. He'd been in trouble again and he needed to cool off. He'll be back. You'll see.'

And then you're going to feel like an idiot, were the unspoken words that hung between them.

Rather that than find his body, Kim thought but realised she was wasting her breath. They were locked into their conviction that Lewis was going to suddenly reappear.

If she wanted a thorough investigation, she was going to have to do it herself.

She stood. 'Okay, guys, thanks. We'll catch up later.'

She headed into their war room, and her team followed behind.

'Well?' Kim asked, standing with her back to the squad room as they took their seats.

'Safe to say we're not gonna be swapping numbers after this, but good old Roy gave me a couple of secret eyerolls, so he definitely thinks I'm in his camp,' Bryant offered.

'And the others?' Kim asked, looking at Stacey and Penn.

'Adil is waiting,' Stacey said. 'He watches everything and is just waiting for someone to put them in their place. For every blow you land, he hides a micro expression of triumph. Carly is uncomfortable. She shifts slightly in her seat a lot as though she wants her chair to fall through the floor. I wouldn't mind a conversation with her.'

'Dickinson is interesting,' Penn continued. 'He's completely unruffled and seems to enjoy the conflict. He's relaxed and happy to be a spectator, but there's a faint look of distaste every time Roy opens his mouth.'

'Any thoughts on potential internal complainants?' she asked.

Everyone shook their heads.

'There's always the chance it's not from inside,' Kim said. 'But keep your eyes peeled. In the meantime, our focus is firmly on Lewis and bringing him home. Stace, I want photos on the board of family, suspects and anyone else of interest, cos right now we're the only ones who seem to care about this kid.'

One way or another, she was going to find out what happened to Lewis, and she intended to return to the people that were supposed to be closest to him.

His family.

SEVENTEEN

'So, has Charlie worked out how to use FaceTime yet?' Bryant asked once they were in the car.

'Kind of but not really,' Kim said honestly.

She'd tried to call him last night to get a look at Barney, and she'd seen just about every part of Charlie's house except where the dog was lying. She could tell the elderly man was getting anxious because he couldn't work it out, so she'd reverted to a good old-fashioned phone call instead, to learn that Barney was being as spoiled as he always was when he stayed with his best friend.

She knew she had nothing to worry about, but she didn't like being so many miles away.

'He'll be fine,' Bryant said, winding through the back streets of Blackpool.

She said nothing. Somehow her colleague always knew when she was thinking of her canine buddy.

'Any more texts from your bestie?'

'Bryant, I dare you to call her that one more time,' she growled.

He laughed in response, and they said nothing more until he pulled up outside the Stevenses' residence.

'Might be a bit early for them, guv,' he said, glancing towards the house.

She too had already noticed that every window was still obscured by drawn curtains.

'It's almost eight, and they have three young children and a missing son. Not sure they're sleeping all that peacefully even if it is half term.'

It was an unfortunate part of any investigation into a missing child that family members had to be investigated too. History and statistics had shown that almost fifty per cent of missing kids that didn't come home had a family member or friend tied up in it somehow. Very few people hadn't heard of the Shannon Matthews case; the twelve-year-old girl had been concealed by a family member with the knowledge of her mother in a bid to get rich from donations.

For the families that were completely innocent, the spotlight cast on them by police questions made the stress of an already heart-breaking situation unbearable. She didn't care very much about the others, and while she wasn't sure which camp certain members of the Stevens family came into, until she had something that said otherwise, they would be treated with consideration and respect.

It took three heavy loud knocks to get an answer, so Kim revised her earlier thought that none of them would be sleeping soundly.

'What the hell?' Bobby Stevens asked when he finally opened the door, rubbing sleep from his eyes and shielding them from the morning light.

A bit strange that he seemed confused about what they were doing there when they could easily have come to tell them their son had been found, an eventuality that wouldn't neces-sarily be confined to office hours.

'May we have a word?'

He stepped aside and beckoned them into a house where all the natural light was shut out.

Bobby immediately started opening curtains and blinds before turning to her with a frown. 'Have you found him?'

Kim shook her head.

'Why the early call then?' he asked without annoyance.

'The sooner we've had a quick chat with the three of you, the quicker we can get back to searching for Lewis.'

'Ssh,' Shirley Stevens said, padding down the stairs.

With three young children, Kim was guessing the woman was already on borrowed time until her day got started for real.

'Three of us?' Bobby asked, just realising what she'd said.

'Yes, we need to speak to Kevin as well.'

Shirley took her phone from her dressing-gown pocket. She rang a number before giving them an irritated look.

'Come downstairs,' Shirley said into the phone. 'Because I said so,' she added before ending the call.

Kim followed them both into a room that bore the signs of a late-night takeaway. Yellow Styrofoam boxes and half-eaten bags of chips littered the surface, even though the family had been in the process of their evening meal when they'd visited the previous day.

It was good to know they were all maintaining healthy appetites.

'Just a couple of follow-up points,' Kim said, sitting at the kitchen table.

Bobby leaned against the fridge freezer with his arms crossed, while Shirley filled the kettle.

'We've been told there was quite the argument the night that Lewis disappeared.'

'Who told you...? Oh, hang on, I can guess,' Bobby said, nodding towards the wall they shared with the neighbours.

Kim didn't confirm or deny. 'Would you mind telling us what the argument was about?'

'Of course. It was about Lewis. They're always about Lewis.'

Kim wished, just once, that she could see one ounce of emotion directed towards his stepson. A child he might never see again.

'Any particular reason?' she asked.

'His cheek, his attitude, his laziness, his fighting, his suspension from school. It was bound to be one of those.'

Kim turned towards Lewis's mother. 'Is he really that much of a problem child?'

Shirley hesitated before answering as though trying to work out the correct response.

'He can be, but I still wish...' Her words faltered.

'Wish what?' Kim pushed.

'That he was here being a pain right now.'

Her eyes filled with tears, and she turned away after displaying the first real emotion Kim had seen. She even detected a shadow of regret pass over Bobby's face. Regret for what?

'You stormed out not long after Lewis left,' Kim said, fixing her gaze on the stepfather.

'So?' he asked, shrugging.

'Did you see him again? Did you catch up with him?'

He shook his head. 'It was a good ten minutes before I went out.'

Ten minutes wasn't that long if you were walking quickly and you knew which way to go.

Although Lewis had entered and exited Coral Island alone, she'd like to know if there'd been any further contact between the two of them once Lewis had left the house. 'Answer my question, please.'

'Never saw him.'

'And where did you go?'

'Hey, hang on. I don't like where this is going. You trying to say I had something to do with his disappearance?'

'As investigators we have to rule out any involvement from family members,' Kim said honestly. 'And I'm really surprised you haven't already been asked.'

He uncrossed his arms and put his hands in his pockets. 'That's the difference when you're dealing with coppers who know you.'

'Was it Red and Roy that came and gave Lewis a stern talking-to?'

He nodded. 'They were doing a follow-up after our break-in. They had a quiet word.'

If they were still arguing about him the night he disappeared, it hadn't done him a lot of good on the behaviour modification front.

'So, if you can just tell me where you went when you left the house,' she reminded him.

'For a walk, down the front. Just to clear my head.'

'Anyone we can check that with?' Kim asked.

He thought for a minute before shaking his head.

'And you returned at what time?'

'Around tenish.'

A good half hour after Lewis had left the amusement arcade.

'That's a lot of head clearing,' she observed.

'Walking ain't a crime, is it?' he said, taking a cuppa offered by his wife.

Kim noted she and Bryant hadn't been offered any kind of refreshment, almost like the Stevenses didn't want police in their home a minute longer than necessary. Unless their names were Red or Roy.

'Okay, if we can just speak to—'

'What is it?' Kevin Stevens asked, entering the kitchen. Obviously hopeful of being able to go right back to bed, he wore pyjama bottoms and no top.

He barely even glanced their way until his mum nodded in their direction.

'Just a question or two and then we'll leave you in peace.'

He yawned and rubbed at his eyes.

'Where did you go the night Lewis went missing?'

'Bedroom, watching telly?' he said as if she would know the correct answer.

'We've been told that you went out.'

'Might have done,' he said, shrugging as though confused as to why it mattered.

'Can you think hard for me, Kevin?' she asked.

He shook his head. 'Definitely stayed in. Nothing to do so I just stayed in.'

Friday night a mile away from one of the most lucrative night-time economies in the country and this teenager couldn't find something to do.

With only the neighbours' recollection to go on, she was unable to push him any further.

Kevin turned to leave the room.

'Hang on, one more thing,' Kim said. 'Is it true that you took your brother somewhere and left him there, as a punishment?'

All three sets of eyes were on her, clearly wondering how she knew about that. She'd bet even Red and Roy were unaware of that one.

He looked to his parents, who were no help at all.

'It was just a joke, a prank. I knew he'd find his way home.'

'So he was on a bus route, and he had money?' Kim asked.

Kevin shrugged.

'How did you do it?' Kim pushed. The boy wasn't old enough to drive.

'Took him for a ride on my bike. Told him my mate wanted to show us his new scrambler. Followed the tram lines for a few miles then went down a few lanes to confuse him.'

'How far?' Bryant asked.

'Dunno. Nine or ten miles. Not far.'

Far enough, Kim thought, for a kid left on his own.

'How did he get home?' she asked.

'Hitchhiked,' Kevin mumbled, making it clear that he'd not been on a bus route and most likely hadn't had any money.

'Was it a joke, or was it a punishment?'

'He was being an arse,' Kevin said defensively.

'Was he being an arse on the day he disappeared?'

Kevin stuck his chin out. 'Probably.'

'And there's no chance you decided to teach him another lesson, except this time something went wrong and he didn't find his way back?'

'I never touched him. I didn't go out that night, I swear.'

Kim knew she couldn't push any further. They were victims and deserved to be treated as such until she found any proof that told her otherwise... but something wasn't right, and she wasn't going to stop digging until she found out what it was.

She thanked them for their time and headed out to the car with a growing sense of sadness.

Whether he was a little shit or not, Lewis didn't seem to have anyone to turn to. Surely he and his older brother should have been a team amidst this new family? They should have had each other's backs at all times. Instead, Lewis appeared to have no one to rely on but himself.

There was a conflict in her mind, splitting her reasoning down the middle. One minute she was convinced that the disappearance of the two boys was linked. She didn't like the coincidence of the timing; it seemed certain that both boys had been abducted. And then her mind would shift once she spoke with the Stevens family and their behaviour caused her to wonder if one of them was responsible for his disappearance.

There was something that she wasn't being told, and she had no clue how she was going to find out what it was.

EIGHTEEN

Stacey found herself still thinking about the exchange between the teams that had taken place in the briefing.

How the boss was keeping hold of her temper she couldn't even imagine, as all the hostility seemed to be aimed at her. The rest of them were being met with mainly silence and strange looks.

That had remained the case once the boss and Bryant had left, with Penn not far behind.

The other team had gradually filtered out of the squad room, this time leaving DS Carly Walsh manning the desk.

Once Penn had left to try and track down Lewis's school form teacher, a task hindered by the half-term holidays, she'd considered trying to find some ruse to strike up a conversation with the woman who was occasionally glancing her way.

Instead, she'd focussed on completing the written application to the amusement arcade for more CCTV footage, from every camera, for the duration of Lewis's time inside plus fifteen minutes before and fifteen minutes after. Not knowing how many cameras they had, she had no clue how long such a task would take.

The only thing that had stopped her from trying to engage Walsh was the possibility of her and Adil comparing notes and finding her approaches suspicious.

She was saved the trouble of giving it any further thought when the woman appeared at her doorway and tapped lightly on the glass.

Stacey motioned for her to enter.

'Wanna cuppa?' Carly asked.

'I'm good,' Stacey answered. 'But I'll come and learn my way round the kitchen while you make one...'

'Don't really want one,' Carly said, remaining in the doorway. 'Just an excuse to come chat.'

Stacey smiled at her honesty and decided to employ some of her own.

'You lot been instructed not to speak to us when the boss is around?'

'More like an implied rule,' Carly answered.

'Ah, got it. I always follow implied rules too. Come to think of it, I follow any rules,' she said, looking down.

'Are you the quiet one of the team?' Carly asked.

'I just keep my head down and do my work. I don't like to make waves. Never a good idea when you're the lowest-ranking member of the crew.'

'But you share your opinions?'

Stacey shrugged. 'Not really. They're all big characters, so I'm easy to ignore,' she said, hoping she was playing her role well. 'I don't mind being on my own most of the time.' She might have been that meek when she'd first joined the team but not any more. 'Nice to have someone to chat to though.'

'I think we're all a bit confused about why you're here,' Carly admitted.

'Pretty simple, I think. You're really busy, we're between cases and our big bosses, who happen to be old training buddies, decided to pool resources.'

'Not sure I believe that,' Carly said, tipping her head.

'If there's anything more to it, you're talking to the wrong end of the totem pole. Not sure what else you think we could be doing.'

Carly shrugged. 'Case review, checking our work, looking for poor performance.'

'Hell no,' Stacey said, shaking her head. 'Don't we have special departments for that? And as I understand it, your boss told us where to focus our efforts. I think she just wants a few extra pairs of hands.'

'We're perfectly capable,' Carly said defensively.

'Hey, I believe you,' Stacey said, throwing open her hands. 'I just go where the boss tells me.'

'Normally behind a desk I've noticed.'

Stacey shrugged. 'It's where I do my best work. You?'

'Hate it, but the boss likes to change us around.'

'Is he decent?' Stacey asked.

Carly shrugged. 'Some days yes and other days an arse. Yours?'

'Same,' Stacey said and immediately felt a jolt of shame for her disloyalty, but she was playing a part.

'You all seem quite tight though.'

'Don't be fooled by appearances. DS Bryant is treading water until retirement, and DS Penn would sell his dog to climb the next rung of the ladder.'

Stacey hated every word that came out of her mouth, but she was hoping Carly would take the information back to her team. It served their purpose better if they appeared at odds with each other.

Carly laughed, visibly relaxing. 'Yeah, I get you. Our Roy is a bit long in the tooth now for modern policing. The bloke gets in his own way with his outdated attitude. Dickinson does whatever he's told cos he doesn't want to be picked on, and

Gonk just puts up with all the shit in the hope he'll be transferred to another team.'

Did no one use Adil's first name? Stacey wondered.

'And you?'

'I can take care of myself,' she said, unfolding her arms.

The response told her that Carly *had* to take care of herself. What she didn't know yet was from what.

'Yeah, being female in the—'

Stacey stopped speaking as Carly's phone rang.

She looked at the screen. 'Sorry, it's the boss – gotta go.'

Stacey nodded her understanding as Carly closed the door behind her.

She hurried back to her desk with the phone clutched tightly to her ear as though she'd been caught with her hand in the cookie jar.

Stacey was distracted from her thoughts by the sound of an email pinging into her inbox.

Fantastic. The footage she'd requested from the amusement arcade was starting to come through. She pulled her keyboard forward and then paused.

Beneath it was a piece of paper no bigger than three inches square.

She knew it hadn't been there last night. She turned it over to see that it wasn't scrap paper at all. It contained three names. Nothing else.

Just three names.

NINETEEN

Kim knew better than to have any preconceptions of what a paedophile and his home would look like.

The stereotype of dirty raincoats and unshaven, unkempt men hiding in dark corners was a myth that had been debunked decades ago. Sex offenders didn't always come from the dregs of society. Some were well educated, living well with decent jobs. Some were successful, established businessmen who were able to afford a decent property with a high wall to prevent the local riff-raff from getting to them.

And that appeared to be the case with Roderick Skidmore.

Stacey's overnight research, shared over breakfast, had informed them the man was forty-two years of age. He'd grown up as an only child of middle-class parents. His mother had been a school counsellor and his father a commercial building inspector.

Not only was he a paedophile, but he was also a pretty intelligent guy who made a very good living designing websites.

He'd served two short terms in prison for possessing indecent images of boys under ten, and although she could understand Red's assumption that Lewis was in the wrong age bracket for this particular paedophile, ten wasn't a million miles away from twelve.

'How is this even possible?' Bryant asked as they approached the intercom.

She knew he was talking about the fancy house and high walls. She wished she had the answer, but the truth was that many thousands of men maintained successful lives and careers while being paedophiles. Sexual deviancy didn't render them incapable of performing well in every other part of their lives.

A smooth, clear voice came through the speaker.

Bryant introduced them both and asked if they could have a word. They heard the sound of a gear engaging before the left leaf of the solid-oak gate began to slide along the wall to reveal the three-storey white house, a modern square block, with a lot of glass. Parked on the gravel drive were a Lexus and a Porsche.

'Two million,' Bryant whispered. 'And I'm not kidding. I could not hate this guy more.'

Kim understood his point. Bryant didn't hate him because he was a man with a Porsche. He hated him because he was a paedophile with a Porsche.

The front door opened once the gate had slid back to the locked position.

The man himself was a fair representation of the property in which he lived. She guessed him to be an inch or two shy of six feet, dressed in plain black trousers and a white shirt, open at the neck. His hair was a sandy colour, cut tidily.

He smiled and held out his hand. She ignored it and, on this occasion, so did Bryant.

'Roderick Skidmore?' she asked.

He retracted his hand with a look of acceptance.

Kim didn't care how much money he had, it wasn't enough for her to shake his hand.

'I assume you're here about Lewis and Noah,' he said, stepping back so they could enter his home.

'You know them?' Kim asked, surprised at the familiarity.

'Not really, no.'

'So, you've been expecting a visit?' she said, stepping into the hallway and wondering how the hell the Blackpool team could write him off without even a conversation.

The man shrugged as he closed the door.

Her gaze was drawn to the artwork on the wall. Nausea hit her immediately. Every piece was black and white, and every one was of a semi-naked prepubescent boy. It wasn't the pictures themselves that made her want to vomit – it was the reason the man had them hanging in his hall.

'Nice,' Kim said sarcastically.

'My house. I make no apology,' he said with an easy shrug.

'May we talk where your artwork is not so prominent?' she asked.

'Kitchen,' he said, leading the way.

From the set of Bryant's jaw, she could see he was struggling just as much as she was. She wasn't sure she'd ever interviewed a paedophile quite like this one.

'There's a distinct lack of shame about your perversion, Mr Skidmore,' Kim observed, unable to leave the subject untouched.

He didn't even wince at the term she'd used.

'I am free to decorate my own home as I like,' he said, pointing to a small table with four chairs. 'I've done nothing wrong that I haven't already been punished for. I had images that I enjoyed. I was neither in the photos, nor did I take them, and I didn't circulate them. I was caught and I was punished. You may not agree with the term I served, but that's your problem, not mine. It's your system.' He paused. 'Please take a seat.'

'I'll stand,' Bryant said, while Kim sat down.

'I won't bother to offer you coffee,' he said, leaning against the countertop. 'You *are* here to ask about the boys?'

Yes, but she had a couple of other questions first.

'Must be annoying to be the first port of call when a child goes missing?' she asked.

He shook his head. 'Not at all. Completely understandable.'

'Must bring the locals knocking at your door with pitchforks and torches?'

He shook his head. 'The locals never bother me. I get the odd email or text message, but they never turn up here,' he said as though the idea was preposterous.

'Why is that?'

'Because I'm rich,' he answered, matter-of-factly.

There was no arrogance or pretence in his tone, and Kim got it. With money came the perception of power. Harassing this man was not like throwing eggs and dog shit at the home of some grubby paedo in a council flat. And yet there was no difference other than the presentation. If it weren't for the photos on the wall and the unapologetic attitude, even she'd be wondering how those images had got on his computer.

'And your business hasn't suffered since your prison term?'

'Trust me, my clients have no interest in my conviction.'

'You design websites?' she asked to make sure she understood. That meant he had to have a company name which would have been out there in public during his trial. What self-respecting business would opt to use his services again after that?

'None that you're likely to see,' he said, sitting back in his chair.

Bryant cleared his throat, signalling his discomfort, and she could understand it. However well he presented himself, he was a sex offender who liked young boys and yet he was living this charmed life. She wanted to know how it was possible.

'I don't design sites for Clearnet,' he explained, and she began to understand.

That was the name given to the regular internet by users of the dark web.

'So tell us how that works, Mr Skidmore,' she asked. There was no better way of finding out the workings of the swamp than asking the people who lived there.

'I'll use the most common example of the iceberg. The normal internet is the part of the iceberg above the water. The deep net is the rest. It's by far the biggest part of the internet. It's where companies run their intranets or where database details are kept. Personal information, bank details. It's where emails are stored, messaging accounts, legal, financial, medical info. The deep web accounts for around ninety per cent of all websites. It's so large that it's impossible to discover exactly how many pages are active at any one time.'

'But that's not where you operate?' Kim asked.

'I work in the dark web, which is a part of the deep web – but a very small part. Much smaller than the Clearnet that you know so well.'

'So, you write websites that support illegal activity?' Kim asked. It always paid to establish someone's level of intelligence, not to mention their access to resources. This man appeared to have an abundance of both. That meant he had the power to make young boys disappear, which made him very interesting to the investigation. A fact that shouldn't have escaped the attention of the local team.

'Not always illegal. Sometimes unsavoury or immoral, but not always illegal,' Skidmore answered.

Bryant coughed again.

'Glass of water?' Skidmore asked.

'I'm good, thanks,' Bryant answered, not moving an inch from the doorway.

Kim realised that Skidmore wasn't attempting to be charming. He wasn't attempting to be anything. He was unashamedly being himself.

'So, to finish my analogy, the dark web would be the bottom of the submerged iceberg.'

'And that's where you spend your time? At the lowest level?' she asked.

'Very passive aggressive, officer.'

'What stops us accessing the bottom of the iceberg and closing you all down?'

She meant the police generally, though she knew that there were teams in place investigating the dark web and that their task was an uphill battle. The place was full of weapons, drugs, pornography, illicit links, extremism and hacking scams.

'First of all, you need to disabuse yourself of the notion that it's like a grubby house with a dark room where you can shine a torch and expose a group of men in the corner on their mobile phones. Unless you know what you're doing, you're not even going to find it.'

'Why not?' Kim asked.

She could just contact Cybercrime and get this information from them, but she was here now, and she didn't know what else she might learn.

'Okay, think of search engines like Google as small fishing boats. They're only able to catch the fish that are closest to the surface. The dark web isn't indexed by regular search engines.'

Kim knew that once you found your way there, the dark web was full of trading sites where people could purchase all kinds of illegal goods and services. She also knew it was the home of keyloggers, botnets, ransomware and phishing schemes.

It reminded Kim of a Ouija board. Although she wasn't particularly sold on the afterlife, she did feel that such an instrument was asking for trouble. Once you opened that door, you couldn't close it again. Once you left your footprint in the dark web, you were susceptible to any kind of scam.

The troubled look on Bryant's face urged her to hurry up. He wanted to be out of this man's presence as soon as possible.

As did she, but she was learning a lot. This man was an expert in doing bad things and knowing how to get away with it.

But how bad were the things he was prepared to do?

'So, your only knowledge of Lewis Stevens and Noah Reid is what you saw in the press?'

'Pretty much,' he answered.

She frowned. 'That's not a definitive yes, Mr Skidmore, which is troubling, as is your use of their first names only when we entered your home. Do you know them or not?'

'I've seen Lewis around. I knew his name. Blackpool isn't a large town.'

'I still don't see how you would know his name.'

'Lewis has been on the news before. It's not the first time he's gone missing, which I assumed was why I hadn't yet been spoken to. Red thinks he's a runaway, doesn't he?'

Did everybody in this town refer to the detective inspector by his nickname?

'Red isn't investigating, we are, and we don't think Lewis has run away.'

Skidmore pushed back his chair. 'Well, you're wasting your time here. He's a little old for me. At twelve, he's practically an adult.'

'Guv,' Bryant growled, and Kim got the message. She was on her final warning with her colleague before he did something they'd both regret.

'Where were you on the night he disappeared?' Kim asked.

'I was here, alone. I never left the house.'

'And Sunday night when Noah disappeared?'

He shrugged. 'Same, I'm afraid.'

No way to prove or disprove his alibis, and he knew it.

She stood. 'Excuse me if I don't thank you for your time,' she said, heading for the door.

Once outside, she locked on to his gaze.

'You've been most informative, and I feel I've learned a lot. Not least that you can dress a piece of shit in finery, a crown and call it king, but at the end of the day it's still just a piece of shit.'

She turned and headed for the car beside Bryant, who finally had a smile on his face.

TWENTY

Penn knocked on the door of a woman named Mrs Perton, Lewis's form teacher. She'd been spoken to by Carly Walsh and James Dickinson when Lewis had first gone missing, but that had been at the school prior to the break-up for half term. Therefore, with no access to details of her home address, he had made contact with the school through their Facebook page. Whoever was monitoring it had responded to say they'd passed his message along. No more than two minutes later, he'd received a call inviting him to her home as she was babysitting her grandchildren.

One of those children was holding the woman's hand when she answered the door. A couple of tendrils of brown hair had escaped what looked like a hastily constructed bun on the back of her head, and her only jewellery was a pair of sapphire stud earrings. He guessed her to be mid-fifties.

'DS Penn,' he said, holding up his identification.

'Brenda Perton, and this is Poppy,' she said, nodding down at the five- or six-year-old hiding behind her legs.

'Hi, Poppy,' he offered in his least-threatening tone.

Her face appeared, but she still eyed him suspiciously.

'Pay no mind – she's a shy little thing. Come in,' Brenda said, guiding the girl out of the way. 'We'll go in the kitchen as the little one is asleep.'

Penn said nothing but followed her past the stairs and the lounge to the kitchen, where an assortment of toys littered the floor.

'Sweetheart, play with your toys for a bit,' she said, grabbing the monitor she was using to watch the sleeping child upstairs.

She set it down on the table between them. 'Any news?' she asked.

Penn shook his head.

The sadness that shadowed her face was genuine.

'Is Lewis a good kid?' Penn asked.

'I wouldn't say that, but I've taught worse.'

'We've heard he likes to fight.'

'Probably more than most, but it's not always his fault. He has a bit of a temper, but he gets bullied a lot. He uses his fists to fight back.'

'Bullied for what?' Penn asked, knowing there didn't always have to be a reason.

'A couple of older kids once saw him rifling through bins, so they called him all kinds of names. Sometimes they have a pop at his parents.'

'And how do you find his parents?'

'Not very easily to be honest. They're always busy with something else.'

'Parent evenings?' he asked.

Brenda shook her head. 'Never come.'

'But he's well cared for?'

'Ah, Sergeant, that's a tricky one to answer. Has his childhood been picture perfect with attention lavished on him? No. Is he beaten and starved on a daily basis? Also no.'

'You think he falls somewhere in between?' Penn asked.

'We all do. Did he occasionally turn up at school with no lunch? Yes, but many kids do.'

'Did you ask his parents about it?'

'Of course. They assured me he'd eaten it on the way to school.'

He waited.

'No, I didn't believe them, but it didn't happen again for a while.'

'Can you give me your honest opinion about him?' Penn asked.

Brenda leaned down to her granddaughter. 'Sweetie, go and watch your sister for a few minutes, eh?'

Poppy turned with a frown. 'She's sleeping.'

'Well, go and make sure she's doing a good job of it while I say some things I don't want you to hear.'

'Okay,' she said, choosing a cuddly toy to take with her.

Once she was out of earshot, Brenda began.

'I think the boy is starved but not necessarily of food. I think he's starved of affection, guidance and general parental involvement. Yes, the lad has learned to use his fists, and he's pretty handy with them. He wins every fight he gets into, but he doesn't go looking for trouble. He's a lonely, solitary figure who gets ignored by pretty much everyone.'

'Except you,' Penn observed.

That wasn't in her statement.

'Yes, I've got a soft spot for him, but I can only do so much. I've got another thirty-one in my class that need looking out for as well.'

And yet, Penn felt that she'd been looking out for Lewis Stevens extra hard.

'He's had a few suspensions. Wasn't there one for stealing glue?'

Many teenagers had tried sniffing glue when he was at school. Solvent abuse had been a quick, cheap way of trying to get a feeling of euphoria. He'd tried it once and had only felt disorientated, but he'd had friends who nicked tubes of glue continually before moving on to household aerosols.

'It's not what you're thinking,' Brenda Perton said with a smile.

He waited. Why else would an angry, lonely, neglected twelve-year-old boy be trying to steal glue?

'He likes making models out of old matchsticks. That's why he was rifling in bins and gutters. They're harder to come by these days, but it was something he liked to do.'

More information that wasn't in her statement.

A clearer picture of Lewis was starting to emerge in his mind.

'And do you think he's run away?' Penn asked. She seemed to know him quite well, and he trusted her judgement.

She shook her head immediately. 'Not that particular weekend.' She nodded towards the countertop, where piles of matchboxes were stocked. 'He was excited for the following Monday,' she said. 'I was going to get the whole class to have a go. He couldn't wait.' She frowned. 'What I don't understand is that I've already told the police this. I've told them there's no chance he would have run away.'

Penn seethed silently. Her opinion on the subject was absolute.

Just one more thing that hadn't been recorded in her statement.

TWENTY-ONE

'And the piece of paper was hidden under your keyboard?' Kim clarified. She and Bryant were sitting in a quiet corner at the back of a café, and she'd put Stacey on loudspeaker.

'Yeah, with just three names on it.'

'And?' Kim asked.

'Can't tell you any more. I only have access to the incident log for Lewis. I don't know who these people are.'

'Or why their names were left on your desk and, most importantly, by who. Any guesses?'

'The whole team was in before we were, so it could have been anyone. But DS Walsh struck up a conversation with me a little while ago.'

'Anything interesting?'

'Nothing yet, but we'll see what happens later. I'm trying to get cracking on this CCTV, but I have got an address for Jasmine Swift if you want it. She's the first name.'

'How did you...?'

'Still got access to the electoral register,' Stacey said, and Kim could hear the smile in her voice.

'Text it to Bryant, and good work,' she said before ending the call.

'Well, I appreciate the gesture, guv,' Bryant said, 'but this cuppa is doing nothing to get rid of the bad taste in my mouth.'

Yeah, she too could have done with nipping back to the hotel for a quick shower after their meeting with Roderick Skidmore. Despite his protest that Lewis was in the wrong age bracket for his attention, she wasn't ruling him out. Most paedophiles had a specific age range that piqued their attention but none were averse to a couple of years either side.

Her colleague's phone sounded the arrival of a text message.

'Come on – let's go see what this is about,' she said. The more time and distance they put between themselves and Skidmore, the cleaner they'd feel.

He plugged in the postcode. 'It's only a couple of miles,' he said, starting up the engine.

Maybe just long enough for Kim to work out how she was going to approach this. She had no idea if the names left on Stacey's desk were linked to the case of missing boys or about the actions of the squad.

One thing it did prove was that a member of Red's team wanted to share information. DCI Miranda Walker was right to be concerned.

Kim found herself thinking of some of the police misconduct cases that had made headlines.

Stephen Cloney from Merseyside had sold addresses of drug dens so his contacts could raid the properties and steal the drugs. He'd been jailed for five years.

In May 2019, PC Benjamin Kemp had been approached by a child with mental health issues. He'd pepper-sprayed her and beat her more than thirty times with a baton. He'd been dismissed from the force but not charged with any offence. Unlike PC Benjamin Monk, who'd tasered Dalian Atkinson for thirty-three seconds and kicked him in the head. He'd been convicted of manslaughter.

Met police officer David Carrick had admitted forty-nine charges. Twenty-four of which were rape.

Her own force wasn't squeaky clean. In the last nine years, over seven officers had been convicted of various offences. Plus there was the infamous Serious Crime Squad that had operated from 1974 to 1989, when it had been disbanded following an investigation into incompetence and abuses of power. The team had been guilty of falsifying confessions, partially suffocating suspects to get confessions, and abusing payments to informants. More than sixty of their convictions were later quashed, including those of the Birmingham Six and the Bridgewater Four.

But that didn't make corruption elsewhere any easier to stomach. They all had a duty to root out and put an end to any behaviour from police officers that went against the code of conduct, and she hoped the first person on the anonymous list would help them with that.

Within a few minutes, Bryant was pulling up in front of a small townhouse with an almost-new electric car on the drive.

'How are we doing this?' he asked as they got out of the car. 'We don't even know why we're here.'

'Minor point,' she said, approaching the front door.

A Ring cam peered at her from the frame.

A woman answered with a single, 'Hello,' through the speaker. Kim had no idea if she was home or not.

'Jasmine Swift?' Kim asked.

'Who are you?' she responded without answering the question.

'Detective Inspector Stone and Detective Sergeant Bryant

from West Midlands police,' she said, holding up her identification.

'Hold it closer, please.'

Kim did so. If the woman was home, she was on her own.

'What do you want?'

'A face-to-face conversation if that's possible.'

There was no verbal response, but she heard footsteps approaching the front door.

It opened on the chain.

'ID again, please.'

Kim was happy to show it again. She preferred people to be cautious, and it was telling her enough to know how to start the conversation.

The woman who opened the door was in her early thirties with a mane of black silky hair tied in a ponytail. Her attractive face was enhanced with just the right amount of make-up so that she looked like she was barely wearing any. She wore a purple V-neck tee shirt cut high enough not to be revealing but low enough to show she didn't mind showing off her body. Her black jeans hugged her frame, showing shapely curves. On her feet were oversize dinosaur-feet slippers with claws.

The woman caught Kim's lingering gaze on the footwear.

'Perks of working from home. Not visible on a Zoom call.'

'Of course,' Kim said, following her through the hallway to the only other room on the ground floor.

In other homes, it might have been a living room, but here it had been converted to an office. A small two-seater sofa stared out at a small back garden, while a drawing board and high stool faced the wall. A bin to the left of the drawing board had boxes leaning against it. Everywhere she looked, clues were staring her in the face.

'You're an architect?' Kim asked, taking a seat.

Jasmine Swift perched on her stool and faced their way. 'I am indeed, but that's not why you're here.'

'You work from home?' Kim asked, fishing for another clue.

'Sometimes, when I really don't want the distraction of interruptions.'

Kim listened for any sense of that being a barbed comment but found nothing.

'I'm sure you're wondering why we're here, Ms Swift.'

'Jasmine, please. And yes, I'm a little curious,' she said, bouncing a pencil off the palm of her left hand.

Kim guessed that was one of her thinking tics which she probably wasn't aware that she was doing.

'We're here about your recent burglary,' Kim said.

'Why would that concern you?' Jasmine asked, and Kim offered a silent thanks that she'd guessed correctly.

The Ring cam was new, as was the chain on the door. Her appearance and demeanour were not those of someone who had been sexually assaulted. She didn't work from home because she was afraid to leave the house. And the box leaning against the waste bin had probably held the new laptop she'd had to buy.

'Have you caught them?' she asked with faint hope.

Kim shook her head, knowing the approach she was going to take. 'We have no involvement in the case. We're part of a new initiative, set up since that Met report came out.'

Jasmine nodded her understanding.

Kim continued, 'Some of us have joined together to provide some interforce quality control. We're given a random case and sent to check that the correct procedures were followed and that everything that could be done was done professionally.'

'Okay,' she said a little doubtfully.

Kim smiled. 'So if you could just talk me through your experience, that'd be great. All feedback is completely anonymous.'

'Of course. I was out with some friends and returned home to find my door kicked in. The place was a mess, and most of my electronics had been taken, even my blender,' she said, rolling her eyes. 'I called the police. Two uniformed officers came first and asked a couple of questions, and then CID turned up.'

Was Kim imagining the tightness that washed over her features?

'Go on,' she urged.

'They were very thorough. Asked me lots of questions.'

'Their names?' Kim asked.

'DI Butler and DS Moss.'

Red and Roy appeared to be joined at the hip.

'They got a forensics person to come, but the place was clean. Not a lot more they could do,' she said. 'They offered me some basic advice about security and that was that.'

Except she was no longer tapping the pencil on her palm but wringing her hands instead.

'So, there was nothing more they could have done to help you?' Kim asked.

'No, no. Definitely not.'

'And they were professional at all times?'

'Yes. Yes. Of course.'

Kim was unsure of the relevance of the repetition in her last two responses. Who was she trying to convince and why?

Was there anything else she could ask that would explain why this name had been dropped to them?

'Okay, Jasmine, thanks for your time,' Kim said, standing.

A hint of indecision washed over the woman's face. It was enough.

'In case I wasn't clear, anything you say is in total confidence, and your name won't be mentioned to anyone.'

'You're sure?' Jasmine asked, giving Kim reason to sit back down.

'Is there something you'd like to share?'

'Only if it will go no further.'

Once Kim gave her word, she wouldn't be able to break it. She nodded.

'It was some stuff that happened after the burglary.'

'Like what?'

'It started with a phone call to check on me; just to see if I was okay. I thought that was great aftercare. Then I got a text message with a link to security cameras.'

'Still helpful,' Kim observed.

'With an offer to come fit them for me.'

'Ah.'

'It made me a bit uncomfortable, to be honest. I thanked him but said I'd made arrangements.'

'Go on,' Kim said. She could tell there was more.

'There were more text messages, so my replies got shorter and shorter... but one night he just knocked the door, said he was passing and wanted to check I was okay.'

Kim felt her blood start to boil. She would bet money they were talking about the sleazebag Roy Moss. He had this type of behaviour written all over him.

'What did you do?'

'I told him my mum was on her way over for supper. He got the hint and left. Next night he texted and asked if I wanted to go for a drink.'

Kim's blood was growing hotter by the second.

She'd heard of cases like this before, where police officers preyed on women they perceived to be vulnerable. Jasmine Swift appeared to be educated, professional, single and, most importantly, she was a victim of a crime.

'And?'

She coloured. 'I asked my brother to pretend to be my boyfriend and answer my phone the next time he called.'

'Did it stop?'

Jasmine nodded.

Kim had just a couple more questions. 'Why did you feel ashamed for asking your brother to step in?'

'Well, I should have been able to handle it myself, shouldn't

I? I've never needed my brother to fight my battles, but I just couldn't react the way I would if some guy was bothering me at the pub.'

'Why not?'

'Because I wasn't sure if I was misreading the signs. Whether he was just checking on me.'

'He wasn't,' Kim said. 'And I bet you I can find a hundred victims of crime who don't look like you who have received no such aftercare.'

Jasmine didn't hide her surprise at Kim's comments.

'Our confidentiality agreement works both ways,' Kim said. 'But you didn't imagine it. His actions were inappropriate. Your instinct knew it, and you were right to ask your brother to intervene. Can I ask why you didn't trust your gut and report him?'

'He's the police. What if I'd read it wrong? My complaint wouldn't have gone anywhere, and what if I'd needed to call for help again? I don't know how he would have handled rejection. No matter how well dressed you—'

'Sorry, Roy Moss?' Kim asked, frowning at the description.

'Oh no,' Jasmine said, shaking her head. 'The man that was a nuisance to me was Detective Inspector Butler.'

TWENTY-TWO

Stanley Park was located one and a half miles from the centre of Blackpool and seemed to be doing a roaring trade on this crisp, bright October day. The swings, climbing frames and round-abouts were full of kids of all ages wrapped up in hats and scarves.

Except for one red-faced kid who looked bigger than the others and was throwing rocks at the metal bin.

Looking around, Penn guessed that was the boy he was here to see and that his mum was the woman on the bench handing a pack of sweets to a younger child.

The younger child ran back towards the seesaw as he approached.

'Mrs Davis?' he asked.

She nodded.

When asked if there was any child in particular Lewis had been close to, his form teacher had mentioned a boy named Danny Davis. Being the helpful woman she was, Brenda had made a call to the boy's mother to see if he could meet up with them for a chat.

'Thanks for seeing me,' he said, taking a seat. He took out his ID automatically.

'I believe you,' she said without looking at it. 'We're between meal deals anyway.'

'Meal deals?'

'We had breakfast at Morrisons where the kids ate for free, and tea will be at Asda where I can get them a hot meal for a pound. In between, if it's not raining, we come here. Not everyone can afford to spend time in town even if they live here.'

Penn couldn't imagine walking around all the shops, arcades and attractions with two kids and no money in your pocket.

'Danny, I assume,' he said, nodding towards the bored-looking kid thirty feet away.

'Yeah, just follow the scowl.'

'May I?' Penn asked.

She nodded for him to continue while she focussed on the younger one, who had now moved to the climbing frame.

Penn approached and sat down on the grass close to the boy.

'You Danny?' he asked, offering his hand.

The boy ignored it and picked up another stone.

'Did your mum tell you why I wanted a chat?'

'To talk about Lewis?'

'Yeah. You're a friend of his?'

Danny shrugged. 'Not really. Lewis hasn't got any friends. The others take the pi— I mean take the mickey cos he messes in bins and smells sometimes.'

'But you talk to him now and again?'

'I sit by him in form. I got no choice,' he said, throwing a stone at the bin. He hit it.

Penn picked up a rock and threw it. He missed. He tried again. And missed.

'You're not doing it right,' Danny said as some of the scowl melted away. 'You gotta focus on the bin and throw beyond it.'

'Ah, okay,' Penn said before trying again. This time he hit it and got himself a warning glance from the boy's mother.

'Everybody says Lewis has run away. Do you think they're right?' Penn asked, dusting off his hands.

Danny shrugged. 'Don't think so.'

'He'd done it before, hadn't he?' Penn asked.

'Yeah, ages ago, but he didn't like it very much. Said he was lonely and a bit scared at night.'

'How long was he gone?'

'Two days, I think. One was a Sunday, so he only missed one day of school. I'd have run away in the week and missed two days of school.'

Lewis had now been gone for so much longer than that, yet everyone still seemed to believe that the kid was going to walk back in the door with dirty clothes, an empty stomach and a mouth full of sorrys.

'Is he happy at home?' Penn asked.

'His brother's a bit of a dick, and his mum ignores him, and his stepdad gets pretty riled up when he fights and stuff.'

'But you don't know of anything that would make him take off again?'

Danny shook his head.

'How about being followed or approached by strangers? Did he mention anything like that?'

'You mean like paedos?'

It was a shame that twelve-year-olds had to know about stuff like that.

'Yeah, that kind of thing.'

Again, Danny shook his head, but for the first time he turned and looked at him. 'He's dead, you know.'

'Wh... what?' Penn asked, astounded.

'He told me his parents wanted him gone.'

Penn calmed down.

'Most kids think that about their parents,' he said. 'You've probably felt the same way. You've probably annoyed them and thought they wanted you gone, eh?'

Danny shrugged and turned away again. 'Yeah, but Lewis actually heard them talking about how they were going to do it.'

TWENTY-THREE

The second name on the list left under Stacey's keyboard belonged to Dean Jackson, who, it turned out, lived above a small café two streets away from the Promenade.

'Now why am I already feeling like this guy probably did something wrong?' Bryant asked as they rang his bell.

'Honestly, you are so judgemental sometimes,' Kim said, but the same thought had crossed her mind. Possibly it was the graffiti scratched into the front door, or the cigarette ends piled up in the corners, or even the presence of recently deposited spit pools on the floor that she was actively trying to avoid.

Knowing she secretly shared his view, he gave her a sideways glance as the door opened.

'And you can just fuck off,' said the man behind it, who had taken one look at them before glowering.

'Excuse me,' Kim said. They hadn't even had a chance to speak.

'I can smell bacon a mile off. Not locally sourced, but you're both still pigs.'

This wasn't starting exactly as she'd hoped because she already wanted to smack him in the mouth.

She guessed Dean Jackson to be mid-twenties. He was tall and gangly and looked like he was crying out for a good meal.

'Whatever you're here for, I didn't do it and I was at my girl-friend's.'

Good to know he had a pre-paid alibi.

'You don't even know why we're here,' Kim protested.

'Nothing good can come from your lot. So unless you've been sent to tell me I've won the lottery and you're my protection from thieving bastards, you can just fuck off.'

The man's hostility was leading nowhere. But it was hardly the first time she'd been faced with an aggressive interviewee.

'Mr Jackson, we just want to ask you a couple of questions.'

'Yeah, course you do. That's how it starts. Well, I ain't falling for that again.'

'We think you can help us with something,' she said. 'And for the record, you haven't done anything wrong.'

He considered for a second.

'May we come inside?' Kim pushed.

'Nope. Ain't going nowhere without witnesses. Plenty folks around at the minute so I'd rather stay in full view.'

This guy had some serious issues when it came to the police, but his words were giving her a clue about how to approach this.

'My colleague and I are from West Midlands police. We've been invited by the local force to review some recent incidents of police contact for the purpose of making improvements going forward.'

His expression was incredulous as he laughed in her face. 'Are you having a fucking giraffe?'

'Sorry?'

'Laugh. Are you having a laugh? First of all, no one would send you my way to discuss police contact, and secondly that's the biggest load of bollocks I've ever heard.'

'It's the official explanation I'm giving to find out what happened between you and the local team,' she said honestly.

'Makes no odds to me why you're asking. I'm happy to talk.'

She nodded towards the café. 'Do you want...?'

'I'm fine, thanks, and this won't take long. Basically, I was hauled in for questioning over a string of robberies. Someone said they saw me in the area when one of them happened. I said I didn't do it, and those bastards were convinced I did. They smacked me around a bit, kicked me in the bollocks and tried to get me to confess. My first three requests for a solicitor were ignored.'

'Did you report it?'

'Course I fucking did, but it went nowhere. They said my bruises were from a physical detainment and that I played up. I didn't at first, but after the second smack I got pretty fucking annoyed.'

'Didn't your solicitor fight the case for you?'

He shook his head in wonder. 'I ain't sure whether you're from the West Midlands or the planet Zog. It was my word against theirs, and CID don't wear bodycams. I got nothing more to say. I'm wasting my breath. Don't know why you're asking but nothing will get done. You lot protect your own. We don't stand a fucking chance.'

'Are you prepared to give me names?'

As she had no access to the local system, she was unable to find out any other way without raising suspicion.

'Sure. It was Butler and Walsh.'

'You mean Moss and Butler?' Kim asked, frowning. This had to be a mistake.

'No, I mean DI Red Butler and DS Carly Walsh. That bitch has got a fucking donkey kick on her. Now if you're done, piss off.'

Kim hid her surprise as the man re-entered his home and slammed the door.

She turned back towards the car and moved right into the

path of Steve Ashworth. Her heart jumped into her mouth as he grinned at her.

'Well, well, well, fancy seeing you here, Inspector.'

'Naff off,' she said, trying to get round him.

He stepped right in front of her.

'Hey, pal,' Bryant said, moving closer.

Kim's expression warned him off.

'What the hell are you doing here?' she growled.

'I go where the story goes, and right now, you're here in sunny Blackpool.'

'You followed us?' she asked incredulously.

'Well, when we last chatted I saw you put an overnight bag into your colleague's car and I thought, oh that looks interesting. Never realised we'd be coming quite so far, but hey, who doesn't like a few days in Blackpool?'

Kim was wracking her brain for any law he'd broken. There was nothing.

'Now, I'm guessing that the local force needs a bit of help, given they keep losing young boys. Why they chose you is beyond me.'

'You don't think the missing boys is a story worth covering?' she asked.

'There's plenty of people on that one, yet there's no one on you. Surprising but I'll take it. Now, would you like to comment on the name I mentioned yesterday?'

'I'm good, thanks,' she said, moving around him.

'Do you know where Amber Rose is now?' Ashworth asked.

Kim ignored him as she waited for Bryant to unlock the car.

'Do you keep in touch with her at all? I'd love to talk to her too.'

Kim continued to ignore him as she slid into the passenger seat.

She moved to close the door, but he leaned down into her space.

'Get away from—'

'One last question, Detective Inspector. Do your colleagues know that you were responsible for the death of an innocent man?'

Kim shoved him out of the way before closing the door.

Bryant pulled away from the kerb quickly but not before she saw the smirk playing on the reporter's face.

'Wanna talk about it?' Bryant asked once they were out of view.

She shook her head. Why would she want to talk about the single biggest mistake of her life?

TWENTY-FOUR

Stacey checked the board one more time before opening up the first batch of CCTV files. She had printed out photos of everyone connected to the case so far. Most of them were family members, and to the right was a photo of Roderick Skidmore. She had decided to work through the footage chronologically and focus on every action she could see from the minute Lewis had approached the amusement arcade.

She located the time stamp for when he entered through the doors opposite McDonald's. Although it was dark beyond the entrance, she was sure she'd be able to pick him up from further in the distance. She moved the cursor to the rewind icon and moved back five seconds, then looked to the middle of the frame and saw Lewis cutting across Central car park on Bonny Street. She moved back a further five seconds to wait for him to come into view at the top of the frame.

She was surprised to see that he was already in shot, just about, but he wasn't moving. His position matched the trajectory of the snippet she'd already watched, but he was seemingly just standing in the middle of the car park. He wasn't looking down, and no light from a mobile phone lit up his face. His hands were in his pockets, and he was still, as though listening. And then he moved further into shot as he started walking towards the arcade.

She went back another five seconds. Already standing at the edge of the frame.

Another five seconds.

Already there.

Another five seconds.

He moved into shot.

Stacey checked the time stamp of him moving away from the spot.

Forty-four seconds.

Who was he standing talking to for forty-four seconds?

She made a note of the time and returned to the footage where Lewis entered the arcade. She continued watching for a minute or so, analysing the expressions of the people who came in behind him.

Her heart stopped as she noticed a figure enter the arcade just a minute after Lewis.

She knew exactly who it was.

His photo was staring at her from the board.

TWENTY-FIVE

'Oh, Jesus,' Kim said, reaching for her phone as Bryant pulled up outside the home of the third person on the list.

They were two streets back from the Promenade, and the house was in a row of four at the end of some boarded-up shops.

'Wassup?' Bryant asked, glancing down at her phone, which had just tinged a message. 'Is it your bestie again?'

'Bryant,' she warned him.

'Okay, sorry. Is it Frost?'

'Yep,' she said with a long sigh.

'What now?'

'She wants to know where I am and what time I'm finishing work.'

'Why?'

'I think the beer and wine glass emojis might be a clue.'

'Guv, I am really trying not to find this situation amusing,' Bryant admitted.

'And failing miserably,' she said, tapping out a response.

'What did you say?'

'Mind your own bloody business,' she said, getting out of

the car. He was enjoying her predicament far too much for her to keep him fully updated.

The reality was she was receiving more messages than she was sharing with Bryant and responding to them too, all because she didn't know how to tell the woman the truth.

She'd think about that later, she resolved as they walked up the path towards what looked like a crack house.

The door was opened before they even reached it.

'You raiding?' asked a guy in his early twenties, wearing only boxer shorts.

Kim shook her head and produced her identification. He didn't even look at it.

'Sallright,' he shouted over his shoulder.

'Pippa Jacobs live here?'

'Should think so – it's her place,' the guy said before calling over his shoulder again. 'Pip, some coppers are here.'

She heard a rustling of movement from the space behind.

He rolled his eyes as he called backwards again. 'They ain't raiding – I already told you once.'

'May we come in?' Kim asked.

'It's not my place,' he said, indicating he wasn't going to move out of the way.

If they were raiding, there were no prizes for guessing what they'd find. The natural police officer in her wanted to storm in and arrest every drug taker in her way, but this wasn't her area and it wasn't her problem to solve. The police clearly knew about it as this woman was the third name on the list – she must have interacted with the CID team.

'Where's the usuals then?' the man asked, looking them up and down.

'Get raided a lot, do you?' Bryant asked.

'Pretty regular. Weekly.'

Kim was prevented from asking the obvious question as a woman appeared behind him. Kim guessed her to be late twenties with a five-year margin either way. Her gaunt frame and prominent cheekbones signalled she was a user. But it was more than that. There was a deadness in her eyes that Kim rarely saw.

'What do you want?' she asked, stepping in front of the man who'd opened the door. 'All right, Chase, go back in.'

He looked directly at Bryant. 'Nah, I'll hang around.'

'I'm good. Bugger off,' she said, nudging him aside.

After a final dark look at Bryant, Chase turned and left the hallway.

Bryant cast Kim a questioning glance. She didn't know what was going on either, but there was a hint of nausea rising in her stomach.

'You get raided much?' Kim asked, repeating her question now that Chase was gone.

'Plenty. What's it to you?'

'On what charges?'

Pippa shrugged. 'No charges. Now what do you want?'

There was a remoteness about her that Kim found unnerving, and it had nothing to do with drugs. She was broken. Something inside her had shrivelled up and died.

'Do you get busted for prostitution or drugs?' Kim asked.

'None of your business. Now ask a different question or fuck off.'

A picture was starting to form in her mind, and it sickened her.

'The same folks keep raiding you?'

Pippa's face hardened, and she nodded before looking down at her feet.

Broken or not, she still felt shame.

'Moss or Butler?' Kim asked.

'Moss, but I don't want no bother. I've got a transfer,' she said, nodding towards the house. 'I'm swapping with a couple who've got a flat in Lytham next week, so I really don't want any hassle.'

Kim nodded her understanding.

'So, what are your questions?' Pippa asked, biting her lip.

'My mistake, Miss Jacobs. I actually have no questions. Sorry to have bothered you and hope your move goes well.'

The woman frowned as they moved away, and she closed the door.

'Well, that was a waste of bloody time, wasn't it? What are you playing at?' Bryant asked as they headed for the car.

'I didn't feel the need to force her to relive it. She feels shitty enough.'

'Guv, I've got no idea what—'

'Think about it. Follow the clues. She's a prostitute. She does it to fund her drug addiction. She gets raided every week by the same person and yet she's not arrested or charged with any crime. Why not?'

'Aww, shit,' Bryant said as the penny dropped. 'He's demanding sexual favours for silence.'

'That's a nice way of putting it. He's threatening her with charges for sex. He's the worst kind of—'

'And you want me to befriend this guy? Act like I've got something in common with him?' he asked, revulsion pouring out of him.

Kim nodded as her phone rang. It wasn't her first choice to put Bryant in the man's company, but it was their best chance of witnessing something that could be used against him.

'Go ahead, Stace,' she answered.

'Boss, you might want to do a revisit. Someone isn't telling you the truth.'

TWENTY-SIX

NOAH

The light through the small dirty window was Noah's only indication of passing time. He thought he'd spent one night sleeping after being given the funny water to drink, but his perception of time was distorted. Then, yesterday, the man called Mister had returned twice, and then darkness had fallen. He thought it might now be Tuesday, but there was no way of knowing for sure. He didn't know how long he'd slept, and more nights might have passed without him knowing.

On the first visit of the day, the man had said his name was Mister. He had said nothing more while emptying the bucket. Noah had shrunk into the corner, wondering if he was going to be examined as he had been the night before. He had shivered with fear as Mister had squeezed and touched his arms, turned him around and pinched his thighs and his calves. Just when he'd thought his bladder might betray him, Mister had loosened his grasp and moved away.

He'd removed the pack of biscuits and left fresh water and a donut with a stern instruction to eat. Noah had tried a mouthful but had vomited it back up within seconds.

He didn't know how many hours passed between the first

and second visit, but when Mister had returned, he'd brought more water and two tablets. Noah had swallowed the tablets while Mister stood over him before checking his mouth. Satisfied the tablets had been swallowed, he'd left the room again. Minutes later, he'd returned with a plastic container on a plate. Steam had risen from what had smelled like some kind of tomato-and-pasta dish.

'Eat up or I'll force it down you,' Mister had said before closing the door behind himself.

Noah had ignored the dish for a few minutes, but the smell of hot food permeating the tiny room had travelled from his nostrils right down into his stomach.

He'd taken a closer look at what appeared to be spaghetti bolognaise, then lifted the plastic fork and taken a bite. He'd smoothed over the gap that had been left, not wanting to give Mister the satisfaction of him doing what he was told. Then he'd looked at the gloopy mess and thought he could probably take another forkful and smooth it back over to make it look untouched.

Four forkfuls later he'd realised that he could no longer hide his appetite and resolved to finish it all but to hang on to the fork. If he had more strength and a weapon, maybe he could escape the next time Mister came in the room.

He'd pushed the plate aside and waited, expecting that the tablets he'd swallowed would make him sleepy. But the drowsiness hadn't come.

He was still wide awake when the door opened for a third time. The window told him it was night-time, and he hadn't expected to see Mister again.

The man nodded approvingly at the plate and picked it up. He held out his hand. 'Fork.'

Noah took the piece of plastic from his pocket and handed it over, trying to still the trembling of his hand.

'Stand up, Noah,' Mister said from behind his mask.

Noah could see that a piece of cloth hung from his pocket.

'Strip to your underpants,' Mister said calmly.

'Wh... what?' Noah asked, feeling a fresh tidal wave of fear.

'Take everything off except your underpants or I'll do it for you.'

The voice was neither kind nor unkind. Just firm.

Noah hesitated.

'I'll give you to the count of five.'

Noah removed his fleece and his tee shirt. The cold circled his bare skin.

He shivered as he pulled his jeans down to his ankles and stepped out of them. He linked his hands together and held them in front of his body. Despite the underpants, he felt completely naked and terrified of whatever was to come next.

'Good boy,' Mister said as he took the blindfold from his pocket and slipped it over Noah's eyes.

TWENTY-SEVEN

Kim hadn't expected to return to the home of Roderick Skidmore quite so soon, and she'd hoped to be carrying a warrant when she did. Unfortunately, she wasn't in a position to carry out a full-scale search on the basis that he'd told her a lie.

He'd been at Coral Island at the exact same time as Lewis and had literally followed him through the door. He hadn't legally done anything wrong by being in the same area, so why had he felt the need to lie about it?

That was the burning question on her lips as they pulled up at the wooden double gates.

Kim got out and pressed on the intercom.

No answer.

She pressed again, holding her finger on the button for a good ten seconds.

'H-Hello...' said a tentative female voice.

'May we speak with Mr Skidmore?'

'He's not here,' said the voice.

'Can you let us in?' Kim asked.

The gate began to slide open. She walked through the gap

while Bryant waited for the opening process to complete so he could follow with the car.

A woman in her late fifties stepped out of the house dressed in plain black trousers, a sweatshirt and a cleaning smock top.

'Is he home?' Kim asked.

She shook her head. 'He called and asked me to come and close up for him.'

'Close up?' Kim asked.

'I clean for him three times a week, but my usual day is tomorrow. He said he was going on a business trip and that he'd forgotten to tell me.'

He'd forgotten to mention it to them earlier as well.

This wasn't planned. It was only a few hours since they'd been here, and he'd shown no signs of being about to go away.

'Did he say how long he'd be gone?' Kim asked.

She shook her head. 'Just said to maintain my usual routine,' she said, showing them a single key with a gate fob attached.

'Any idea where?'

'Other business trips have involved Thailand. He has a place there.'

Yes, what self-respecting paedophile of considerable means didn't have a hideaway in Thailand?

Despite its beauty, the country was one of the top five worst countries for child prostitution, along with Sri Lanka, Brazil, America and Canada.

She'd read that due to the hidden nature of the business, accurate figures were hard to come by, although it was estimated that in Thailand some thirty to forty thousand children were being exploited as prostitutes. Where else would the bastard have a holiday home?

'And is this rare?' Kim asked.

'Not his trips. He goes once, maybe twice every month, but I normally know about it ahead of time.'

So, what had spooked him into leaving so suddenly? Had he suspected they were going to be paying him another visit?

'How long have you worked for him?' Kim asked.

Maybe it wouldn't be a totally wasted journey if this woman could tell them more about Skidmore.

'Four years.'

'And you don't mind...?'

'Of course I mind, but I've got a kid with special needs. This way I don't have to leave him for twelve hours a day to afford to take care of him.'

Obviously, the man paid well enough for her to put a pause on her principles. Kim couldn't really judge her. She had bills to pay – and expensive ones by the sound of it.

'My family don't know though,' she admitted, putting her hands in her pockets.

Yeah, it was nothing to shout about either.

But since she'd worked for him for four years, Skidmore had to have some kind of trust in her.

'Have you ever seen or heard anything that makes you uncomfortable?' Kim asked.

'God, no, and if it wasn't for the sex offenders' register and those pictures on the wall, you'd never know that...' She pulled a face. 'You get my drift.'

'Okay, thanks for your time,' Kim said, turning away. Her questions were just going to have to wait.

'No problem, but...'

'What?' Kim asked, turning back.

'I shouldn't really say, but there's a cellar. He keeps it padlocked, and I never clean it. I don't know what he does down there, but whatever it is, he doesn't want anyone to see.'

'Okay, thanks,' Kim said, heading for the car as she took out her phone.

Red answered almost immediately.

'We need a warrant,' she said, getting into the car. In an

ideal world, she would have applied for the search warrant herself, but this wasn't her force, and all official channels had to be navigated by the home team.

'For where?' he asked.

'The home of Roderick Skidmore. He's got a secret room, and he's done a runner. He's looking—'

'I'm not wasting my time,' Red said, cutting her off before she'd even told him the best bit.

She felt her features wrinkle in confusion. 'Did you hear what I just said? He also followed Lewis into the arcade, and now he's disappeared.'

'I heard you. It's not as compelling as you think it is. The man likes to play the poker games at the arcade, and having a locked room in your home isn't a crime.'

Kim couldn't believe what she was hearing. 'Have you seen the artwork in his house? And I know you know about his conviction.'

'I don't need to see it to know it's not going to be Impressionist masterpieces, but it still isn't gonna get me to ask for a warrant. Leave it alone. He's not our man,' Red said before ending the call.

Kim stared at her phone in disbelief. A known paedophile who seemed familiar with both boys had been proven to be in the same area when the first of them went missing and that didn't deserve immediate attention from the senior investigating officer?

Red's refusal to obtain a warrant coupled with the gaping holes in the investigation were sounding alarm bells in her head. She was beginning to think that Detective Inspector Butler didn't really want these young boys found at all.

TWENTY-EIGHT

Stacey's timeline of Lewis's movements was starting to come together after trawling through fifty-six cameras.

The hours she'd spent interrogating the footage meant she now had a good idea of camera sequence and location, so she could follow someone's movements. There was a logic to the system that enabled her to move around it efficiently.

Lewis had been in the arcade for half an hour, and so far she had trailed his every movement for twenty-four of those thirty minutes.

He had walked through the arcade in no great rush. He'd glanced at some of the machines, paused by others. The whole time his right hand had been deep in his pocket as though clutching his five pounds tightly.

At the bottom of the ramp that led to the lower level, he'd put the five-pound note into a machine to get change.

He'd wandered into an enclosed space and had a few plays on a fruit machine and then wandered out again, before approaching the window that displayed the prizes that could be won from the ticket machines.

Stacey had been able to track his every move, and he'd spoken to no one.

He'd then dawdled back up the ramp and entered the café area, where he'd bought a can of Coke and sat at a table close to the window.

At this point, he'd been sitting alone for four minutes, sipping his drink. Stacey wondered if she'd ever seen a lonelier-looking kid. He certainly didn't look like the troublemaker they were being told about.

She knew he left the arcade in six minutes' time, but she refused to skip ahead. She wanted to be able to account for every second he was in that arcade. What she was failing to understand right now was how this hadn't already been done.

'Yo, comrade,' Penn said, entering the war room.

'Anything?' Stacey asked.

'Yeah, the kid likes making matchstick models.'

Stacey waited.

'Not many friends, respectful to teachers, doesn't go looking for fights but always wins them, and he seemed to think his family were planning on getting rid of him.'

'Blimey, not bad,' she said, trying to reconcile the matchstick-model maker with the terror that his family had portrayed.

'Yeah, and the boss wants me looking at flights to Thailand. Looks like Skidmore might be on one of them. Any luck with the footage?' Penn asked, taking two cans of Coke from his man bag. He slid one across the table towards her.

'Nothing so far, but...' Her words trailed away as she glanced back at the screen. In the few seconds since she'd looked away, someone had slid into the booth opposite Lewis.

It was Kevin. The fifteen-year-old brother who said he hadn't seen Lewis once he'd left the house.

The older boy leaned forward, elbows on the table. Lewis took another sip of his pop and stared down at it.

Despite not being able to hear the words, it was easy to see that Kevin was doing all the talking – and quite loudly. His posture was forward and animated. Occasionally, Lewis would shake his head, but he continued to stare at his drink. Kevin paused for breath now and then or to look around the café, but then went right back into his urgent speech.

Lewis only offered head shakes and shrugs as responses.

Kevin took something from his pocket and thrust it at Lewis. It was a phone.

Lewis refused to take it, shaking his head vigorously.

Kevin also shook his head with what appeared to be despair as he put the phone back in his pocket.

He pushed himself up and stood at the end of the table as though giving Lewis one last chance.

Lewis didn't move a muscle, not even when his brother passed by him, balled his fist and gave him a good smack on the side of his head.

Given what Penn had just said, Stacey couldn't help but wonder which member of his family had wanted to see him gone.

TWENTY-NINE

It always felt surreal to Kim when they visited the same property at both ends of the day.

Their meeting with the Stevens family had been their first of the day. Darkness was now falling around them, yet they still didn't have a clue where Lewis was.

'Gonna start charging you lot rent,' Bobby Stevens grumbled, stepping aside for them to enter.

Kim was doing her absolute best to keep in mind that this was the family of a missing boy. Either her empathy tank was running on fumes, or the vibes they were giving off didn't match the distraught and concerned family dynamic she usually encountered.

'No, we haven't found him yet,' Kim said pointedly, entering the home. 'I'm sure that was going to be your next question.'

'Not really. I've already said that he'll be found when he wants to be.'

'Mr Stevens, why are you so convinced he'll turn up safe and sound?'

'He's a resourceful kid,' he said, heading into the kitchen.

Unlike the day before, they appeared to have caught the tail end of teatime. Shirley was putting away the dishes, and Kim could hear the younger kids squabbling over the remote control in the other room.

Free to speak openly, Kim continued. 'But did he take anything? Clothes, shoes, money, valuables? When kids run away, they normally take a few bare essentials, even if it's just some bags of crisps and a chocolate bar.'

She was no longer content to let Lewis's parents bury themselves in ignorance.

Bobby Stevens shrugged as Shirley turned and leaned against the countertop.

'You want to destroy our hope of getting him back?' she asked.

'I want you to be realistic about where he is. Most runaways, even the ones that return quickly, undertake some kind of planning. Maybe they pack one bag with some favourite things; they definitely take a few items of clothing. Lewis took nothing. He walked out of the arcade and just disappeared.'

'Red and Roy agree with us,' Shirley defended herself.

After the day Kim had had, those were two names she didn't really want to hear, and the statement was no recommendation.

'Did you know there was a known paedophile in Coral Island at the exact same time as Lewis?'

'Wh... what?' Shirley asked.

'Not that fucking Skidmore bloke?' Bobby asked. 'He's in that arcade all the time. He'd have no interest in Lewis.'

Kim wasn't yet prepared to reveal that they knew Lewis had had an exchange with someone in the car park, but she was having trouble stomaching everyone's dismissal of a known sex offender. If they could get a shot of Skidmore anywhere near the car park, she'd haul him in herself with or without Red's authorisation.

'We haven't yet established any contact between them... But that's not actually why we're here.'

'Why then?' Shirley asked, frowning.

'Could we just speak to Kevin for a minute?' Kim asked.

Bobby stepped into the hallway and called the boy's name.

'Why can't you ask us?' Bobby asked as footsteps sounded on the stairs.

This man clearly liked to know everything that was going on. It was as though he wanted to answer questions directed to every member of the household. Why would he need that level of control over what his family might happen to say? Kim wondered. She ignored his efforts to control the interview and said nothing in response.

Kevin appeared in the doorway but didn't come into the room.

'Got a minute, Kevin?' she asked.

He nodded.

'Do you want to do this with or without your parents?'

'It's fine,' he said after just a second's hesitation, giving Kim the impression he might prefer without. But as he was a minor, she was on dodgy ground trying to insist. Especially as he'd now stated he wanted them present and from the looks on their faces they weren't going anywhere.

'Okay, Kevin, why didn't you tell us you saw Lewis again after he left the house?'

His parents looked at each other and then at Kevin, eager to hear the answer.

'I just wanted to talk some sense into him. He was being a little shit.'

'Is that why you hit him?' Kim asked.

She was rewarded with expressions of surprise on all three faces.

Kevin had to know now that the whole exchange had been caught on camera.

'I hit him cos he wouldn't listen. He kept saying he was gonna run away,' he said, looking to his parents.

'Told you,' Bobby said.

'He was talking about running away at that table and you didn't bother to tell anyone?' Kim asked.

'Bloody knew it,' Bobby heckled again.

'Everybody assumed it anyway so there was no point,' Kevin said, chewing his lower lip.

Kim wasn't finding this story particularly believable.

'Why did you offer him your phone?' she asked.

The question caught him off guard.

'I, err... told him to call a taxi if he wanted to run away that badly.'

His story wasn't getting any more believable.

'How was he supposed to afford that?' Kim asked. 'He had less than a fiver in his pocket.'

Kevin shrugged and stared at the ground.

'And you never saw him again once you left the café?'

He shook his head.

Kim was all out of questions, but she was sure she hadn't got all the right answers.

She stood to leave.

'Hey, make sure you're back in time to tuck us in,' Bobby joked as she headed for the front door.

For some reason, she thought she detected a note of relief in his tone.

As the door closed behind them, Kim knew she had to consider that Kevin had played some role in his brother's disappearance. He'd been angry enough to strike him, and he could have been waiting for him somewhere along the route home. It wasn't like he hadn't taken his brother off somewhere before.

But then why had Bobby sounded relieved after her exchange with Kevin, as though he was pleased that the boy hadn't revealed something?

Why hadn't Kevin told either his parents or the police that he'd seen Lewis again?

And why had he blatantly lied about the conversation that had taken place between them in the amusement arcade?

Yes, it was official – she now had more questions than she'd had when she'd got there.

THIRTY

Kim timed their return to the station to ensure she'd be able to have a briefing with her own team before they joined Red Butler's team for theirs.

Penn had just updated them all on his meetings with Lewis's form teacher and his friend Danny.

'Danny said Lewis never told him exactly what he overheard, but he said Lewis definitely heard his family talking about getting rid of him.'

Kim considered this admission and found there was little they could do with it. She wasn't as surprised as she should have been, but without knowing exactly what Lewis overheard, they had no idea where to start. She wasn't sure the statement of a twelve-year-old boy who couldn't remember the exact wording of what his friend heard was going to hold weight with anyone she needed to convince. She needed something more concrete before Red would consider there was something deeply suspicious about the Stevens family.

'And I've checked with Thai Airways, the most popular airline for that destination, and Skidmore isn't booked on any of their flights. But there are still a few airlines to check.'

'Stay on it, Penn,' Kim said. Roderick Skidmore may have packed a bag and told his cleaner of his plans, but she wasn't totally convinced he was leaving the country. Her gut said they'd been fed that story so they wouldn't look for him anywhere else. Especially once they found out he'd lied about being at Coral Island.

'I didn't see him anywhere near Lewis inside the arcade,' Stacey said as though reading her mind.

'Doesn't mean he wasn't the person in the car park and the reason Lewis didn't move for almost a minute,' Bryant offered.

'True,' Stacey admitted. 'Next I want to interrogate every camera on that side of the building to see if anything that far back on the car park is visible.'

Kim nodded her agreement. They needed to do everything possible to find out who Lewis had been talking to before entering the arcade.

She glanced into the main squad room before speaking again. The local team was starting to drip into the room.

'Okay, the three names that were left under Stacey's keyboard all have a story to tell about this team. Jasmine Swift felt intimidated by Butler after a burglary. He got a bit too familiar and made a nuisance of himself. She handled it herself with the help of her brother, and he hasn't bothered her since. No way in hell she's raking it up again, so we have no current complainant there. Dean Jackson says he was smacked around by two of the team. Already tried to complain and it went nowhere.'

'Butler and Moss?' Penn asked.

'Butler and Carly Walsh apparently.'

'Wow,' Stacey said, obviously fighting the urge to look Carly's way.

They all knew that eighty-two per cent of officers referred forward to misconduct proceedings were male. That still left eighteen per cent of the total complaints being about women.

'And finally, we have Pippa Jacobs, a prostitute and drug addict who is being harassed for sex in exchange for not facing charges.'

'Gotta be Moss,' Penn and Stacey said together as the man himself entered the squad room, followed by his boss.

'No chance of a complaint from her. She's got a house exchange to Lytham next week and just wants to get away from him.'

'You taking any of this to the chief?' Stacey asked.

'We've got nothing,' Kim said. 'Not one complainant on the record. We gotta go deeper. But right now we've got a briefing to crash,' she said as DC Dickinson sauntered in to complete the Blackpool team.

She turned to her colleague. 'Bryant, please don't take offence at what I'm about to do.'

'Okay.'

She headed for the door, and her team followed.

'Hope you don't mind us joining the party,' Kim said. 'You'll make the drinks, won't you, Bryant?'

His face tensed as he headed towards the kitchen.

Exactly as she'd hoped.

THIRTY-ONE

Bryant wasn't surprised when Roy Moss sidled in behind him. It was what the boss had been hoping for.

'Fucking hell, mate. That bitch treats you like shit. Wouldn't you just love to smack her one?'

'Just treading water, mate,' Bryant replied without looking at him. If he could pull this off, he'd be making an application to drama school. The only person he wanted to smack right now was the man getting mugs out of the cupboard. Every atom of his being despised Moss's thoughts, actions and attitude, and having to bite his tongue was proving near impossible, even though they needed Moss to do it to expose him. So far he'd indirectly insulted both Stacey and the guv, leaving only Penn up for grabs... but being a straight white male, he wasn't going to warrant too much attention.

Moss followed his lead and lined up the mugs for his own team, then frowned. 'Shit, don't really know if they have sugar or not. Carly always makes them.'

Of course she did, Bryant thought.

Bryant knew he wasn't perfect when it came to police conduct. Over the years, he'd laughed at inappropriate jokes or failed to speak up on someone's behalf when maybe he should have done, but as the system had improved and evolved, he'd been more than happy to evolve with it. And never, not once, had he abused his position as a police officer for his own gain, either with his team or with the public.

They'd been given the names of three people to speak to, and it was Moss who was involved in the worst of those three cases.

The broken demeanour of Pippa Jacobs would stay with Bryant for a very long time.

He wanted to run to the chief himself and lay bare what they'd learned, but he knew the guv was right. They didn't have enough, and they had no one to back them up.

'Hey, I know what'll cheer you up,' Roy said, taking out his phone.

Bryant continued to make drinks for his team.

'Feast your eyes on this,' Moss said, looking around furtively before showing Bryant the screen.

On it was the image of a woman in her mid-twenties. Her trousers were around her ankles, and her shirt had been ripped open, exposing her breasts. She was lying amongst dead leaves and weeds. And she was dead.

Bryant worked hard to keep his rage from boiling over and forced his face to remain impassive. He stared at the screen not because he wanted to but because he honestly couldn't believe what he was seeing.

'Last big case. Rape and murder. Not much of a looker but great tits.'

Bryant thought he was going to throw up.

He nodded in agreement before looking away as a wave of self-loathing swept over him. He had to focus on the bigger picture. If he knocked the guy out right now, he'd be removed from the case and robbed of the chance to find something that would definitely send this bastard down.

'Did you catch him?' Bryant asked, stirring the tea.

'Nah, nothing physical left behind. Bastard got away with it.'

'What was her name?' he asked, trying desperately to uncover just one shred of humanity in the bloke.

'Dunno. Layla, Lucy or something.'

'Got any more?' Bryant asked, praying for him to say no.

'I only take the good ones. Gotta have something to remember them by, and you gotta make your own fun in this job. You?' Moss asked.

'I'm shit at not getting caught,' Bryant said, trying to put the image out of his mind. He couldn't bear the thought of the victim's family not even knowing that their loved one was suffering this final indignity. 'My boss would catch me if she was half a mile away. Got eyes in the back of her head.'

'Yeah, doesn't surprise me,' Moss said, pouring water into the mugs in front of him. 'She wouldn't last long if she was my boss,' he added as Bryant picked up the tray.

Bryant bit his lip hard to prevent any retort coming out of his mouth, then headed back into the squad room, wondering how the hell he was going to keep this up.

THIRTY-TWO

Kim could tell from her colleague's hard stare that something had happened in the kitchen. She wondered briefly what it was costing him to maintain this charade. She'd check on him once the briefing was over.

'Hope you don't mind me jumping in,' she said, moving to the front of the room. 'But we really need to merge these investigations and assume the disappearance of Lewis and Noah is linked,' she went on, even though she wasn't totally convinced they were. The Stevens family were hiding something to do with Lewis, which suggested otherwise, but there was a nagging feeling in her stomach that the two cases were connected somehow. Additionally, linking the investigations would allow her to keep closer tabs on the Blackpool team.

Red began to shake his head. 'You gotta trust us on this. Lewis is a runaway. We've investigated—'

'And you've identified the person Lewis talked to in the car park for more than thirty seconds?'

This time Red looked at Adil, Dickinson and Carly, who all remained silent.

'And you absolutely have to know that Kevin, the brother

who already dumped him somewhere in the past as a punishment, caught up with Lewis in the arcade café, shouted at him and smacked him before storming off?'

Red was saved from answering when his phone rang. He held up his hand to excuse himself and took the phone into their mini squad room, closing the door behind himself.

Kim stole a glance at Stacey, who gave a slight shake of the head to indicate that nothing concerning the three names they'd been sent was on show.

Red paced back and forth a couple of times while looking their way.

'Don't think anything you've said is grounds to change the way we're investigating,' Roy said, folding his arms over his stomach.

'Sorry, Roy, didn't hear your boss temporarily promote you while he stepped out to take a call,' Kim said, meeting his gaze. His expression left her in no doubt about his feelings for her and she couldn't care less.

'That was Bobby Stevens,' Red said, rejoining them. 'Kevin left the house after being grounded, and they can't reach him on his mobile phone.'

Roy started to clap. 'Bravo, Inspector. Two for the price of one. That poor family now has two missing boys.'

'Shut up, Roy,' Red snapped at him, surprising everyone in the room, before looking her way again. 'They don't want you to visit them again.'

'You don't find that suspicious?' Kim asked. 'And since when did we take instruction from suspects?'

'They're not suspected of anything. They're missing one child, and now they're missing another. For the time being, I'd prefer you didn't contact—'

'Hang on. We've uncovered more about Lewis's disappearance in twenty-four hours than—'

'Wait one minute,' Red said as his entire team gave her

daggers. 'Let's not get personal and keep this about the case. Whatever their reasons, the Stevenses are still victims right now, and we'll honour their request.'

The atmosphere in the room was charged.

Kim was guessing she wasn't popular with any members of the local team right now and that was okay with her. As long as the rest of her team remained open and approachable, there was a chance they could finish what they'd come here to do.

'Right, let's call it a night,' Red said as Iris walked in with her vacuum cleaner. 'Temperatures are way too high. Dickinson is stopping by the Reids on the way home, and we'll debrief about Noah first thing. I'll consider your suggestion that the cases are linked, but for now I need to go and ask uniforms to keep an eye out for Kevin Stevens.'

'Mind if Penn tags along to the Reids'?' Kim shot out. 'He's very good with families.'

Red hesitated before shrugging. Good, she'd hoped he was done battling for one night. And it would be useful for one of her team to get a read on the other family while spending some time with one of the quietest members of the home team.

Dickinson stood, and Penn took his cue, following the Blackpool detective constable out the door.

The rest of the local team filed out with silence and dark looks.

'And the Miss Congeniality award once more goes to Detective Inspector Stone,' Bryant said, once they were alone. 'What I don't get is why you should have all the fun?'

'Perks of the job,' she said, checking the time on her watch. 'Okay, guys, nothing more we can do until they let us into Noah's case tomorrow. Back to the hotel, get a good meal and a good night's sleep. The only question I've got left is what happened in the kitchen, Bryant?'

'Crime scene photos on his phone. Young female, raped and murdered.'

'Bloody hell,' Stacey said, shaking her head.

Bryant was struggling to speak in full sentences, as though he wanted the filthy words out of his mouth as quickly as possible.

'He didn't even know her fucking name,' he said as his voice rose. 'What kind of man, never mind police officer, attends the scene of a girl raped and murdered and can't even remember her fucking name?'

Stacey was busying herself with something on her screen. No one liked it when Bryant lost control of his anger.

'Bryant, calm—'

'No offence, guv, but being told to calm down has never induced someone to actually calm down.'

Kim showed no reaction, but his language and his tone told her he was having an extreme reaction to Moss. Completely understandable, especially as he was father to a daughter himself.

She agreed that Moss's actions were beyond despicable. No victim or their family deserved that kind of indignity. But if it was a single incident, it wasn't going to get him thrown off the force, and that was exactly what they needed to do.

'Stace, head down to the car,' Kim instructed.

Stacey gathered her belongings in record time. Kim only spoke again once she'd left the room.

'Bryant, if you haven't got the stomach for this, tell me now. I won't judge you, and I'll send you back down to our patch.'

He didn't answer immediately, and when he did it was barely more than a whisper.

'Let me sleep on it, guv. You'll have my answer in the morning,' he said, heading towards the door.

She followed him silently down to the car.

She could ask no more of him than that.

THIRTY-THREE

Kevin backed into the shadows as the detectives who had visited his house a few times left the building. Even though they couldn't see him, his heart was beating hard in his chest. He was sure they knew he was there.

He'd turned off his phone. His mum and Bobby had been blowing it up, wanting to know where he was.

He was making them nervous because he knew everything.

He'd tried to stop it all from happening, but his brother wouldn't listen. He'd only needed to make one phone call and it probably would have all ended there and then.

Ever since he could remember, he'd tried to look out for Lewis. It had always been just the two of them after their dad left. He'd been upset himself, but Lewis had been just six years old and had taken it worse.

They didn't only lose their dad. A big part of their mum left too. There was no more fun, no more games or silliness or laughter. He didn't understand at the time that she'd been focussed on working and making enough money to support them. The mum they knew had been swallowed up by stretching money, cutting costs, doing extra shifts and paying bills. There had been no time or energy for having fun. So they'd made their own fun and had grown closer than ever.

And then their mum had started to smile again. They'd catch her humming in the kitchen or putting on a bit of perfume. She was happier and the whole house was lighter. She started chasing them to their rooms again, buying them little treats and taking them to the park.

And then she'd brought Bobby home.

At first, Bobby had been amazing. He'd showered them with love, time and presents. They'd lapped it up. Their mum had been happy and laughing and even better than the mum she'd been before.

It was after the wedding that everything started to change.

Bobby moved into their house and the fun times stopped. Both he and Lewis had realised that it had all been an act to get what he wanted. He wasn't overly mean, just disinterested. He rarely engaged with them and seemed to want them out of the way.

Then his first new brother had come along and the arguing had started.

Kevin came to realise over time that his stepdad was just plain lazy. He did nothing around the house, did nothing to help with the babies as they came along, and struggled to hold down a job.

Their mum was once more reduced to the quiet, penny-pinching shadow of herself as she worried about making ends meet, while Bobby seemingly worried about nothing.

Once the third new child came along, neither he nor Lewis got any time with their mum.

At the same time, Lewis started getting into fights and their parents started being contacted by the school. Each time something happened, their mum looked at Lewis as though he was just one more problem she could do without.

And yes, he had taken Lewis to Lytham and dumped him, but not for the reasons everyone thought.

He'd wanted his mum to worry about his brother. He'd wanted her to miss him and grow concerned, but it hadn't worked that way. She'd almost been relieved that she didn't have to think about him for a while.

Lewis had returned a few hours later, got a telling-off and not one thing had changed.

And then there'd been the burglary.

Out of nowhere, Bobby had decided to treat them all to the cinema.

When they'd returned, the house had been done over. Very little damage to the back door, minimal mess, but a lot of stuff taken – all the electrical items and most of their mum's jewellery.

The insurance payout had replaced the items with a fair bit left over. But that money had run out, leaving the family once again broke with no signs of Bobby getting a job again any time soon.

It was the burglary that had first brought the detectives to their door. They'd been honest about the likelihood of catching the thieves, and Bobby hadn't been too worried about it.

During their second visit, Bobby had asked them to have a word with Lewis. Tell him about the possible consequences of his behaviour, basically scare the shit out of him.

It hadn't worked. Then Kevin had started hearing his parents having hushed conversations that ended abruptly when he entered the room. From the snippets he heard, he understood the plan, but he hadn't ever thought they'd go through with it.

Not until the night they gave Lewis some money and sent him out of the house.

He'd tried to stop it. He really had. But now his brother was gone and he didn't know what to do.

He'd wondered if he could trust that new copper his parents didn't like. That was why he'd come to the station. To see if he could catch her on her own. He sensed she felt something wasn't right.

Then he saw her, and his courage deserted him.

She was heading towards the car with that other detective.

Thoughts started crashing through his mind. What if she didn't believe him? What if she told his parents what he'd done? What if she told the other detectives what he'd said?

But his biggest fear – and the thing that stopped his feet moving in their direction – was the final question.

What if she was as bad as the rest of them?

THIRTY-FOUR

Penn knew that his task with Dickinson was two-fold. No one had managed to get a read on this particular officer yet. He spent a great deal of time listening but not much talking. And the second objective was to observe Noah's parents and see if anything stood out as suspicious.

Thinking of suspicious behaviour, Penn decided to remain quiet on the journey to the Reid family home. If the moment they were alone he started firing questions at Dickinson, there was a chance he could blow their whole cover. He also had to take time to slide into the persona he'd been instructed to adopt.

The role of ambitious young officer wasn't as big a stretch of the imagination as the one Bryant was being asked to convey, but it was still pretty alien. Ambition had never been part of his make-up. He'd never been competitive and had always focussed on the journey, not the destination. If he enjoyed something, he did it, but he didn't feel the need to win at it.

So far, Dickinson had hardly spoken to any member of the team, barely even looking their way unless he had to. Penn had to tread carefully.

No words had been exchanged by the time Dickinson

pulled up outside a semi-detached property with a double drive just three miles out of Blackpool.

'Let me do the talking, okay?' Dickinson said as they got out of the car.

'Of course,' Penn answered. He knew next to nothing about the case anyway.

The door was answered before they got anywhere near it.

'Mr Reid,' Dickinson said, holding out his hand.

The man shook it while never taking his eyes from Dickinson's face.

Dickinson shook his head as Mrs Reid appeared beside her husband. A small sob escaped from the woman's lips as they let him into the house. They followed them down the corridor into the kitchen, Dickinson introducing Penn as they went.

'Why would someone from Birmingham be interested in Noah?' Mr Reid asked as he reached for the kettle.

'Not for me,' Dickinson said, holding up his hand. 'It's more of an observation exercise. The Birmingham team have little to do with Noah's case. That's being handled by the officers you know.'

Both parents appeared reassured by that fact, and Penn fought the urge to clarify that the Black Country was not Birmingham. Although factually correct, Noah's parents wouldn't give a shit.

'I just wanted to drop in and catch up. Are you sure you won't consider a family liaison officer? They could...'

'No,' Mrs Reid said emphatically. 'I don't want a stranger in my house. The place feels weird enough.'

From the photos on the wall, it appeared that Noah was an only child, so unlike with the Stevens family, there wasn't even the distraction of other children running around.

Dickinson took a seat at the kitchen table opposite Mrs Reid, while Mr Reid remained close to the kettle. Making drinks was the most common displacement activity, regardless of the situation.

'He's going to be out there again tonight, isn't he?' Mrs Reid said, glancing towards the kitchen window, where darkness had now fallen.

Dickinson neither denied nor confirmed it. 'Every officer working is looking out for him, and our enquiries continue through the night. We have people talking to shop and restaurant staff, and we're uncovering more potential witnesses all the time. It only takes one person to have seen something, and—'

'I still don't get it,' Mr Reid said, shaking his head. 'You say he left the pier and we were right across the road. How could he just disappear?'

Penn didn't feel like the man was expecting an answer to the thoughts he was letting come out of his mouth.

'He's not going to do well, you know,' Mrs Reid said, clasping her hands together. 'He's not a tough boy. He's never had to fend for himself. He's eleven. He only just started high school. He's never even been camping.' Tears were gathering in her eyes.

Mr Reid left the kettle and took a seat beside his wife, his face full of concern and fear. 'It's okay, love. They'll find him. And he's stronger than you think,' he soothed her, taking her hand.

'But this'll be his third night,' she said, turning towards her husband. 'He's never been away from us for that—'

Her words were cut off as Mr Reid pulled his wife into his chest and allowed her to sob against him.

'We won't intrude any further,' Dickinson said, getting to his feet. 'I just wanted to reassure you again that we are doing everything we can to find Noah and to let you know we're here to support you too. The minute we find out anything, you'll be the first to know.'

Mrs Reid removed her head from her husband's chest. 'Thank you.'

'We're going to find him, Mrs Reid,' Dickinson said, touching her arm lightly before stepping out of the room.

Penn followed the detective out of the house, wondering if that was the kind of promise he should be making. But what else was one to say in this situation?

As he got in the car, Penn observed that there seemed to be a marked difference between the treatment of the Stevens family and the Reids. To his knowledge, there was no nightly visit to offer an update to the Stevens family, nor even regular phone calls. He had to wonder where that directive had come from.

Nothing in that house had troubled the hackles on the back of his neck. The parents' appearance was in stark contrast to that of Bobby and Shirley Stevens's behaviour, but so was the treatment being afforded them.

He'd pass on his observations to his boss in the morning, but in the meantime he had a second task to attend to.

Once Dickinson pulled away from the house, Penn took out his phone and began to scroll. 'Damn,' he cursed under his breath.

'Everything okay?'

Penn sighed and put his phone away. 'Yeah, just missed a deadline on a job opportunity.'

'You not happy where you are?' Dickinson asked, taking the bait.

He shrugged. 'They're not bad, but I'm not emotionally attached if that's what you mean. No room for upward movement, and it's getting a bit stale.' He was trying hard not to overplay his hand and let Dickinson do some of the heavy lifting.

'You want DI?' Dickinson asked.

'Of course. Don't you?'

Now it was Dickinson's turn to shrug. 'I'm thirty-two. I've got plenty of time.'

'Nah, I can't be thinking like that,' Penn said. 'I want DI by thirty-five and DCI by forty. Never gonna happen if I spend too much time in one place.'

'You seem pretty tight with Wood though,' Dickinson said.

Penn laughed. 'I'm tight with anyone who suits my purpose, and I try to keep on the good side of my boss. A recommendation from my DI would go a long way, so I've gotta keep her sweet.'

Penn could see from the pinched expression on the other man's face that this was going nowhere. Dickinson wasn't identifying with the character he was playing.

'It's not for everyone,' Penn continued. 'Some folks don't want the added paperwork or headaches. I kinda wish I'd found a team where I wanted to stay long term.'

'Sometimes acceptance amongst the majority of your colleagues means more than a few extra quid in your pocket.'

'Oh yeah, couldn't agree more,' Penn said, reading between the lines. He suspected Dickinson was gay, and his team knew it. His first impression of the man had played into the stereotype, which had made him careful not to attach any label to the guy. Taking good care of your hair and skin didn't automatically mean the man was gay, but it seemed that, on this occasion, his gaydar had been tuned in well.

Secretly, he totally understood the comfort and security of finding such a team, but he couldn't admit that in the role he was playing. 'Good for you. Moss doesn't seem much like the accepting kind though.'

'Roy doesn't know everything about everybody,' Dickinson said tightly, telling Penn that he knew exactly how Moss would react to the news and that he'd never have a minute's peace going forward.

'Yeah, we've all got our old-school coppers, but they're all gonna die off eventually,' he offered as Dickinson pulled into the Blackpool station car park.

'Not totally convinced we should have to wait for bigotry and racism to retire,' Dickinson replied with an edge to his voice.

'Yep, there should be a better way. But while they're clean and doing a decent job...'

'And what if they're not?' Dickinson asked, pulling alongside Penn's car.

'Then I suppose we've all gotta do what we gotta do,' Penn said, opening the car door.

He stepped out and pushed the door shut, waving as Dickinson pulled away, but the detective seemed focussed only on driving.

Penn opened the door to his own car and couldn't help wondering one thing after that conversation. He'd discovered that, on the face of it, Dickinson was a loyal team member who didn't have the stomach for bad policing.

But was there any chance at all that he'd just found their snitch?

THIRTY-FIVE

Keats hated calls to water more than any other kind. It was one of the worst environments to find bodies in. Often, the waxy, bloated appearance made the victim look like a grotesque version of their former selves.

He also felt that he was getting too old for these five o'clock callouts.

It wasn't looking good for his behaviour towards the investigating officer, he thought as he approached the Dudley canal basin. And he knew which one he was hoping for. It was always a bonus if he could work out some of his aggravation by poking at his most adversarial detective inspector. His jibing released his pent-up frustration and ensured he could do his job more efficiently, for which everyone else around him was grateful.

But there was no sign of her presence as he approached the group of high-vis jackets watching the body being removed from the water.

The dive team of six had encased the body in a waterproof body bag to preserve any trace evidence that might still be present. The body bag had then been placed onto a float and was being gently pushed to the edge of the basin.

Amongst the uniforms, Keats spotted one man dressed in a suit and a three-quarter-length jacket. His name was Detective Inspector Waines, and he was known for wearing the camel overcoat on all but the hottest of days.

'And here's our resident pathologist looking bright-eyed and bushy-tailed,' Waines said, slapping him on the shoulder.

Keats didn't like him very much, not least because he hadn't bothered to read the memo about not touching your colleagues.

Although that wasn't the main reason he disliked the inspector. He was bland, vanilla. He offered no moments of brilliance or creativity. He asked no questions and issued no challenge. Keats couldn't bounce off him like he could other officers. There was no entertainment value. Keats knew his humour would go right over the detective's head.

'Sorry we disturbed your morning cereal, Keats,' Waines continued with a smirk that said he was nothing of the sort.

Keats ignored him and moved forward to Inspector Plant.

'Who called it in?' he asked.

'A jogger.'

He offered Plant a look. 'Sorry. Never understood the fascination.'

Plant laughed. 'Me neither. I'm not keen on any form of exercise that gets me out of bed in the dark before I'm ready to start my shift. Not to mention they're always finding bodies. This guy bent down to tighten his laces and saw a limb caught on that branch.'

Keats glanced across. Waines was heading towards the jogger, a man in his late twenties.

'Why's Waines here?' he asked. 'This is Halesowen's remit, isn't it?'

'Yeah, but the whole of Halesowen CID is off on a jolly to Blackpool, I heard.'

Keats frowned. He was pretty sure they wouldn't have all

gone to see the lights together, but it was nothing to do with him.

'Hey, Keats, they're coming out,' Mitch called to him.

He went to the side of the basin as the dive team lifted the body bag out.

He kneeled down and slowly unzipped the bag. His gaze swept over the victim as horror hit him right in the chest. Instantly, he knew three things:

The victim had not died by drowning.

The body had not been in the water for very long.

And there was only one person he trusted to work this case.

He took out his phone and made a call.

THIRTY-SIX

It was six thirty before Kim joined her team for breakfast in the hotel restaurant. She had news, and she wasn't sure how they were going to feel about it. But first she wanted an update.

'Learn anything last night?' she asked as Penn sat down with a full English.

'Family seems genuine. I don't think they're involved,' Penn said, trying to find the rip line in a ketchup sachet. 'No other children, and Noah appears to be the centre of their world.'

'And Dickinson?'

'Empathetic to the family, caring and considerate. Treated them well and reassured them the team was doing everything possible to bring the boy home.' He turned the sachet up the other way. 'Gotta be honest, boss, the Reids are getting way better treatment than Lewis's family.'

Stacey took the sachet from his hands, ripped it open and handed it back to him.

Kim shook her head with despair. 'It's this bloody fixation on him running away. It's stopping them from considering the family's suspicious behaviour or the fact the cases could be linked.'

'They just won't consider any other option,' Stacey noted.

Kim nodded before turning back to Penn. 'And what did you learn about Dickinson himself?'

'Pretty sure he's gay and that most of the team know it and couldn't care less, except Roy.'

'He definitely doesn't know,' Bryant added. 'He'd never shut up about it. And he wouldn't be saying anything Dickinson would want to hear.'

'He seems loyal to his team and has no great ambition to move up. Came across as straight up and doesn't think bad coppers should be tolerated.'

Kim's interest was piqued. 'Is he our source?'

Penn shrugged. 'I couldn't say, boss. He was only sharing his opinion, but I get the feeling that if he knew anything, he'd likely do something about it.'

'Okay, keep an eye on him. In other news, I've gotta head back home, folks,' Kim said. 'Keats has got a body and he won't tell me anything else, only that he's not handing this to anyone else.'

'But, boss...' Stacey protested.

Kim held up her hand. She'd already guessed there would be some objections.

'I understand we're all invested in trying to find Lewis, which is why we're not all going back. Two of us will stay here to—'

'I'd like to stay, guv,' Bryant said without hesitation.

'You sure?' she asked. Last night, he hadn't been sure whether he could stomach one more minute in the company of Roy Moss. Perhaps some alone time and a call to Jenny had recharged his batteries.

'I'm positive,' he said and sounded it.

'Me too, boss,' Stacey said, and Kim understood her reasoning. She'd made decent contact with two members of the local team, so removing her and installing Penn in her stead would put them back to square one.

'I'm easy on,' Penn said with a shrug.

'Guess you'll be driving us back then.' She paused. 'I've informed Woody that we're splitting the team up, and he was okay to a point. He wants to help his old training partner, but a murder trumps a missing boy, so expect a call any time. If I need you down there, that'll be the end of it.'

They both nodded their understanding.

'And you'll probably be folded into the team working under Red's supervision, so I can't allot tasks, but you both know what you're looking for?'

Bryant and Stacey looked at each other and nodded again. Kim could see how passionate they were about trying to find Lewis, as well as uncovering the depth of the corruption and protecting whichever team member had made the complaints.

Kim couldn't shake the feeling she was abandoning her team. They were grown adults undertaking a serious and responsible job, but for some reason she felt like she was throwing them into the middle of a pack of wolves.

THIRTY-SEVEN

'How do you reckon this is gonna go?' Stacey asked as they walked into the building.

Bryant had been wondering the same thing himself. It wasn't that they needed the guv for protection, but their team had been cut in half. In fairness, they had both chosen to stay, so they had to be prepared for whatever came their way.

He'd done exactly what he'd told the guv he would do. He'd slept on it. Part of him had wanted to ask to be sent back so that he'd never have to lay eyes on Roy Moss again. But the man had no place on the force, and he knew if there was any way he could contribute to exposing him, he had no choice but to swallow down the bile that now lived in his mouth and get on with it.

'Just one thing, Stace,' he said as they made their way to the squad room. 'If Moss says anything even remotely out of place, you tell me.'

'Jeez, Bryant, I can—'

'I'm not pulling any kind of macho, misogynistic crap on you, or implying you can't take care of yourself, but the man is a racist, sexist pig.'

'Yeah, cos I've never come across one of those before,' she said with a smile.

'He's on another level. I wouldn't put anything past—'

'Okay,' she said, cutting him off. 'I'll let you know.'

He breathed a sigh of relief as he opened the door into the squad room for Stacey to step through.

All eyes fixed on them. Bryant felt like they were the new kids in class.

'Sorry, you got stuck with us,' he said with what he hoped was a disarming smile. 'The guv had an urgent case back home.'

Red waved for them to sit down. 'No point in keeping everything separate with just the two of you.'

'So, you think the two cases could be linked?' Bryant asked pleasantly, taking a seat. Maybe what they'd uncovered yesterday had shocked some sense into them.

'Not really, and the focus is still going to be on Noah, but if we come across anything compelling, we'll consider it.'

Bryant mused that he'd simply traded one pig-headed boss for another; although, in fairness to his real boss, she was never arrogant enough to hinder an investigation rather than admit she was wrong. He wasn't sure what could be more compelling than the facts they'd uncovered yesterday – but the guv had made it clear. Red was in charge.

'Okay, quick update on Noah for those at the back. Noah Reid is eleven years old and was out with his parents on Sunday night for his birthday treat. Mum and Dad popped over to Wetherspoons to grab a table, leaving Noah to spend his last few pounds on South Pier. He should only have been a few minutes behind, so after twenty minutes Dad went looking, and after another hour of frantic searching, we got the call. CCTV at Spoons show the parents' actions matching their account, and an attendant recalls seeing them all together at the basketball hoops earlier as they claimed, so they've been ruled out.' He paused for breath. 'So far we've interviewed over forty people and no one saw a child being manhandled. There's no CCTV on the pier, and the properties across the road are too far away to have caught anything.

'One report from a street vendor said there was some kind of electrical contractor van parked up on the pavement close by, which we're looking into, and we're still interviewing tram and bus drivers who might have been passing by at the time.'

So, this was how they conducted an investigation when they hadn't made the assumption they were dealing with a runaway, Bryant thought. The time and effort being spent on Noah was in stark contrast to the attention given to Lewis.

'I'm gonna mix things up today to get fresh eyes on the Noah case. Roy, you're with DS Bryant.'

Bryant covered his internal groan with a nod. It was what he'd both dreaded and hoped for.

'Wood, you'll be given access to the current case files, so have a good look over everything. Walsh, you're with me at the tram depot, and Dickinson and Gonk, keep chasing up the electrical contractors. Roy, take Bryant with you to interview the last couple of staff members on the pier.'

Everyone nodded their understanding.

'Oh, and folks in dispatch know we've got extra pairs of hands, so don't be surprised if you get a call trying to task you to other incidents. You know what trumps the case we're working, so if you get any shit, just tell me.'

Red headed back to his desk, and everyone started to gather their stuff.

Roy was first on his feet, and Bryant followed.

He stole a quick glance at Stacey, who nodded that she was fine, before following Moss out the door.

What the hell was he going to find out today?

THIRTY-EIGHT

NOAH

The straw was no more comfortable on his bare skin now than it had been the night before when he'd first been moved.

Mister had tied the blindfold and guided him wordlessly out of the house. He had understood why he'd been allowed to keep his shoes on when he felt the cool night air on his skin and gravel crunching beneath his feet.

'Stay quiet,' Mister had said. After less than a minute, he'd felt the surface beneath his feet change. He was now walking on concrete, and the air was warmer. There had been a smell that reminded him of when his mum had taken him to see the beach donkeys.

Noah had heard something open before he was pushed forward, then he'd felt the sharp straw scratch against his ankles.

'Sit down,' Mister had said calmly.

Noah had done as he was told.

Mister had taken his right hand and held it flat to the ground, then a chain had been pulled around his wrist. He'd instinctively recoiled from the cold metal and tugged his arm away. Mister had grabbed it again but rougher this time and slammed his palm to the ground.

'No talking,' Mister had said as he'd removed the blindfold.

Noah had watched him leave through the gate of the pen he'd been placed in. It was smaller than the box room, and there was a brick wall to his left and a breeze-block wall to his right. In front of him was a wooden fence and the gate. It reminded him of an animal pen from when his dad had taken him to a petting zoo. He couldn't stand, but it looked like a similar pen was directly opposite.

The overhead lights had gone out, and he had fallen asleep.

It was now Wednesday morning, as far as he could guess. He hadn't seen his parents in three days.

He suddenly heard rustling and froze in terror. What other animals were in here with him? Could they get to him through the fencing? Did they bite?

For some reason, Noah felt even more frightened than he had before. His parents hadn't found him yet, and there was something about this move that felt more permanent, as though he wasn't going to be leaving here for a while and his captors knew it.

The realisation that his parents might never find him hit him hard. A sob escaped from his lips, and once it did a torrent followed. He couldn't stop the tears that flowed over his cheeks. These strangers had taken him, and he didn't know why. They weren't nice, and he didn't know what they were going to do with him. He just knew he was losing hope of ever seeing his parents again.

A cry caught in his throat as he heard a sneeze. And another.

Someone else was in here with him.

He felt both hope and fear at the same time.

'Who's there?' he called out.

'Shush,' he heard from across the space.

'Where are you?' he called.

'Shut up,' came the terse response. 'You can't talk or we get no food.'

'Please, just tell me—'

'You gotta shut up. Do you wanna get us killed?'

Noah shook his head as he heard the barn door open.

He didn't know where he was or what they wanted him for, but at least now he knew that he wasn't the only one.

THIRTY-NINE

Despite Penn's car looking as though it was held together by masking tape, superglue and a prayer, it had got them down the hundred plus miles of motorway in good time, landing them at Russell's Hall Hospital just after 9 a.m.

Admittedly, it wasn't as comfortable a ride as Bryant's Astra Estate, she mused as they headed towards the morgue, but she'd been more preoccupied with what had prompted Keats to summon her specifically despite her being over a hundred miles away. There were other detectives, and one would have been assigned immediately, so there had to be a reason Keats had requested her, and she doubted it was just for his own amusement.

Jimmy, Keats's assistant, opened the door as they approached. The pathologist was scrubbing up in the anteroom.

'Okay, Keats, explain yourself,' she said, reaching for the protective clothing that was already laid out.

'Good morning, Inspector. I heard you were all up in Blackpool, so I'll curb my curiosity as to why we have young Penn here instead of Bryant. I am sorry to disturb your holiday, but I have a body.'

'Only one?' she asked. She'd been thinking it was some kind of triple murder.

'Yes, only one but—'

'There's no one else that could have handled it?' she asked, thinking about the rest of her team left to the mercy of the Blackpool squad.

'They sent me Waines,' he offered by way of an explanation.

'Competent,' she said, although she'd never worked with him herself.

'I want better than competent for this poor soul. I want dynamic, engaged, passionate and persistent. In the absence of those things, I'll take you.'

'Hang on,' Kim said, raising an eyebrow. 'Back up a minute. Is that some kind of compliment?'

'If you're that desperate for praise, take it how you will. In the meantime, follow me.'

Kim did as she was asked and followed the pathologist to the first metal table in the row of three. A sheet still covered the form.

'Are you ready?' he asked.

She nodded.

He peeled back the sheet to reveal sandy blonde hair, then a face, a young face, narrow shoulders, an emaciated frame, dirty boxer shorts, pronounced hip bones, thin legs and bony feet.

Kim remained silent for a minute as she took in the scene before her.

She guessed the boy to be no older than fifteen.

It wasn't only his young age which saddened her, but as Keats had uncovered the body a bit at a time, he had revealed more and more areas of bruising. The skin was a canvas of yellow, purple and red bruises. This boy had been beaten relentlessly.

'This is how he was found?' she asked.

Keats nodded. 'At the Dudley Canal basin. No other clothing was found, but he didn't drown. I'd say this was the culprit,' he said, pointing to a line of bruising that stretched all around the boy's neck.

Kim frowned. The body looked barely touched by water. She'd seen plenty of drowned victims in her time.

'Not very long, is the answer to your next question.'

Kim waited.

'I'd say he'd been in the water barely longer than an hour,' Keats answered. 'I can't tell you yet exactly how long before that he was murdered, but I'll try and offer something a bit tighter once I've had a chance to chat with him further.'

Kim knew Keats's 'chat' entailed the dissection of every major organ in the quest for answers. She also knew that every step of that process would be carried out with respect and sensitivity.

'Anything else for now?' she asked, taking one more look at the body.

'Nothing, except for the fact that you have to find whoever did this.'

She left the morgue and headed into the anteroom with Penn two steps behind her.

Was it chance that she was helping to investigate the disappearance of two pre-teen boys and had been called back home to the body of what looked like a fifteen-year-old boy?

Yes, there was a few years' difference between the boys, but she didn't believe in this kind of coincidence.

Keats popped his head into the room as she removed the protective slippers.

'Your case then?'

She nodded. 'Yes, Keats, this time you were right to give me a call.'

FORTY

It didn't take long for Bryant to realise that Roy did everything as though he was the only person that existed.

They had barely travelled a mile before their car had been honked at and shown the finger more than once.

'Bet you can't believe the bitch has been called back, eh?' Roy asked. 'Sometimes you just gotta believe in God, eh?'

It was surreal to hear the man refer to God in any way. He had to be the least God-fearing man Bryant had ever met. But today he was better prepared to play along.

'Oh, yeah, gives me the chance to do some real police work, and maybe have a bit of fun at the same time,' he said, slipping into his despicable character. Although he had the guv's permission to play this part, he still felt a stab of guilt every time he badmouthed her.

Roy laughed. 'If it's fun you're after, I've got a doss house that needs raiding later. That'll brighten your day.'

Bryant glanced out of the window to hide the tension that had shot into his face as a picture of Pippa Jacobs's lifeless eyes, broken spirit and fearful demeanour came into his mind.

He was pretty sure she wasn't having any fun.

'Listen, we're not gonna get a lot from these on-the-pier guys, so we'll chat for half an hour then go find somewhere out of the way for a cuppa.'

'You don't think they can help find Noah?'

'Nah.'

'His parents must be going out of their minds,' Bryant said – a not-so-subtle reminder of the job at hand.

'Shoulda thought about that before they left the kid alone. Their negligence means a ball-ache for us. If the kid ends up dead, who do you think is gonna get the blame – us or the two grown adults that left him on his own? Seriously, it pisses me the fuck off when folks have kids and make 'em somebody else's prob—' He stopped speaking as his phone rang.

No surprise that he took it from his pocket, answered it and held it to his ear while driving with one hand.

He listened for a few seconds.

'Where?' he asked.

In response to the answer, he replied that they were on their way before ending the call.

'Change of plan, my man,' he said, pulling into a private drive to turn the car around.

Bryant held on to the side of his seat.

'Boss said we might get a call, and this is a big one. Gonna show you folks how we do it up here.'

Yeah, please show me how you can investigate poorly in a haphazard manner, Bryant thought as he held on for dear life.

A sense of relief coursed through Bryant when Roy finally pulled the car to a screeching halt at the cordon tape serving as a barrier to an industrial estate.

Every head, from members of the public to police officers, turned. He was reminded of the opening credits to the old seventies cop shows where the main characters zoomed in to save the day.

Seeing who it was, the police officers quickly lost interest, but the public were still watching them closely as Roy barged his way through the crowd.

The officer keeping the log managed to nod at Roy without even looking up.

All activity was focussed on a small industrial unit which appeared to be unused.

Roy spoke to no one as he approached. A man whom Bryant assumed to be the pathologist appeared to curse under his breath.

This wasn't his case, meaning he was free to observe the reactions of the people around him, and he'd yet to spot anyone pleased to see Roy Moss.

'Step aside,' Roy said to no one in particular.

They did so, and Bryant found himself frozen to the spot.

His gaze had landed on the figure of a woman in her late twenties.

Her jeans were pulled down around her ankles and her underwear pulled down to her calves. Her sweatshirt was rolled up, exposing her bra. A single line had been cut across her neck; the wound had bled down to her breastbone and into her black hair.

'Shit,' Roy said, running a hand through his hair. 'I know this woman.'

'Oh yeah,' Bryant croaked out, trying desperately not to give himself away.

He knew her too.

The face he was looking at belonged to Jasmine Swift. The woman they'd visited the day before. The woman who'd reported a burglary and then been harassed by DI Red Butler.

Bryant had to turn his face away to hide the shock written

all over it. He was sure Roy would know in an instant that he wasn't looking down into the face of a stranger.

How was it possible that a woman they'd just spoken to was now lying raped and murdered not five feet away from him? Had they caused this? Did someone know they'd spoken with her? Was someone covering their tracks?

His first instinct was to take out his phone and call the guv. This young, vibrant woman was dead, and he didn't know if they were the cause of it. But he had to hold his nerve. There was nothing the guv could do to help Jasmine right now, and any strange behaviour on his part would only appear suspicious.

Only when he was sure he could keep his expression impassive did he turn back to the body at his feet.

The similarities to the crime scene photo Roy had shown him were astounding.

'Looks similar to...'

'Yeah, yeah, exactly what I was thinking,' Roy said, stroking his chin.

'How long's she been dead?' Roy asked, looking at the pathologist with whom he had exchanged not one civil word.

Dealings between his boss and Keats were hardly warm and fuzzy, but at least they were cordial to each other.

'Twelve hours or thereabouts,' the pathologist said, glancing at Bryant as though waiting for an introduction.

'Anything else I need?' Roy asked, completely devoid of manners.

Bryant could see the pathologist bristling at the sergeant's manner. Rather than answering, he turned away to consult with one of the forensic technicians.

'Now's your chance,' Roy hissed in his ear as he took out his own phone.

Hell no, Bryant thought. The very idea of taking a photo made him nauseous, but he took out his phone anyway. As he raised it, he knocked his elbow into Roy's hand, sending his phone clattering to the ground.

The pathologist turned and gave Roy a hard stare.

Roy mumbled his apologies and retrieved his phone, but the moment was lost. The pathologist's attention was now firmly back on the victim.

Small triumphs, Bryant told himself. The man was as despicable as they came, not to mention rude, insensitive and arrogant, but at least he wouldn't be poring over any photos of this poor soul any time soon.

'Fuck me, man,' Roy said as they headed back towards the car after what must have been Bryant's shortest ever crime scene visit.

'Yeah, I bloody told you. I always get caught.'

'Crime scene ones won't be anywhere near as good. I had the perfect angle to see right up—'

'So, where now?' Bryant asked hurriedly.

'Ah, well, I already know a bit about this lovely lady, so I think we'll start with her ex-boyfriend.'

'Not her family?' Bryant asked. Surely her next of kin were the first people to contact?

'Yeah, we'll let someone else do that. First line of suspicion has to be the ex, and I know exactly where he lives.'

'But surely—'

'My man, you gotta throw away the book you're living by. Up here, we do real police work, and you should already have realised, Toto, that you ain't in Kansas any more.'

FORTY-ONE

'Anything?' Kim asked, placing a cuppa on Penn's desk.

'I've gone back two months so far and there's nothing that fits the age or description of our victim.'

She'd left Penn to interrogate the missing persons reports while briefing Woody. Although he wasn't thrilled that Keats had summoned her, he understood her decision to return. He also supported her resolve that if she needed to, she'd summon the rest of her team back in a heartbeat.

Right now, her priority was in putting a name to the face she'd looked down on at the morgue. Learning someone's identity was always a priority, not least so the family could be informed, but also because everyone deserved to be referred to by name rather than as a body, or a corpse, or a victim. She knew her compulsion stemmed from spending years as a nameless, faceless part of the care system as a child.

She took a seat at Stacey's computer and logged in. Penn was taking the logical approach and working backwards. She really didn't have that kind of time to find out if there was any chance of his death being linked to the investigation up north.

If her age estimate was right, then the boy in the morgue was around fifteen years of age.

Lewis was twelve years old. Noah was eleven.

She entered the *from* date search field and entered *January 2020*. In the *end* search she entered *December 2022* to cut the search in half. Penn would be working his way back towards her.

Kim began flicking through the records, glancing at the photos, confident that she would recognise the boy in the morgue. Seventeen records in and she stopped dead.

There he was.

'Got him,' she said.

Penn wheeled his chair around and nodded immediately at the image on the screen.

'Joshua Lucas, twelve years old when he went missing on the fourteenth of September of twenty-one,' Kim said as Penn took down the address.

She sat back in her chair. Joshua had been abducted three years ago and allowed to live.

Why?

And more importantly, what had been done to him during those three years?

FORTY-TWO

Having never visited the seaside resort before, Stacey was still trying to work out if she liked Blackpool or not.

She'd spent the last twenty minutes walking around armed with Google Maps and a few postcodes.

Her travels had taken her along a selection of back streets that had probably been thriving in the town's heyday. Empty properties still bore the signs of what had once been inside: markets, craft shops and cafés. The last back street had spat her out on a long road that, according to Google, would lead her all the way to Coral Island, but she didn't really want to go that far, just far enough to see with her own eyes where Lewis had disappeared from the view of the camera.

The bed and breakfast establishments on her right were gradually giving way to gift shops and knick-knack stores, chip shops and burger bars as she neared the centre.

The car park Lewis had crossed was coming into view, and now she began to pay attention. She saw from the sign that the space held over three hundred car parking spaces, and right now, at 10 a.m., it was almost full.

She continued along the road, looking at the premises on her right and then over to the car park.

A sinking feeling grew in her stomach as she neared the spot on the pavement that lined up with where Lewis had stopped to chat with someone. So far, she hadn't seen one camera on any of the nearby premises that would be any use to her.

She walked another fifty feet and guessed she was now probably level with the exact spot. Behind and to her left was a tiny café, no camera. Directly behind was a dry cleaner's, no camera. To her right was a kebab shop... and in the top corner, above the sign, was a camera.

Please, please, please don't be a dummy device, Stacey prayed as she knocked on the door. A light shining in the back of the premises told her that someone was there despite it not yet being open.

A dark-skinned male with an apron, a mop and a face full of irritation headed towards the door.

Stacey already had her identification in her hand.

'Police,' she said, choosing to omit mentioning the force she worked for.

He frowned at her.

She smiled. 'You're not in any trouble, but can I just have a quick word?'

'Go head,' he said, putting his mop against the door.

'Is that a dummy?' she asked, pointing up at the front of the shop.

'Dummy?' he asked, scratching his head.

'Sorry, decoy, for show?' she answered, trying to make herself clear.

He shook his head. 'Is real.'

Her despondency got a swift kick of hope.

'Do you have footage?' she asked, not realising she was making signs with her hands which were probably confusing him more. 'Video?' she clarified.

He nodded and stepped aside.

Only then did Stacey realise her vulnerability in this situation. She was in a strange town about to enter unknown premises with a man she had never met before. The boss was always telling them to be aware of their surroundings, but as she spent most of her day at a desk, she didn't always realise the potential for harm.

Seeing the hesitation on her face and understanding her predicament, the man handed her the keys that he was carrying.

She smiled her thanks before following him through to the back area. Stacked boxes forced her to move crab like through the space.

Beyond the storage area was a small kitchen full of old cabinets. The sink and food-prep area was spotless and seemed new, as did a floor-to-ceiling cabinet next to a freezer.

He made a motion with his hands, and she realised he wanted the keys.

She held them out.

He chose one and handed them back to her before pointing to the cabinet.

'Thank you,' she said, putting the key in the lock.

The cabinet opened to reveal a pull-out shelf holding a keyboard and a mouse. The shelf above held a flat-screen monitor, and on the floor was a hard drive. The whole setup looked reasonably new.

'How many cameras?' she asked, grabbing a chair.

He held up three fingers.

'Back, shop, front,' he said, pointing in various directions.

She fired up the hard drive before turning to the man again.

'Do you know how long the recordings go back?'

He shook his head.

'Why the one out front?' Stacey asked.

'My son, watches car, late night,' he said, pointing again to the front.

Was there a chance the camera was positioned to watch the car park?

'All good?' he asked, heading out of the room.

She nodded. She was certainly beginning to hope so.

FORTY-THREE

'What a memory,' Bryant said as Roy parked the car on double yellow lines in front of Jasmine's boyfriend's house.

'Wasn't so long ago we were here having a chat with him. Jasmine thought he might have had something to do with the robbery I told you about.'

Bryant had to keep reminding himself that as far as Roy was concerned he'd never met Jasmine.

'Why's that?' he asked.

'One of the items taken was an Alexa or something that she'd refused to give back when they split up.'

'And was he responsible for the burglary?' Bryant asked, getting out of the car.

'Dunno. We never found the culprits. He's a bit of a loser to be honest.'

Bryant followed him to the front door of a slim mid-terrace, a couple of miles out of the town centre.

The door was opened by a man who instantly reminded him of Penn, with curly blonde hair almost to the shoulder. His open expression clouded slightly when he saw Roy.

'I've told you already, it wasn't me.'

'It's all right, Justin, we're here about something else. Can we come in?'

Justin appeared surprised by Roy's gentle tone, but not as surprised as Bryant was. He wouldn't have thought that the sergeant had an ounce of empathy in him, for anyone.

The minute Bryant stepped into the small house, he could see why it hadn't worked out between this man and the woman he'd met the previous day.

Jasmine Swift had her shit together as the Americans liked to say. She had a nice home, a good job and an attractive, personable demeanour. He had to mentally shake himself to remember that she was the same woman he'd seen dead less than an hour ago; a confident, accomplished woman reduced to an object – debased, humiliated, exposed.

He clenched his fists and fought the images away.

He wondered again what they were doing here. There was no way this guy had murdered anyone. It looked like he barely had the gumption to haul himself out of bed.

'Justin, can you sit down a minute?' Roy said gently.

He did so without moving the pile of clothes on the arm of the chair.

'I've got some bad news for you, mate. Jasmine is dead.'

The man just stared at Roy as the sergeant took a seat beside him.

'D... dead?' he spluttered.

'Afraid so. What I'm going to tell you is going to be hard to hear. She was raped and murdered sometime last night.'

Bryant was unsure why Roy had delivered so much information so soon into the conversation. The guy looked like he was going to vomit.

'I'll get you some water,' Bryant said, heading for the kitchen positioned directly off the front room.

'It's all right, mate. I understand,' Roy said. 'It's a shock. You're going to need some time to process it.'

'I c... can't— I mean, are you sure it's her?'

Roy patted his arm as Bryant came back into the room. 'We're sure, mate.'

Bryant handed Justin a glass of water.

He took it with trembling hands. He didn't take a sip; he just stared at it.

'Listen, it's just a formality, mate, but I gotta ask where you were last night.'

His head shot around and water sloshed from the glass. 'You can't think I did it.'

Bryant took the water back and placed it on the coffee table.

'Not for a minute, mate,' Roy soothed. 'But as her last known partner, we have to ask.'

'I was playing pool with my mates down the Buzby club.'

'Until what time?' Roy pushed.

'Ten, half past.'

'And then?'

'I came back here with a pizza.'

Bryant could see the box on the countertop.

'And you didn't go out again?' Roy asked in the same gentle, soothing tone.

Bryant saw the panic start to rise on Justin's face.

'Nah, I never left, but I wouldn't hurt— Oh God, I could never hurt Jas. I loved her, mate – you gotta believe me.'

'It's all right, pal, I believe you. Now just calm down, eh? You've had quite the shock.'

The young man took a couple of deep breaths, looking relieved that Roy believed him.

'Told you, just a formality. Now do you mind if I use the loo before I go?'

'Course not,' Justin said, waving towards the kitchen. 'Just through there.'

'Is she really dead?' he asked, once Roy had left the room.

'I'm afraid so,' Bryant said, shoving his hands in his pockets.

He was still struggling to understand what they were doing here before Jasmine's next of kin had been informed.

'That's better,' Roy said, coming back into the room. 'Okay, mate, sorry to have brought you shitty news. If you need anything, give us a shout.' He walked straight past Justin to the door. 'Oh, and don't go making any calls to family members until they've had a chance to absorb the news, okay?'

Justin nodded as Roy let himself out of the room.

Bryant had the feeling a whirlwind had just swept through this man's life.

He wasn't sure that either he or his boss would have been happy to leave this guy unattended so soon, but Roy's gait indicated that they'd done what they were here to do and it was time to move on.

Nevertheless, he felt the need to offer something.

'Deeply sorry for your loss,' he said, squeezing the man's shoulder as he walked past.

He closed the front door quietly behind himself.

'You don't think we should have called a relative to comfort him?' Bryant asked, getting back into Roy's car.

'Nah, mate, not our job, and our family liaisons don't stretch to the ex-boyfriends of the deceased. That's best saved for the family. He'll be all right.'

And yet the ex-boyfriend was the person they'd visited first.

'Family next?' Bryant asked, clipping in his seat belt.

Roy shook his head as he pulled away from the kerb. 'Nah, someone else is taking that call. There's somewhere else we need to be.'

'Oh, yeah?' Bryant said.

'The morgue,' Roy answered before turning his attention back to the road.

Bryant frowned. They'd seen the body less than an hour ago. Why the hell did they need to see it again? What was Roy up to?

FORTY-FOUR

Gornal Wood was one of the three small villages, along with Upper and Lower Gornal, forming the larger Gornal area.

Located on the western boundary of the Dudley Metropolitan Borough, it contained a small shopping area and was the location of the Crooked House pub, a famous landmark due to its wonky appearance as a result of mining subsidence, and notoriously destroyed by fire in 2023.

The area also housed the Straits Estate, a housing conurbation built in the early sixties.

Kim still found it amusing that all the streets within the Straits were named after famous poets and writers. She smiled as they took a left on Chaucer Avenue to turn into Kipling Road.

Her smile disappeared as she remembered what they were here to do.

The vast majority of the houses they'd passed were semi-detached and well kept.

'I think this is it,' Penn said, parking at the bottom of a sloping red-brick drive that ended at a single-car garage to the right of the house.

Kim squeezed between the two small cars on the drive to reach the front door. She took a deep breath and readied herself before knocking on it. Informing family members of a death didn't get any easier with practice, especially in the case of a child.

The door opened and for a second her heart stopped.

She did a double take. Any doubt she'd had about being in the right place evaporated.

Standing before her was Josh Lucas's double. Well, Josh Lucas if he'd been alive, fit, healthy, well nourished and not covered in a hundred bruises.

'Hi, is your mum home?' Kim asked.

'Well, one of them is,' the teenage boy offered with a smile.

Kim smiled back in response. There was something engaging about this kid.

She was reaching for her identification when a casually dressed woman appeared behind him.

The smile instantly froze on her face.

Kim left her identification where it was. She didn't need it. The woman knew exactly who they were.

'May we come in?' Kim asked gently as the colour began to drain from the woman's face.

The boy looked from one to the other. 'Is this about Josh?' he asked.

Kim said nothing.

'Harry, go to your room,' the woman said without looking at him.

'I'd rather stay,' he said, stepping back and taking his mother's hand.

She regarded him for just a second before squeezing his fingers and motioning for them to enter.

'Clare Lucas?' Kim asked as they followed through to the lounge. Clare Lucas was the person who had reported her son missing.

The woman nodded and waved towards one of the sofas as she and her son took the other chairs.

'Is there anyone you'd like to call?' Kim asked, taking a glance at the photos that graced the walls.

Although randomly placed, Kim could see a timeline that appeared to start when the boys were six or seven years old. There were photos of the four of them until the twins were eleven or twelve. After that, Harry was the only child in the photos.

Sadness for the story represented in the images washed over her, hitting her right in the stomach. Josh would never return to complete this family again.

Clare shook her head in answer to Kim's question. 'My wife is in hospital – kidney removal.' She paused. 'Have you found him?'

Her expression said that every word in that sentence travelled up her throat with razor blades. She didn't want to utter the words, and yet it was the only question she wanted to ask. Once the question was answered there would be no return to the place of limbo, the place of hope.

Kim nodded as Harry scooted closer to his mum and took her hand again.

'Mrs Lucas, it's—'

'Clare, please call me Clare,' she said.

Kim understood. She didn't want to hear the inevitable words, the news she'd been dreading for years, from someone formally addressing her by her full name.

'Clare, it's not good news,' Kim warned her.

The woman swallowed and nodded for her to continue.

'Josh's body was found earlier today at—'

Clare cried out as Harry buried his head against his mother's arm.

'I'm so sorry for your loss,' Kim offered, knowing that every sorry in the world wasn't going to lessen her pain.

Kim waited while mother and son absorbed the news, holding on tightly to each other.

Her gaze swept over Harry, a boy with whom she had more in common than any other person in the room and whose pain she understood better than anyone.

Clare had lost a son and there was no refuting the depth of that pain, but Harry had lost the other half of himself, and she knew from experience that loss would affect him for his whole life.

Finally, Clare raised red eyes to meet her gaze. Kim could see many questions forming there. The answers to which were going to help no one's grieving process, but least of all Harry's.

She began to turn to her colleague, but he was one step ahead of her.

'Hey, bud, mind showing me to the kitchen?' Penn asked.

Harry looked to his mother, who patted his arm and nodded.

'Lovely photos of the boys,' Kim said, casting her gaze around the room.

The time would come soon enough for the details she would need to reveal.

Clare fixed her gaze on a photo of the two boys dressed in matching outfits. Kim noticed that was the only one where the boys were wearing the same clothes.

'We never did that again,' Clare said as a pain-filled smile passed over her face. 'Josh made it clear he didn't like it.'

Looking closer, Kim could see a frown on one of the boys' faces.

'He told me in no uncertain terms that he liked blue and his brother liked green.' She shook her head. 'He was always the most outspoken one. The one who liked to fill in the details of what they liked and didn't like. Harry didn't talk very much at first.'

'They were adopted?' Kim asked.

Clare nodded. 'We always knew we wanted to adopt, and we didn't want babies. We wanted kids that were hard to place. We knew we had the love and strength to do it. We heard about the boys. Their father had died in a hit-and-run, and their mother had taken her own life a week after the funeral. Not surprisingly, they were difficult kids. They were confused, grieving and terrified. After the third foster home returned them, we stepped in. They were six and a half years old.'

Kim admired the woman immediately. Taking on two young boys full of grief and anger was not a task for the faint-hearted.

She raised an eyebrow, and Clare understood.

'Not even for a second did we regret it. The harder they fought, the more determined we were to give them the love and stability they needed. The adoption agreement was for life, and they are our children.'

Kim said nothing, allowing the woman to just talk.

'Harry warmed to us first. It was joyful watching him come out of his shell and learn to trust us. It gave us the confidence that we were doing something right. Josh was a tougher nut to crack,' she said as a tear slid unnoticed over her cheek. 'It was Jacks – Jaqueline, my wife – who cracked him in the end. Ever the pragmatist, she called a family meeting, right before their seventh birthday, and asked him directly why he couldn't accept our love. I'll never forget it.' She wiped at her cheek.

'Go on,' Kim urged as though trying to give her a buffer of good memories before she had to break her heart.

'He said we were only linked by a piece of paper, not blood, and so we could give them back any time. He said he wasn't going to get comfortable because it was only temporary.'

Kim's heart ached for the little boy full of doubt and fear.

'Jacks immediately knew what to do. She fetched a needle and pricked everyone's thumbs. Once we'd all pressed our thumbs together, she said, "See, now your blood runs in our veins and ours runs in yours. We will never give you up."' A fresh wave of tears escaped. 'So simple a gesture, but it worked. From that day on, he allowed himself to trust in our love and our family.'

Kim choked back the emotion. She had very nearly had that family herself.

'I want to know everything,' Clare said, wringing her hands together. 'And yet I don't. Once I know the details, I'll have to accept it's real.'

Kim understood. The words of finality hadn't yet been spoken. They were not out there yet. He was still a missing child.

'Can you just run me through that last day again?' Kim asked. It had been four years, but she guessed the memory of it had never faded.

'It was a Tuesday, changeover day.'

Kim frowned.

'I work Saturday to Tuesday; Jacks works Tuesday to Friday. Tuesdays were always a bit of a juggle, not least because it was Josh's night playing badminton. I was running late to pick him up but still had plenty of time. There was a small fire in a bin at the gym, everybody was evacuated and Josh disappeared. The guys at the gym assumed he'd decided to head home early, since it's less than a mile away, and I assumed the same when I pulled up and was told about the fire. I drove home the way he'd walk, but he was nowhere in sight. Not one soul saw him walking home that night. It's like he just vanished.' She met Kim's gaze. 'But he didn't, did he?'

The question meant she was ready for some answers.

Kim shook her head.

'Are you absolutely sure it's Josh?' Clare asked.

'I was the moment I saw Harry.'

The penny dropped quickly, and horror filled her face. 'He's been alive all this time?'

Kim nodded.

'Oh God, no,' she said, covering her face as though trying to keep that knowledge from reaching her. 'Oh God, no,' she repeated, putting her hand over her heart. 'I've always comforted myself with the notion that any suffering was over quickly, that he wasn't having to miss us as much as we were missing him, that he was at peace. It was how I was able to pick myself up and carry on.'

The tears continued to fall down her cheeks as the realisation hit. 'We continued living. We had to. There were times we laughed, adventures we went on thinking that Josh was at peace. We grieved but we also lived, and the guilt of that will never...'

Kim said nothing, unable to give her that comfort.

'When did he...?' she asked, struggling to say that final word.

'Recently. Days,' Kim confirmed.

'Can I see him?' she asked hopefully, as though the act would bring him back to life.

'We will need you to confirm that it's Josh,' Kim said. 'But you need to be ready. He hasn't been taken care of by the people that abducted him.'

Clare closed her eyes against the pain of that knowledge. 'He's suffered, hasn't he?'

Kim nodded. How much wouldn't be clear until Keats had had a better chat with him.

'If only I hadn't been late. If only the gym hadn't had that fire,' Clare said, again burying her head in her hands.

Kim wished she could offer some kind of comfort to the grieving mother, but all she could do was try and find the people responsible for her son's death.

And one of the 'if onlys' that Clare had mentioned definitely needed a closer look.

FORTY-FIVE

After explaining to the owner of the kebab shop what she was doing, Stacey finally found the footage she was seeking.

The camera had a great view of the first row of cars in the car park and specifically the eight-year-old Porsche she assumed belonged to the owner of the kebab shop. As a consequence, she could see the second row of parked vehicles and the gap in between.

Determined not to miss anything, she watched the footage for fifteen minutes before the time Lewis sauntered into the car park.

In that time, none of the cars parked on the front row moved. On the row behind, some type of estate car reversed out and left. Three minutes later, the space was filled by a dark-coloured transit van.

Seven minutes later, Lewis appeared in the top left of the screen, walking between the two rows of cars.

A figure appeared and stopped him.

The person was dressed in dark trousers and a long dark jacket, wearing a hoody beneath the coat.

From this angle, Stacey could see the nuances in Lewis's body language that were unavailable from the arcade's footage.

Initially, Lewis seemed startled. His reaction didn't have any sense of familiarity. His limbs were still and rigid. He was listening to what the figure was saying, but there was no easy movement, no looseness in his joints.

The figure talked animatedly. Lewis shook his head.

The figure held out something.

Stacey couldn't see what it was, but Lewis stared down, shook his head and took a step to the side.

The figure blocked him from moving forward, and Lewis stiffened. He glanced around him, and Stacey could see that he was looking to see if there was anyone else nearby.

There wasn't.

He shook his head again and stepped around the figure.

From the distant camera of the arcade, this had looked like a harmless exchange, like he was being asked for directions, or for the location of a particular attraction, but on closer inspection it wasn't that at all. It looked more like he was being propositioned for something and he was turning it down.

Stacey felt unease begin in her stomach. It was far too coincidental that this meeting had taken place the night the boy disappeared.

She continued to stare at the van as the minutes ticked along. She already knew what Lewis had been doing. She'd tracked his every move inside the arcade, but now she was interested in this vehicle. The figure had got back into the driver's seat, and the van remained stationary.

Why? she wondered as the minutes ticked along. Any reason that made sense to her disappeared the longer the van remained immobile. A couple of cars came and left, but nothing else happened until 8.37 p.m., two minutes after Lewis left Coral Island, undoubtedly to head home.

She could picture him entering the car park to take the shortcut through.

The rear lights on the vehicle switched on, indicating the engine had been started. The figure got out of the driver's side just as Lewis came into view again.

Stacey's heart began to pound as three things happened at once.

Lewis tried to sidestep the figure.

They grabbed Lewis by the arm.

The rear door of the van opened.

Arms reached out and hauled the boy into the back of the van.

'Jesus,' Stacey whispered to herself, knowing she might just have witnessed Lewis's last few moments alive.

She watched it back with the urgency of someone who felt they could do something to stop it.

Three seconds. That was the amount of time it had taken to get Lewis into the back of the van. There were no missteps; there was no clumsiness, no hesitation. It was quick and efficient, and she now understood how no one had seen a thing.

Stacey wanted to sound the alarm, make calls, inform everyone. She wanted to create the urgency that had been lacking while everyone concerned had been convinced that Lewis had run away.

The urgency came from what she'd just learned. They were ten days past the actual event, and the van was long gone.

What more could she glean from this footage?

She already knew she hadn't got the number plate, but she went back and watched every second from the moment the van came into view.

She watched the interaction between the figure and Lewis over and over again, focussing only on the figure. The more she did so, the more she became convinced of one important fact.

The figure clad in black from head to toe was definitely a woman.

FORTY-SIX

It was almost midday when Bryant followed Roy Moss into the morgue at Blackpool Victoria Hospital, and he still had no idea why they were there.

The pathologist was waiting for them at the inner door.

'Sorry but no entry until I get a proper introduction. I don't let any Tom, Dick or Harry in here.'

Bryant held out his hand and gave his name and rank. 'Not here to tread on any toes,' he added. 'Just here to assist with the missing boys investigation.'

'Richard Wade,' the pathologist said, shaking Bryant's hand. 'Although I'm not sure why either of you are here. I've not yet finished prepping the body.'

Bryant tried not to cringe. Over the years, he'd become spoiled by Keats referring to victims as though they were still alive, using pronouns, salutations, even endearments as though they could hear him. He wasn't sure he'd ever heard the man refer to any victim as 'the body'.

'Ah, no probs, bud,' Roy said affably. 'Just wanted to check something real quick. Is that her?' He pointed through the glass.

Wade frowned, and Bryant could offer nothing. Roy hadn't let him in on the purpose of the visit either.

'Okay, well suit up and—'

'Fuck me, I'll only be a minute,' Roy blustered, pushing his way into the sterile room.

Bryant was learning more and more about Roy with every interaction the man had with both himself and other people.

He gave the pathologist a wry smile.

'Who did you piss off to get this assignment?' Wade asked.

'Just my bad luck, I guess, but I suppose if the guy gets results...'

'Wasn't sure he did,' Wade said. 'I'm afraid to say that no one around here is sure why the man still has a job. It's certainly not due to his charm and charisma.'

Bryant tuned out for a minute as his focus shifted to his peripheral vision and Roy's movements in the morgue.

He had approached the body on the trolley and peeled back the sheet to reveal the head and neck. As Wade continued to talk, Roy leaned over the body as though inspecting it for something.

'You know the saying about lying down with dogs,' Wade said, pulling his attention back.

'Hey, no choice, I've been assigned,' Bryant explained as Moss re-entered the anteroom.

'False alarm but it was worth a shot.'

Wade said nothing, waiting for an explanation.

'There was a recent case up in Glasgow. Similar circumstances but with bruising to the back of the neck. Just wanted to see if our girl had anything similar.'

'Trying to offload your case onto someone else, Moss?' Wade asked.

'You know me, pal – work smarter not harder.'

Wade allowed the repulsion to show on his face as Moss headed for the door.

Bryant would have liked longer to talk to the pathologist. He felt he could have learned a lot, although it would probably have been anecdotal. From Wade's demeanour, if he'd had anything concrete, he would have shared it before, and Bryant had to be careful of not blowing his cover. Even to Wade, he needed to appear as the disillusioned, disaffected copper just treading water until retirement.

'What's the case in Glasgow?' Bryant asked as they approached the car.

'Ah, nothing you'd know about,' Roy said, getting into the driver's seat.

He rubbed his hands together as though they were cold.

'Buckle up, buddy. Time for a little distraction. There's a girl named Pippa I'd like you to meet, and I know you're gonna love her just as much as I do.'

Bryant said nothing as he turned to stare out of the window. He needed to think hard on this.

How the hell was he going to get out of this one?

FORTY-SEVEN

Hours after getting back to the station, Kim was still thinking about the family she'd left. Although Clare had refused the offer of a family liaison officer at first, Kim had strongly urged her to reconsider. The woman's wife was in hospital recovering from surgery and she had a teenage son to console as well. She needed some support.

She'd left the Lucas home wishing she could have done more, but she supposed the best thing she could do was find out what had happened to their son.

And that thought had brought them back to the office.

Penn was busy checking with other forces about missing boys. With forty-four other police forces in the UK, it wasn't a five-minute job. She'd limited him to a three-year timeline or they'd still be collating information next week.

For herself, she wanted to pore over the case file of Josh Lucas. How had his disappearance been handled by the Dudley team? Had they lifted every stone to try and find him, and how had a twelve-year-old boy simply disappeared?

She was almost finished with the file and hadn't yet found

anything to give her pause about the quality of the work that had been done.

The missing person's report had come in at 9 p.m. The family had been interviewed at 9.30 p.m. and by 10 p.m. the initial search had begun with more than fifty pairs of shoes on the ground.

A photo and description had been circulated around the force within three hours and to neighbouring forces by hour six.

The parents had been discreetly investigated, the local paedophiles had been questioned, neighbours interviewed, bodies of water checked. Every resident of every property that lay between the gym and the boy's home had been spoken to, appeals had been made on local television and a reconstruction had been filmed two weeks after Josh had disappeared. The grand total of leads generated was absolutely zero.

In her opinion, Dudley hadn't put a foot wrong. There was not one single thing she'd have done differently.

It really was as though the boy had vanished into thin air, or that he'd never left the gym at all.

The appendix indicated that CCTV footage was available.

Having taken up residence at Bryant's desk, she logged into the system from there. Penn placed a fresh mug of coffee on the desk.

'You, okay?' she asked. She'd sensed a vibe since they'd returned to the office.

'Yeah, fine,' he said, retaking his seat.

He hadn't poured himself a drink.

'Stop it,' she said, seeing the pensive expression on his face.

In the time since they'd left Blackpool, Penn had tried to fill every spare minute with questions or idle conversation. He'd kept her supplied with an endless stream of coffee that she was now beginning to feel the effects of.

'You can't replace them both, so stop trying,' she said with a smile.

There were two CCTV files available, and both CCTV clips were from the gym.

The first showed a view of the lobby and recorded all exits and entrances. The footage totalled four minutes and captured everyone inside heading out of the building at speed due to the small fire. She would imagine the fire alarm had been blaring.

She instantly recognised Josh's blonde hair as he made his way out with the others, but unlike most of the others, Josh already had his sports bag slung over his back.

She switched to the second file and opened it.

This camera was on the front door, aimed down at the pavement. The angle offered a narrow view and caught people only once they were directly underneath it. The camera had no peripheral view at all, and Kim found herself looking at the top of a lot of heads.

She watched the same people file out of the building that she'd just seen in the lobby, but the view was so narrow that she could barely tell the direction in which they were walking, never mind being able to glean any further clues.

Kim sat back in frustration, her fingers tapping on the desk.

She hadn't expected to discover a smoking gun in the CCTV footage. The Dudley team had been much too thorough for that. But there was a seed of uncertainty in her stomach.

She knew for certain that Josh had left the gym. There was no reason to doubt what they'd been told by the gym manager: that Josh had simply carried on towards home when his mum wasn't there to pick him up.

He'd walked out with his hands in his pockets, looking completely comfortable and relaxed.

Everything she'd been told was true, and everything she'd seen on the footage was expected.

Only one thing bothered her. The angle of the external camera. It made no sense.

She knew the area well, and directly outside the gym was a small parking area, a row of bins and a grass verge onto the road.

It wasn't logical for the camera to cover just the two square metres of space below it when it could have been monitoring the whole outside area.

She always stopped to question things that didn't make sense.

She typed the name of the gym into her phone and got a number.

The call was answered on the second ring.

'Hey, I'm hoping you can help me,' Kim said.

'I'll try,' said a pleasant voice on the other end.

'I parked right outside your place last night and my wing mirror got damaged. You wouldn't have any CCTV, would you? Only I saw a camera above your door.'

'Sorry, I can't help you with that directly, but if you report it to the police, they'll request the footage, and we can pass what we have to them.'

'Ugh,' Kim groaned. 'I don't wanna go to all that hassle if your camera doesn't cover that area. I might as well just buy—'

'The camera covers the car park. If your car was damaged there, we'll definitely have caught it, but I can't give the footage to you directly.'

'Okay, thanks for your help,' Kim said before ending the call.

She now had a very big question.

Why had that camera been moved?

FORTY-EIGHT

Stacey hadn't yet revealed to anyone what she'd found on the CCTV at the kebab shop.

It wasn't like there was anyone to talk to anyway. The rest of the team had been deployed on other tasks, and she was sitting in an office on her own. Normal day really, except if she leaned back in her seat far enough, she could see the top of Blackpool Tower.

Before sharing her findings, she wanted to scour the CCTV collected for Noah to see if she could spot a similar vehicle around the time he vanished.

Until she had incontrovertible proof that the cases were connected, she suspected the Blackpool team would try to convince her that Lewis had thrown himself into the back of the van as part of an elaborate running-away plan.

She opened the CCTV file within the Noah case file and was pleased to see it labelled clearly. She was sure that Adil was responsible for the organisation.

She clicked onto the pier footage first. Ten seconds in, she saw Noah leaving through the front doors of the pier onto the

Promenade. He was noticeably shorter than Lewis, who appeared tall and gangly for his twelve years.

Noah was a half foot smaller and carried a little more weight. Having been kept away from the case, it was the first time she'd laid eyes on a moving image of the boy.

She watched as he hesitated, as though unsure where Wetherspoons was.

He came forward and began walking to the right. Stacey could see the edge of the crossing, and he walked past it, obviously choosing to cross the road without the help of the flashing green man.

From what she'd seen, the pub was literally across the road.

He'd come out of the pier but hadn't made it across the road to the pub on the other side. How was that even possible?

Stacey returned to the folder and saw that the majority of the remaining footage was from the trams.

She clicked into a word document titled 'Tram CCTV'.

She read the short paragraph that explained that many of the trams had been fitted with an Obstacle Detection Assistance System, basically a camera that detected obstructions on the line ahead and then knew to apply the service brake to avoid collisions.

She could see from the files that Adil had collected all the relevant footage and labelled it in time order. Obviously, he would have checked them all, but he wouldn't have known what to look for. Adil hadn't known about the van that had abducted Lewis.

She knew from the pier footage that Noah exited it at 9.31 p.m.

She located the file nearest to that time, labelled as '9.23'. She opened the file and was immediately transported to the front of the tram as though she was driving it herself.

Her heart stopped as she saw a dark-coloured transit van

parked at the tip of the taxi rank, right where Noah would have crossed the road.

She scoured the files for the next tram that had passed through.

That file was labelled as '9.37'. She clicked into it.

The van was gone and likely so was Noah.

She sat back in her chair, knowing she didn't have solid proof that it was the same van or that the people inside had abducted Noah... but the coincidence didn't sit well in her stomach.

She was wondering what to do with the information when her phone dinged.

She frowned as she read the short message Bryant had sent her.

What the hell was he up to now?

FORTY-NINE

Bryant worked hard to keep his face neutral as Moss parked the car in front of the property he'd visited the day before.

The face of the woman who lived here had remained in his head in the hours since. As soon as he'd known for sure they were heading here, he'd considered every option available. More than anything he wanted to march into the DCI's office and call out this man for the disgusting piece of shit that he was.

The only problem was that he had no proof. The best he'd got was an unauthorised photo taken at a crime scene. That wasn't going to put Moss in front of the people who could throw him off the force.

Bryant knew he had to witness him doing something irrefutably against the code of conduct, or downright illegal, and he was about to see one of those things right now.

'What's this place?' Bryant asked as they approached the front door.

'Stress relief,' Moss offered with a wink and a smile.

Bryant thought he was going to throw up, but he managed to hide his revulsion. He took care to position himself one step behind Moss so the man couldn't see his face.

The door was opened by Pippa, whose face instantly filled with loathing and fear.

She glanced his way and frowned. He met her gaze and shook his head.

'Oh, don't mind him,' Moss said, misreading the question in her eyes. 'He's a friend of mine who needs loosening up.'

Her eyes questioned Bryant again as he followed Moss into the house.

He said nothing. He knew that if he was the kind of officer with a tougher stomach, he'd finally have some tangible proof against the man.

'How's things, Pip?' Moss asked, leaning against the banister that led up the stairs.

'Nothing new,' she said, taking a box of smokes and a lighter from her pocket.

There was a visible tremble as the flame danced around the edge of the cigarette.

Bryant had no idea how many times she'd been forced to do this, but it clearly hadn't got any easier over time.

It was clear to Bryant that she loathed this man almost as much as she loathed herself.

'Well, your insurance is due, Pip, so I'm here to collect your premium. And this week it's double,' he said, smirking Bryant's way. 'But I'm first in line.'

The way Pippa nodded her acceptance and just looked at the ground all but broke his heart. This young woman had not one ounce of fight left in her.

'Come on – we ain't got all day,' Moss said, heading up the stairs.

Pippa stepped past him without looking him in the eye.

She slowly began to mount the stairs behind him.

Come on, Stace, Bryant prayed silently. *Do what I asked you to do.*

Moss was now at the top of the stairs, and Pippa was

halfway up. The protest was building inside his body, but if he had any chance at all of getting this man locked up, he had to maintain his cover. Three more steps and it would be out of his hands. He wondered how much more abuse this woman could take before her spirit was broken forever.

She was at the top step.

His heart was beating out of his chest.

He opened his mouth.

His phone rang.

He reached into his pocket. The sound had been enough to make Pippa pause.

'Hey, Stace,' he said loudly.

'You asked me to call,' Stacey answered.

'You're sure?' he asked, raising his voice.

'Bryant, what the hell is going on?' Stacey whispered on the other end of the phone.

'Bloody hell, Stace. Okay, no problem. We'll head back to you now.'

He ended the call before she had a chance to respond. The conversation had brought Moss back to the top of the stairs.

'Gotta get back, mate,' Bryant said, shrugging. 'Stacey's got something she needs us to see.'

He saw the indecision cross Moss's face.

'I can call her back and send her to Red if you want,' he bluffed.

'Fuck it,' he said, heading back down the stairs and out of the front door.

Pippa frowned again, but this time her expression held a glimmer of curiosity.

He'd known in the car he didn't have the stomach to allow Moss to abuse Pippa again, even if allowing the act would give him the proof that he needed. A simple text to his colleague had ensured he'd be able to interrupt the whole thing.

Somehow, and he didn't yet know how, he would make sure that Roy Moss never had the chance to abuse her again.

FIFTY

Although the gym looked small from the outside, it opened to an expansive area that encompassed a boxing ring, equipment area, and a partition that led to a badminton court and a dance studio.

They were approached immediately by a man wearing a red tee shirt that sported the name of the gym on the left-hand breast.

Kim held up her identification.

'That was bloody quick,' he said, offering a smile. When she said nothing, he continued, 'I assume you're here about the smashed wing mirror out front. I'm Warren. I spoke to the woman who—'

'Not exactly why we're here, Warren. How long have you worked here?' she asked.

'Almost seven years. How can I help?'

'Remember the young boy who went missing?'

The memory didn't come easily to him, but eventually he nodded. 'Jake... err...'

'Josh Lucas,' she reminded him.

'Yeah, yeah, I remember him. Nice kid.'

'Were you on duty that night?'

Warren glanced over at the door as it opened and nodded a greeting to two teenagers with duffel bags.

'Wanna step over here?' he asked, pointing them to two worn leather sofas on the edge of the boxing ring.

As they sat down, a couple of guys in their early twenties got into the ring.

'Yeah, I was on duty. There was a small fire in a bin out back. Fire alarm went off. Everyone headed outside, and Josh went home. That's it.'

'Well, that's not it, is it, Warren, because Josh never made it home. You were probably one of the last people to see him.'

'I wasn't really paying attention. I was trying to make sure everyone was safe.'

'From the fire, which was caused by...?'

'Oh, just a small bin fire in the kitchen. A bowl of water sorted it out.'

'And the cause?' she asked.

'Dunno. Just one of those things.'

To Kim's knowledge, fires didn't just start in bins for no reason.

'And you saw Josh leave the building?' she asked.

'Yeah, and the cameras caught it too. I don't know what this is about, but we didn't do anything wrong. The kid had left, and we don't walk 'em all home.'

'Talking of cameras, that one out front that covers the parking and the bins?'

'Yeah?'

'It wasn't covering that area the night Josh disappeared.'

'Yeah, some bloody contractors came to clean and service all the cameras the day before. It got knocked askew. We didn't even know until your guys came to look for the footage.'

Kim was growing uncomfortable with the number of coincidences that had come together to produce one huge shitshow and a boy that no one saw disappear.

A small bin fire that caused no damage or injury, but major disruption. A camera that was conveniently looking the other way.

'It was sorted the next day, but...'

'Not a lot of help to us,' Kim said, deciding to change direction. 'Do you remember anything different with Josh that night?' she asked.

'No, we went over this at the time. He was in here doing what he always did.'

Kim could feel her impatience growing. The kid hadn't walked into a black hole.

'Do you know who he was playing badminton with?'

Warren frowned. 'He didn't come here to play badminton. Josh came here to fight.'

'To what?' Kim asked, not hiding her surprise. Her first thought was that his mother hadn't known. She had told them that he came to the gym to play in the badminton league.

'Boxing. He came here wanting to learn how to fight. He was getting shit at school over having two mums. He wanted to defend himself. The kid had quite a knack for it.'

'At eleven?' Kim asked, having learned that was when Josh had first started visiting the gym.

'Nothing wrong with it. It ain't illegal for a kid to box. They gotta be eighteen to take part in a professional boxing match, but they can practise at any age.'

'You don't think there's anything disturbing about encouraging kids to take part in a sport where hurting your opponent is the only goal?'

He shook his head. 'It's not just about the fighting. It's about training, using the bags, teaching reflexes and repetitive punching skills. They learn how to jab, cross, hook, uppercut. We teach 'em defence, slipping, bobbing, blocking, cover up, clinching, footwork, pulling away. It's a skill. It's good for kids – it increases muscle tone. They get strong bones and ligaments, cardiovascular fitness, muscular endurance, improved core stability, co-ordination, body awareness, stress relief, self-esteem.'

'But you're talking about a child,' Kim insisted.

'There are plenty of governing bodies, and there are rules in place. Hand wraps are used at all times; mouthguards and helmets are—'

'Headgear doesn't prevent brain damage,' Penn interrupted. 'From 1980 to 2007, more than two hundred boxers died due to ring or training injuries. Isn't that why it's banned in some countries?'

Not for the first time, Kim had to wonder where Penn stored the facts and figures he quoted out of nowhere. One of these times she'd check his facts with Google.

'Yeah, sex before marriage is banned in some countries too, but it ain't gonna stop the rest of the world doing it.'

'What about drugs? You pump 'em full of steroids too?' Kim asked.

'Nah, no pumpers or gym candy coming in here. I've told you. Josh liked to fight and he was—'

Warren stopped speaking as Kim's phone rang.

It was Keats. He gave her no chance to speak.

'I need you to come back here. There's something you really need to see.'

The call ended, and Kim stood. The tone of his voice said it all. He'd found something that she wasn't going to want to hear.

FIFTY-ONE

The first thing Bryant noticed upon entering the squad room was that Red was back.

The second thing he noticed was the state of him.

His whole body was transmitting tension like sonar. His face was pinched and flushed, and his gaze was aimed squarely at Moss.

'What the fuck did you think you were doing, Roy?'

Moss appeared to be unperturbed as he took his seat.

Bryant slid into the chair beside Stacey as Walsh headed their way.

'Wanna sort some drinks?' she asked in a blatant attempt to give the two men privacy.

'Nah, I'm good thanks,' Bryant replied as Stacey shook her head.

Red had his own office, and if he couldn't be arsed to act in a professional manner and take the man out of earshot, Bryant was totally here for it. If it had been any other member of the team, Bryant would have followed Walsh's respectful lead, but it didn't look like Red was going to notice either way.

Bryant stretched out his legs and folded his arms.

'Do you wanna fucking explain?' Red shouted.

Roy shrugged. 'We got the call. How was I to know it hadn't come through you?'

'Because then I'd have fucking called. I told you we'd likely get a call, and you should have referred it back to me instead of taking it upon yourself to attend the crime scene.'

'You're busy,' Roy said, showing no embarrassment at being bollocked in full view.

'Not too busy to decide which cases my team members are working.'

'Sorry, I just assumed the instruction had come via dispatch from you, and that you'd tasked me to attend. I think it's dispatch that fucked up. All I did was—'

'What you did was offer first response on a case you can't continue to work, putting the SIO at a fucking disadvantage before they've even started.'

'Come on, Red – a body trumps any missing—'

'Not when it's a kid we're still hoping to find alive.'

Bryant seriously wished he'd got a bag of popcorn for this show.

'I ain't bailing you out of this one, Roy. You fucked up, so you'd best get over to DI Crawford and explain your actions.'

'She got the case?' Roy asked in disgust.

'Yeah, and she's already behind the ball thanks to you. Go tell her what you did minute by minute, and don't be surprised if she bawls you out as well.'

For the first time, Roy looked uncomfortable with the conversation.

Bryant was willing to bet it was because he now had to explain himself to a woman of all things. And a woman who held a more senior rank than he did.

Roy pushed back his chair with force and glowered at his boss.

Red glared back. 'And once you're done with the handover to Crawford, get off home. I don't want to see you again today.'

Both his face and his demeanour brooked no argument.

Roy almost knocked over Dickinson and Adil as they walked in the door. They looked to Red for some kind of explanation, while Bryant glanced at Stacey, who was working hard to keep the amusement out of her face.

Finally realising he wasn't alone, Red looked their way as Carly re-entered the room with a full tray of drinks. She set one down on Roy's desk even though he was no longer there.

'Sorry you had to witness that,' Red said.

'No problem,' Bryant said, waving his hand. 'Understandable. Roy said it was someone you both knew. Kinda hinted you especially,' he added to gauge Red's reaction.

Stacey kept a good poker face, even though she didn't have a clue what he was talking about. He hadn't yet had a chance to update her on the identity of the victim.

'Jasmine was a target of a burglary some time back,' Red said as a flush began to creep up his neck. 'I knew her no better than Roy, but you're right that it hits harder if it's someone you've met.'

'Of course. Any clue who...?'

'As I told Roy, it's not our case. We're not going down that rabbit hole.'

'Roy seemed to think the ex-boyfriend looked good for it,' Bryant said, not willing to let him off the hook that easy. According to Jasmine, the man in front of him had crossed a line and paid her way more attention than he should have.

Red frowned and started to tense up a bit.

'Didn't seem like the sort to me, but...' Bryant said, shrugging.

'How would you know anything about Justin?' Red asked.

'Sorry, my mistake. I thought Roy had let you know that we

paid a quick visit to the guy to tell him about Jasmine,' he said, throwing Roy under the bus and driving over him.

'Jesus Christ,' Red said, rubbing his hand through his hair.

Bryant shrugged again, deciding to keep the morgue visit to himself for now. 'I'm sure he'll update the SIO with everything when he gets there.'

Red looked as though he wanted to shout some more, but the object of his rage was no longer in the room.

The man visibly composed himself before speaking again.

'Okay, back to our own case.'

'Cases,' Stacey interrupted.

Red rolled his eyes. 'Not that again.'

Even Bryant wondered where Stacey was going with that claim. These folks were determined to believe that Lewis was not connected to Noah.

'I've got proof.'

Carly groaned. Dickinson folded his arms. Adil sat up straighter, and Red took a seat at Roy's desk.

'There's a camera,' Stacey said. 'Opposite the car park, above a kebab shop. It captured Lewis being physically bundled into a van.'

'What?' they all said together, including Bryant. He'd had no chance to catch up with Stacey since returning.

If what she said was true, she'd had a much more productive day than he'd had.

'Here,' she said as every team member came to stand behind her.

'There's Lewis talking to someone before going into the arcade,' she said, playing a video that lasted a few minutes.

Even Bryant could tell that Lewis was uncomfortable and eager to get away.

No one spoke.

'And this is when he came back,' she said, clicking on another clip.

They all watched in horror as Lewis was forcibly bundled into the van that hadn't moved an inch.

'Shit,' Red said, straightening. 'We were convinced that Lewis ran away.'

'But why?' Bryant asked.

'Our own theory, constantly reinforced by the family,' Carly answered, still looking at the screen as Stacey played it again.

'Yeah, but why?' Bryant asked. What did they have to gain?

Red seemed to allow that question to enter his brain before turning back to Stacey. 'Is there more?'

Stacey nodded, and Bryant felt a rush of pride surge through him. As a team, they were dead lucky to have her.

'Here's tram footage before and after Noah crossed the road.'

She played both clips.

'Same van,' Adil noted.

'Hang on, we can't be totally sure of that,' Red said. 'It certainly looks similar, but—'

'It's the same van,' Adil said with confidence. 'Go back to the second car-park clip,' he instructed Stacey.

She did as she was told.

He pointed at the screen. 'Rear left light is shining brighter than the right.'

It wasn't something Bryant had noticed, but now it had been pointed out, it was unmistakeable. Stacey clearly hadn't noted it either. She looked impressed.

'Bring up the first tram footage,' Adil said.

Stacey did so, and they all saw it immediately.

'New bulb must have been fitted recently,' Adil said. 'Probably a different manufacturer. It burns slightly brighter.'

'Bloody hell,' Dickinson said. 'What are we gonna do?'

'What we always do,' Red answered, taking off his jacket. 'We go back to the beginning and talk to everyone we've interviewed. We ask them again about that night.'

He turned to Adil. 'Gonk, I want you up and down both streets looking for more CCTV. Now we know what we're looking for, we might find just one Ring camera to give us a partial plate.' He paused. 'Dickinson, I want you trying to track down anyone who was parked in Central car park that night. I'm talking staff members from the shops and arcades. Somebody might have seen something.'

'I've studied the video, and I might be wrong, but I think the person talking to Lewis is a woman,' Stacey offered.

Red didn't agree or disagree. Carly was frowning, listening closely to something on the radio.

'You may be right, so we know we're definitely looking for two— Carly, turn that—'

'Sorry, boss, but it's DI Crawford's team. They're heading out to make an arrest for the Jasmine Swift murder.'

Red's face drained of all colour as he grabbed his jacket. 'What the fuck is going on?'

Bryant was sure he saw dust rise from the floor as Red stormed out of the office.

An arrest for Jasmine Swift, so soon? He was definitely wondering about that, although that wasn't the question foremost in his mind.

Two pre-teen boys had been bundled into the same van within ten days.

His biggest question was why?

FIFTY-TWO

The first thing Kim noticed when she entered the morgue was that Josh Lucas's body was still on the table and that the white sheet had been pulled up to his neck as though he'd been tucked in for sleep.

Keats offered compassion and respect to all his charges, but there seemed to be an added element of tenderness employed on this occasion.

'Okay, Keats, what we got?' she asked, coming to stand beside the body.

'More injuries than I can count at the minute.'

'Go on,' Kim said, stepping back and leaning against the countertop. Penn remained standing beside the body as though he couldn't be so presumptuous.

'General health first. It's clear to anyone that the boy is undernourished. The weight range for his age is between a hundred and two pounds to one hundred and seventy-two pounds. Josh weighs in at ninety-four pounds.'

'Six and a half stone?' Kim asked.

Keats nodded. 'But it's important to note this hasn't always been the case. Neither his organs nor his digestive system show signs of long-term starvation. This is recent.'

Why would he have been kept in good condition for years and then suddenly starved? Kim wondered.

'There are no remnants of solid food in his stomach, and his last meal was some kind of health shake.'

Kim took a moment to process the information before nodding for him to continue.

'The boy has had many broken bones over the years. Every fracture leaves a trace, and I've counted seventy-six separate injuries. Some are scattered around his body, a couple of toes, three in the ribs, but by far the highest concentration, forty-four to be exact, are in his hands.'

'Boxing?' Kim asked.

'Yes, and not the good kind. Actually, there is no good kind, and the sport should have been outlawed years ago.'

'The guy at the gym told us there are safeguards though?' Penn said.

'Oh, dear boy, let me take a minute to disabuse you of that opinion. Do tell me what regulating body can foresee whether knocking a person unconscious will cause a concussion or permanent brain damage. Tell me how they regulate the force needed to knock a person out or kill them. Name me one governing body that can predict the later onset of a degenerative brain disease called chronic traumatic encephalopathy, which has no cure and which begins gently enough with mood and personality changes and then turns to memory loss, confusion and problems with movement.'

'But boxers know—'

'Did he know?' Keats shouted, making Penn jump as he pointed to Josh.

Her colleague hadn't read the signs.

The summons back from Keats with as few words as possible.

The absence of banter at Kim's expense.

The thoughtfulness extended to the victim.

Very few cases got to Keats emotionally, but this one had.

'You said this was the bad kind?' Kim asked, feeling that Penn had suffered enough.

'Bare-knuckle boxing. You see, early fighting had no written rules. Head-butting, eye-gouging, chokes, et cetera were all permitted. Bare-knuckle boxing originated in England and had a resurgence as we came into the twenty-first century.'

'But he's a kid,' Kim whispered, wondering what kind of sick individual wanted to watch kids beat the shit out of each other.

'There'll be money behind it somewhere, just like the legal stuff. It's big betting, but you won't find the odds at William Hill.'

'Underground,' Kim said.

'Probably fixtures and a league,' Penn added.

Given the number of boys missing in recent years, she couldn't help but wonder what the hell they'd stumbled upon.

'Okay, Keats, thanks for—'

'Yeah, that's actually not why I called you. You were probably minutes away from figuring that much out yourself.'

He stood at the foot of the body and gently pulled the sheet down to the toes.

'In addition to the multiple fractures to every phalanx in his hands, there is one recent fracture to both the triquetral and the hamate.'

She frowned, and he grabbed her by the hand and then squeezed at the point where her hand met her wrist.

'Okay,' she said, pulling her hand away.

'Bear that in mind as you take another look at his bruises.'

Kim said nothing. The extensive bruising looked exactly as it had when she'd seen it earlier.

'He'd had a really bad fight?' Kim asked.

Keats moved around the table, talking as he went. 'A bruise starts off red as the blood appears under the skin. In one to two days, the haemoglobin in the blood changes, and the bruise looks blueish, purple or black.

'Bruises turn green or yellow somewhere between five to ten days. After ten to fourteen days, they are yellowish brown or just brown. Mild bruises can last a few days to a week. Severe ones can last several weeks or longer.'

'That's a lot of fights,' Kim said, seeing the timeline of the bruises everywhere on this young boy's body.

'Take a look at his wrists and remember what I said about the most recent injury.'

Kim saw what looked like rope marks on both wrists.

'That injury to his hand meant he couldn't fight,' Kim said as Keats's discovery began to dawn on her.

'He wouldn't even have been able to make a fist.'

'Oh, Jesus,' Kim said, putting together the clues Keats had laid out for her. The malnutrition, the injury, the wrists, the bruises.

'I don't get it,' Penn said, looking from one to the other.

Kim had to swallow down nausea before answering.

'He was no use to his captors as a fighter, but he had one last purpose as he slowly starved to death.'

She took a breath before saying the words that told her they were dealing with monsters.

'He was tied up and used as a punching bag.'

FIFTY-THREE

It was almost seven before Bryant had a moment to chat to Stacey alone.

As instructed, Roy had never returned, and just ten minutes earlier Red had called to stand them all down.

Slowly, Dickinson, Adil and finally Carly had filtered out, right before Iris had entered with her cleaning trolley.

'What are we doing here, Bryant?' Stacey asked, sitting back in her chair.

'Trying to find two missing boys and some bad apples,' he said as his phone dinged receipt of a text message.

He took it out and read it with a smile. 'Guv wants to know if we're back at the hotel yet.'

He began typing a response.

'Ah, still looking after us even though she's not here,' Stacey said.

'Nah, Stace. She means she hopes we're not slacking off.'

He finished his reply and put his phone down.

'What did you say?'

'Told her we'd just got off the Big Dipper and we're heading towards the bumper cars.'

Stacey chuckled before continuing. 'Do you think they'll pay any more attention to Lewis now?'

'I definitely think that's gonna happen after seeing what you uncovered today. Bloody good work by the way.'

'Thanks for that,' she said, rubbing at her eyes. 'But I'm more worried about you. What the hell was Roy playing at today?'

'Dunno. We attended the crime scene. Bastard tried to get me to take a photo. Went to see Jasmine's ex-boyfriend, then to the morgue and then over to Pippa's for a bit of stress relief.'

He considered sharing his suspicions about Jasmine's murder and the visit to her ex-boyfriend, but he wanted to get the thoughts straight in his head first, and the exhaustion of the day was just starting to catch up with him.

'Aah yes, Pippa and the cryptic call. Did it work?' Stacey asked.

'Yeah, this time, but how about the next time? Who's going to stop it happening then?'

'You haven't got enough to go to the chief?' Stacey asked, stifling a yawn.

He shook his head. 'I've got no proof of him actually doing anything with Pippa, and she's not going to make a statement. She's terrified of him – she's moving just to get out of his reach. We've got to nail him for something big. We've got to make sure he can't hurt anyone else again.'

'How are we gonna do that?' she asked.

'I really have no idea.'

'Bryant, do you think we're in too deep here without the boss?'

He'd wondered the same thing himself. Every time he'd had a free minute, he'd considered calling the guv to discuss Jasmine's murder with her, and every time he'd reached the same conclusion before activating his phone.

'Trouble is, she's been called back to deal with a body. We gotta try and keep things moving in her absence.'

'Yeah, but if she knew we needed her back here...'

'Let's sleep on it, eh?' he said, standing up. It had been an exhausting day, and he needed some time alone to think.

Stacey grabbed her jacket and satchel as Iris headed their way.

They both already knew better than to hang around when Iris wanted to get things done.

She was dusting the keyboards before they'd even reached the door.

They were almost at the bottom of the stairs when Bryant heard a familiar voice.

'I haven't done anything,' the voice cried. 'I'd never hurt Jasmine. I swear to you I've done nothing wrong. Ask Roy – he'll tell you.'

Bryant pushed through the doors to the booking desk.

A female DI and a bunch of uniforms were booking someone in for the murder of Jasmine Swift.

The man in handcuffs was none other than her ex-boyfriend Justin Holmes.

FIFTY-FOUR

At 8.40 p.m., Kim finally lifted her weary legs onto the sofa. She had eventually stood herself and Penn down after the trip to the morgue. She had wanted nothing more than to collect Barney and spend a little quality time with her companion.

Even though she'd only been gone a couple of days, it had clearly felt much longer for both of them. She found it hard to believe that first thing this morning she'd been in Blackpool with the rest of her team.

'Come on, boy,' she said, patting the sofa beside her. He jumped up and nestled into the curve of her leg. Her hand instinctively reached for the back of his head, his favourite tickling spot. As though in sync, they both let out a long sigh.

'Yeah, I missed you too, buddy,' she said, letting her head rest on the back of the sofa.

Her brain was still whizzing with all that she'd learned in this one day. Her thoughts moved between the sorrowful sight of Josh on the cold metal table, beaten half to death, to the picture of a small family forced to accept that the missing part of their whole would never return.

The revulsion over what she'd learned today wouldn't leave

her. She had this horrific image of Josh being trussed up at the wrists and hung like a cattle carcass for the purpose of other kids practising on him, being kept barely alive with liquids so that he could be punched repeatedly.

She felt the anger rising within her again. As did Barney, who raised his head to find out why there was now tension flowing out of her fingertips. Anyone who told her that dogs couldn't read their owner's emotions had clearly never had a dog.

To distract her mind, she reached for her phone and wondered how she was going to solve another one of her problems.

She'd received three messages from Frost today. The first was a Paddy and Murphy joke, accompanied by a row of laughing emojis. The second was a clip of a little girl singing a Celine Dion song brilliantly for some televised talent show. A row of teary emojis had accompanied that one. The third had been an invitation to grab coffee after work.

As she was holding her phone, it beeped the receipt of another message. Kim shook her head. Text message number four had just landed. She clicked into it.

Hey, are you watching the TV? Taskmaster is bloody hilarious tonight!!!!

Kim clicked out of the message quickly, almost like Frost could trap her there. She would not respond at all to that one. Her one-word responses without emojis were obviously doing nothing to get the message across. The next day it all just started again. Kim idly wondered if another bang to the head might put it right. Then she shuddered at the thought of it, remembering the pool of blood in which they'd found the reporter.

No, she'd have to find another way to let Frost know the truth.

She put her phone down on the arm of the chair as Barney placed his entire body across her legs.

'You know, don't you?' she asked, giving his head a vigorous rub.

He pushed his head into her hand as she reached for her phone again. She couldn't rid herself of the suspicion that there was now another boy hanging where Josh had hung, being beaten for practice. Just the thought of that possibility was enough to keep the adrenaline pulsing around her body.

She pressed on her colleague's number. He answered on the second ring.

'Penn, I can't rest. I'm heading back to the station.'

'No probs. I'll get the kettle on.'

'What?' she asked, pushing herself up from the sofa.

'I'll make us a pot. It's no bother seeing as I'm already here.'

Kim ended the call with a hint of a smile as she attached Barney's lead.

Some days her team just blew her away.

FIFTY-FIVE

It had been almost nine when Bryant parked the car. It was now twelve minutes past, and he still hadn't got out.

He and Stacey had shared a quick meal in silence at the hotel before heading off to their rooms.

Once there, he'd been unable to settle after calling Jenny, convinced that Roy Moss would head back to Pippa Jacobs's house. And with one of the three names on the anonymous list already dead, it wasn't only the sex that was the problem. An even worse fate could befall her.

So what exactly was he going to do now? Sit here and watch the house all night? The plan in his mind hadn't been that detailed. All he knew was that just over there lived an empty, broken woman who never knew when the door was going to be knocked for someone to sexually assault her again. He didn't care if she was running a doss house or not; she didn't deserve that.

He got out of the car.

There was something inside him that needed to let her know that she had a friend, and that not all police officers were like Roy.

For some reason, he found himself looking around before he knocked on the door. An involuntary shiver crept up his spine, causing him to look again, but there was nothing except parked cars as far as his eyes could see.

Pippa opened the door and immediately her eyes filled with disgust and a hint of disappointment.

'Suppose you're here to—'

'Absolutely not,' Bryant said, shaking his head vigorously. 'In fact, the complete opposite.'

She frowned and stepped aside to let him in. She closed the door behind him. 'Go on.'

'I want you to take my number. I'm not sure how much longer I'll be around, but if he comes knocking, I want you to call me.'

'Why?' she asked, folding her arms. Was it too late for this young woman? Would she forever view any act of kindness with suspicion?

'Because I'd like to find a way to stop him from assaulting you again.'

'You gonna break down the door?' she asked with a wry smile.

'If I have to,' he said, returning the smile. 'We're not all like him.'

'So, you know what he's like?'

'We're getting a pretty good idea.'

'Yet he's still knocking my door and bringing his new buddies along too?'

'He will be stopped. I promise you that.'

She let out a long breath. 'I know you mean well...'

'Pippa, why have you never reported him?'

'You know why. My word against his. They'll never believe me. They didn't the last time.'

'What time?' Bryant asked, having no knowledge of any time at all.

'You seen my record?' she asked, pushing her hands into her pockets.

He nodded. 'I know you're an addict. I know there are other addicts here. But that still doesn't give him the right to—'

'You've read my record and think you know everything about me, which kind of proves my point. I'm clean. I've been clean for almost eighteen months. This house is now open only to people trying to get clean.'

Bryant was confused. 'You were only inside for possession seven months ago.'

'I was indeed. Moss came and I said no. I found the courage to tell him to fuck off. Coincidentally, I was raided that night and drugs were found in my room. A lot of drugs.'

'Jesus,' Bryant said, running his hand through his hair. He didn't doubt Pippa's story for a second.

'So, you'll understand why, much as I appreciate you trying to protect me, I know he's a step ahead. I just want to keep my head down and move out of this house. Then I'll be free.'

Bryant said nothing, wondering if she knew how easy it would be for Moss to find her if he wanted to. He was guessing that she just hoped he wouldn't be arsed to put in the effort.

'Look, I'll take your number, and I appreciate you taking the time and trouble to come here. I think you mean well. Now I want to return the favour and tell you to be careful. Roy might seem like your mate, but he isn't. It might seem like you've got him bang to rights, but you probably haven't.'

'Whatever it is, there's a reason he brought you here today, and it wasn't for a blow job between interviews. There's a bigger reason than that. Be careful.'

'Okay, thanks,' he said, giving her the card with his number.

He stepped out of the house, and the door closed behind him.

He stood for a moment, weighing Pippa's words. They seemed melodramatic but also plausible.

He stepped off the pavement as a vehicle further down the stretch of road pulled out and sped away, giving him no time to see the make or model of the car.

Probably just a boy racer or someone in a rush, he told himself as he approached his car.

Trouble was that neither his brain nor his gut believed it.

FIFTY-SIX

Penn was true to his word, and a fresh pot of coffee had brewed by the time she got there.

A bribe in the form of a pack of donuts for Jack on the desk had secured Barney's admission into the station.

'I just can't stop thinking about it,' Penn said. 'We're talking about kids taken from their families and forced to fight.'

'Or worse,' Kim added, picturing Josh being used in the most barbaric way. 'What do the numbers say?' she went on, taking a seat opposite Penn with her cuppa.

'Hard to get a clear picture based on all the forces, but by narrowing the age range to pre-teen, we're looking at approximately thirty to fifty boys who go missing each year and are never seen again.'

'Definitely enough for some kind of sick league, but how the hell would we find out?'

'Gotta be on the dark web somewhere,' Penn offered. 'Any network needs a hub to communicate.'

'But Cybercrime are crawling over that place. How have they not come across it?'

Penn shrugged. 'We already know there are search engines

that allow users to connect without fear of being tracked. We also know there are trading sites where people can purchase illegal goods and services.'

The idea of it always gave Kim the image of masked men parked up in dark, unsavoury areas with their car boots open. If only the dark web was no more sinister than folks selling stolen or counterfeit goods out the back of vans.

Even she had heard of sites like Silk Road, a kind of Amazon for drugs, fake drivers' licences and countless other illegal products. Although shut down by the FBI in 2014, it had continued to raise its head in various forms over the years.

'So, can we just search the dark web for anything to do with illegal child fighting?' Kim asked, trying to picture it as a filthy Google.

'Tried it,' Penn said. 'No joy. It's either dressed up as something else, or we're going to have to get more creative and go deeper to find where it's hiding.'

'What do you mean about being dressed up as something else?'

'I mean it's like buying something and it not being what you thought. I suppose it's like wearing a mask. Like a place that's advertising itself as a sweet shop in its store window, but when you get in there, they're selling drugs. The site could be masquerading as something else, and we need a search engine that can go deeper into the code to give us what we want.'

Kim scratched her head. 'Bloody hell, Penn, you're losing me.'

'It gets worse. If the hub of the league is hiding as something else, it may not only be on the shop front.'

'Go on,' Kim said after groaning loudly. Every sentence he uttered pushed them further away from finding these monsters.

Penn wasn't put off as a soft snore came from Barney at her feet.

'Okay, back to our sweet shop analogy. Let's say we're

looking for the word cocaine in the IP address. We're not gonna find it because the IP address is listed as Haribo, but we don't believe it and we access the site anyway. And now we're in, we can search for cocaine, right?'

'Yeah,' Kim agreed.

'But what if cocaine is listed as lemon sherbet or fruit burst. Heroin could be listed as—'

'Okay, I got it. So, you're saying that trying to find this on the dark web is virtually impossible unless we know the codes they use?'

'Pretty much,' he said, pushing away his keyboard.

Kim thought for a moment.

'Not so fast with the defeatist attitude. If we're right, we're talking about a network.'

'Correct.'

'Well, networks were around a long time before the internet, so maybe this one existed before then too. And good old networking starts how?' Kim asked, pushing back her chair.

'Talking, word of mouth, newsletters.'

'Exactly. Grab your coat. I know precisely where we need to start.'

Penn followed her and Barney down to the car park, where a familiar vehicle pulled up alongside them. They barely had a second to respond before Steve Ashworth was out of the car and blocking their way.

'Detective Inspector, long time no see.'

Yes, it had been over twenty-four hours, and she'd felt it was too good to be true.

'Had lunch with Lydia today. You remember Lydia, don't you? The wife of the man you—'

'Oh, fuck off,' she snapped, trying to walk around him.

He stepped right in front of her, and she had to stop short so as not to touch him. She could imagine what he'd make of that. Barney growled, straining on the lead.

'Aah, losing your cool now, Inspector?' Ashworth goaded. 'Probably not the first time. It'll come as no surprise to learn that Lydia really, really hates you. So damn helpful she was. Gave me lots of dates, times. She still has them after all these years. Makes for very interesting reading.'

She attempted to step around him again as Penn looked to her for guidance.

'Oh, and I found Amber Rose. She's twenty-eight now, and life hasn't been all that—'

'I'm not interested,' Kim growled.

'Oh but you were interested, Inspector. Interested enough to cause a man's death.'

Kim stepped into his face. 'Ashworth, so help me God, I'll tear every—'

'One of those pages from your notebook,' Penn finished, getting in the middle of them. He then stepped back, forcing her away from the reporter and giving her a second to regain her sanity.

Ashworth met her gaze with a look of triumph that he'd broken through her composure and got the reaction he'd been waiting for.

He offered her one last smirk before he got back into the car.

'Damn it,' she cursed under her breath as she got into Penn's car.

Her colleague said nothing as he pulled out of the car park, but he'd done her a huge favour.

If he hadn't got in between them, there was no telling what she would have done.

FIFTY-SEVEN

LEWIS

Lewis had lost track of the days he'd been here. He was sure it had been longer than a week, but for all he knew it might have been two.

He'd tried to keep track of time when he was in the small room, and again when he'd been brought to the stables, but sometimes the pills made him drowsy and sometimes they didn't, meaning he didn't know if he'd slept for a few hours or straight through the night.

He had known within an hour in the stables that he wasn't in there alone. Within ten minutes of being chained to the ground, he'd heard a cough. He'd tried to make contact just like the new boy this morning had, and he'd been told the consequences of speaking by one of the others. First talking offence got you no food for twenty-four hours. Get caught a second time, you lost both the food and the privilege of being taken to the toilet. No one wanted to sit in their own mess.

He didn't know how many others there were, but he wondered if they'd been caught the same way he had. Had they been offered money as well? Had they been told that it was like a summer camp where they'd learn to fight? Had the others refused because they'd already heard their parents talking about sending them away like he had? Not that it had mattered. He hadn't noticed the van was still there as he'd headed home, and they'd just grabbed him anyway.

He wished he knew how many others there were, but all he could see through the wooden fencing was that there appeared to be an identical pen on the other side of the walkway. He hadn't been able to see more of the building, as he was blind-folded every time he was taken out and brought back. He heard others being taken out and brought back too, and he sometimes heard the low whispers of Mister and Missus, the people who had abducted him, but he hadn't been able to keep track of how many other boys were imprisoned alongside him.

On one of the days, he'd started thinking about trying to escape. He'd thought of trying to overpower Mister during one of the toilet trips. That same day, one of the others must have tried it. He'd heard a scream and some swear words from Mister before hearing something being thrown against the wall. More angry words had followed, and the sound of someone in pain had echoed around the building before Mister had left and turned out the light. Lewis had heard pained cries for the next few hours. The following day, he'd seen a bite mark on Mister's hand when he'd brought in the food.

Every time he was taken out, Lewis had tried to form an escape plan. He counted the steps on the hard gravel until he was shoved into an outside toilet. He had seventeen steps to try and make his escape. But he was blindfolded and naked except for his underpants. He had no clue where he was and knew he didn't have the stamina to outrun Mister. There had to be a way though. It was just waiting until the right moment came along.

His thoughts were interrupted by the barn door opening. Food was coming, and however much he hated his captors and his conditions, he was grateful that it was time to eat.

Mister appeared at the gate to his enclosure, and his heart sank when he saw what was in the man's hand.

This was a real plate. On it was steaming meat, vegetables and mashed potatoes. His stomach rumbled in response, even though the feeling of dread had started to form. This had only happened one other time. He knew what it meant.

'Okay, Lewis,' Mister said, sitting on the ground beside him.

The plate also held a knife and fork that he would never get to touch.

Mister cut off a piece of the steak. 'Come on, Lewis, eat up. You're fighting tomorrow night.'

Despite the dread in his stomach, his body still craved the food.

He'd been taken to fight only once before, and it was an experience he'd never forget. The first fight had been between a couple of boys older than him. They had gone at it for a good fifteen minutes before one of the boys was knocked out cold. He had watched as well-dressed men jeered and cheered throughout the bouts. He'd watched money change hands all around the ring. And he'd watched when, after attempts to revive the unconscious boy had failed, he'd been dragged out of sight. He'd overheard Mister say 'dead' and knew that he'd been talking about the unconscious boy.

He didn't want to fight. From what he'd seen, none of them wanted to fight. But it was survival.

Lewis opened his mouth to receive the food. He had to be as strong as possible or the next person being dragged out dead could be him.

FIFTY-EIGHT

Warren was just closing the door to the gym when they got there.

Kim placed her toe against the frame as an extra measure of insurance.

'Hey, buddy, got a minute?' she asked with more manners than she felt. The confrontation with Steve Ashworth was still rattling her nerves.

He looked down at her foot, the positioning of which belied the fact he had a choice.

She forced the reporter from her mind. She was watching Warren's micro expressions more closely this time and detected a shadow of fear. She liked that. People who were nervous had something to hide, which meant that there was something he didn't want her to know. That made her even more determined to find out what it was.

He stepped back into the gym and flicked a switch that illuminated only the lobby area, leaving the rest of the vast building in eerie darkness.

'So, how do you pick 'em?' Kim asked, taking a seat on the sofa.

'Sorry? Pick what?'

'The kids who are good enough for the league?'

'What league?' he asked without enough confusion in his voice.

Kim sighed. 'Warren, you are going to have to assume that we've come back here with a lot more information than we had earlier.'

'I honestly don't have a—'

'Fella, we know for a fact that Josh's time away from his family was spent fighting. We also know he didn't go willingly. The kid was walking home. As it's unlikely he spent four years fighting with himself, we can assume there's another kid involved. And why stop at two when you can just lift anyone off the streets or arrange to have them abducted.'

Warren swallowed loudly, telling her a lot. He knew something, and he was terrified.

'You know kids are going missing, and that kids are turning up dead and beaten. From abduction to murder, I'm working out how many crimes I can arrest you for.'

'I don't do anything, I swear,' he said, almost falling onto the sofa.

For his legs to fold on him so easily, Kim believed him.

'But you know stuff, so let's start there.'

'I can't. They'll know. They'll hurt me.'

'We can do this down at the station if you'd feel safer.'

'God, no, definitely not. I just can't put my family in that kind of—'

'Everyone's got a family, Warren. But okay, let's talk hypotheticals.'

He nodded.

'Is it possible that boys from this gym have been trafficked into an underground fighting league?'

'It's possible,' he said, looking behind him even though the place was in darkness.

'And is it possible that your boss, the gym owner, might be heavily involved?'

Warren nodded.

'Was the fire a set-up? A distraction to make Josh's abduction easier?'

Again, he nodded.

'When did you know?'

'I didn't know for certain,' Warren said as the air seemed to leave his body. His flesh crumpled in on itself. 'I got suspicious that something had happened when I questioned the camera angle the following day. The same company's been servicing them for years. They'd never left one positioned like that before.'

'You think your boss moved it?'

Warren nodded.

'Why Josh?' Kim asked. There must have been hundreds of boys passing through these doors.

'Josh had talent. He had skill from the minute he stepped into the ring. He had a gift that couldn't be taught and the right amount of anger to go with it. He could have been a professional,' Warren said with fondness in his tone.

Kim took out her phone and thrust it towards him.

'That's Josh now.'

Warren's mouth dropped open as his face drained of all colour.

Kim could see that he wanted to look away but couldn't. Not until his own body betrayed him and he turned to the side and vomited.

Penn grabbed a wastepaper bin and placed it beside him.

'Okay, okay, put it away,' he begged before making more retching noises.

Kim waited.

'Th... that's not boxing.'

'Oh, he boxed all right. Did it for years, and he's got the

broken bones to prove it. But poor Josh, who had such a gift for it, sustained an injury that put him out of action, so they used him as a punching bag instead before strangling him and throwing his body in the canal.'

Warren turned and puked again, but Kim wasn't prepared to go easy on him. He'd known something about Josh's disappearance and had chosen to do nothing. Josh could have been home safe and sound if this man had spoken up about what he knew.

'Imagine having to go and explain that to his family, Warren.'

Warren raised his head. There were tears streaming over his cheeks.

'You mentioned your family, so I'm gonna take a wild guess that you've got kids. I'd like you, for the purpose of true empathy and understanding, to imagine one of your children being hung up like a dead animal: terrified, alone, starving, wondering why you haven't rescued them from being punched repeatedly until their internal organs pop inside their—'

'Okay, I'll tell you everything I know, I swear.'

Kim sat back and waited.

For the first time she actually believed him.

FIFTY-NINE

The feeling of unease hadn't left Bryant all night. Even the bacon he was putting on his plate held no appeal despite the fact he was able to enjoy it without Jenny's gentle disapproval.

He took a seat opposite Stacey and buttered a slice of toast, but that held little appeal either. He was happy to put it back on the plate when his phone sounded receipt of a message.

'Guess who?' he asked, rolling his eyes.

'What's she say?' Stacey asked before spooning more cereal into her mouth.

'To stop dawdling over breakfast cos time's a wasting.'

'You think she's taking this awful boss act a bit far?' Stacey chuckled.

'Oh yeah, she's got into character, all right.'

Though he wanted to nail Roy Moss, there was a part of him that wished he'd retuned to the Black Country with the guv. After what Pippa had said to him, he wondered if he really had bitten off more than he could chew. He wished he had the boss to bounce off some of the stuff in his head.

Much as he hated to admit it, there were times when her objective, unapologetic opinion cleared the forest so that he could see the wood for the trees. Another part of him knew that the equilibrium of the team was severely damaged when they were separated and two entire skill sets were missing from the tool shed. He even missed Penn a little bit.

He took a bite of the cold toast and sat back in his chair.

'Hey, Stace, don't you just wish she was—?'

'Hey, team, did ya miss us?'

Bryant's head snapped round as the guv and Penn headed their way.

He blinked to make sure his imagination hadn't conjured up a mirage, but they were definitely real.

'Why, you been somewhere?' he asked with a smile. The relief that flooded through him was immense.

The guv nudged him as she took a seat and reached for a piece of toast.

Stacey looked as pleased to see them as he was and was quick to pour Penn a fresh cup of tea.

'Case solved already?' he asked. Even without knowing what the case was it would still have been some kind of record.

'Not yet but getting closer. Pretty certain it's linked to what's going on up here.'

Stacey put down her fork. 'We know Lewis and Noah were taken by the same people.'

The guv nodded. 'Without a doubt. Our boy back home, Josh, was abducted four years ago from a local gym. He'd be fifteen now.'

Bryant could feel the lines linking the dots. 'Fighting?'

'Yep, the bare-knuckle, no-rules kind.'

'But they're kids,' Stacey said with a hint of doubt.

'No, they're entertainment and big business. The guy who vomited, literally, the information to us last night knew that Josh had been abducted for that purpose, but it's his boss who arranged it. Our informant is now in custody being questioned more fully and unable to give his boss the heads-up that we're on to them.'

'And where's his boss?' Bryant asked.

'Up north somewhere.'

Ah, now he understood the reason for the guv's return.

'We're pretty sure there's some kind of league which could include as many as a hundred boys nationwide.'

'Bloody hell,' Bryant said, blowing out air. The guv had barely got her legs under the breakfast table and they'd moved from two missing boys to possibly a hundred caught up in an illegal fighting racket.

'So, what now?' Stacey asked.

'We talk to Red and see if we can get everyone moving in the same direction.'

'Good luck with that,' Stacey groaned. 'It took some persuading that Noah and Lewis were taken by the same people, and that was with video evidence.'

'You found something on CCTV?' the guv asked.

'Yep, got Lewis being forced into the back of a van and what looks like the same van in the area at the exact same time that Noah disappeared.'

'Jesus, good work, Stace. What about you?' she asked, turning Bryant's way.

'I just spent the day with the biggest piece of shit in the police force.'

'Anything we can use?' she said, getting straight to the point.

He shook his head. 'Nothing that will guarantee his removal, but something you need to know. Jasmine Swift was found raped and murdered yesterday morning,' he said and felt instant relief that the words were out of his mouth. In the hours since he'd visited the crime scene, he'd questioned his decision not to tell her, but ultimately there would have been little she could do from back home.

'Jesus Christ,' she said, taking a minute to digest the information.

No one spoke as they all finished their breakfast.

He understood the thoughts that would be going through her mind because they'd been with him ever since he'd turned up at the crime scene. Had they somehow precipitated her murder by speaking with her about Red?

Eventually the guv broke the silence. 'So, not only do we think we might have stumbled upon a national illegal fighting ring with heavy ties to the north, but someone who could have made a complaint about corruption in the local force turns up raped and murdered?'

They all nodded.

'That's not all, guv,' Bryant said before finishing his cuppa. 'Pretty sure I watched Roy Moss frame Jasmine's ex-boyfriend for the crime.'

'Bloody hell, looks like I came back in the nick of time.'

SIXTY

'Not a chance,' Red said, shaking his head. 'Sounds a bit far-fetched, and I'm not throwing resources at it. A fighting ring, for God's sake.'

Kim kept her temper in check. It was the response she'd expected, but she'd hoped she was wrong. Was this man ever going to stop blocking their progress?

'If the owner of the gym is up here, then there's a good chance there's going to be some kind of fight. We have the opportunity to try and—'

'Inspector, how you choose to manage your own team is your own affair, but now we know our two boys are linked, we're going to focus on widening our net on sex offenders.'

Kim groaned. His view was as narrow as looking through a kitchen-roll tube. It had taken three days and a mountain of evidence provided by her team to prove to him that the disappearances of the boys were linked at all, and now he couldn't even fathom that this thing went wider than Lewis and Noah.

'Shall we?' he asked, pointing to the door that led to the squad room where both teams were waiting.

Kim conceded defeat and stood. It wasn't that she doubted

the correct direction of the investigation, but now she knew it would be her team alone following it.

'And I'm sorry to hear about the rape and murder of Jasmine Swift. Roy said you knew her,' she offered as he opened the door.

He visibly bristled. 'I knew her as the victim of a crime, nothing more.'

'Of course,' Kim said in a tone that said she'd never thought otherwise.

Not a subject he was eager to discuss, she noted as they exited his office. Bryant had filled her in on the events of the day before, and like him she found the whole thing highly suspicious. Why had Roy attended the crime scene? But more importantly why had he visited the ex-boyfriend and then returned to the morgue? She had a pretty good idea, but now wasn't the time to bring it up. They needed more information before bringing it to anyone's attention.

'Okay, people,' Red said, standing at the head of the room. 'We're splitting the investigations again. The away team are working their own leads on a case unconnected to ours, and we're going to be chasing down local paedos.'

'So, you'll be getting off home then?' Roy asked, turning to her.

'Not your business, Roy,' Red snapped. 'But their case might have links this end of the country, so they're free to use the office space assigned to them until the chief says otherwise.'

Kim caught both underlying messages. First, separate yourself and don't distract the home team. Second, he'd be lobbying for the chief to make that call sooner rather than later.

'Sounds like a long day ahead,' Roy said, tapping his fingers on the desk. 'Hope everyone got a good night's sleep.'

His glance settled on Bryant, who looked away. An alarm of unease rose in her stomach.

'What's happening with the Jasmine Swift case?' Bryant asked, looking directly at Red.

'An arrest has been made, but our involvement with that case is over.'

'Who was arrested?' he pushed, despite knowing exactly who it was. She guessed that he wanted to hear Red say it, and he wanted to see Roy's reaction when he did.

'Not our business, pal, so it's certainly none of yours,' Red snapped.

'Okay, guys,' Kim said, shepherding her team into their own war room. 'Clearly, we're on our own,' she went on once the door was closed. 'So we play nice to hang on to the office space and the logs. Red is convinced there's no link to our boy Josh, but we still need to have access to the regional reports.'

They all nodded their understanding.

'Stace, I want you looking for any links between Lewis and Noah. We know Lewis was probably chosen because he was a fighter, but how did these people know that? How did they know about Noah, or was that an opportunistic grab?'

'Got it, boss.'

Kim turned to Penn. 'I want you going as deep as possible into the dark web. If our gym owner is up this way, there's a good chance there's an event happening soon. We need to be at that fight.'

'Try my best, boss,' Penn said.

Kim turned back to the detective constable. 'Stace?'

'Just sending it through now, boss.'

Kim waited for her phone to sound receipt of the message before standing.

The video had shocked her. Seeing Lewis being bundled into the van so blatantly had boiled her blood.

Lewis had been propositioned first. He'd refused, but then they'd taken him anyway.

Given the attitude of his parents and the interaction between Kevin and Lewis in the arcade, this thing had been planned. At least one of the three of them had known about it.

SIXTY-ONE

'Would now be a good time for you to share anything you haven't told me?' Kim asked once she and Bryant were in the car.

'Roy Moss is a bent bastard.'

'Or something I didn't already know? Roy doesn't say anything for nothing, so why the quip about you getting enough sleep?'

He shrugged. She knew him well enough to know he'd never lie to her, but that was different to not telling her the whole truth.

'Okay, let's do this another way. I want a blow by blow account of your day with him yesterday.'

'We attended the crime scene of Jasmine Swift, where he tried to take a photo of the body. I accidentally knocked the phone from his hand.'

Kim smiled. Of course he had.

'Next, we went to see Jasmine's ex-boyfriend before going back to the morgue because he wanted to check something.'

'Okay,' she said. She knew that and already knew what their

next step was going to be on that matter, but there was clearly something her colleague hadn't yet told her.

'Next, we paid a visit to Pippa Jacobs for some stress relief.'

Kim rubbed at her forehead. This was new information and helped to explain why Bryant was coiled like a spring. He'd spent the day watching a man be everything he despised.

'How did you manage to...?'

'A timely call from Stacey got us out of there in time. Got back to the station, where Red ripped Roy a new one for getting involved in the Jasmine Swift case.'

But was he really that angry? Kim wondered. It was mightily convenient that someone with a potential complaint against him would now never get the chance to speak. Had Red found some way to silence her either himself or with help?

'And that was the end of the day?' she asked, pushing her suspicions to the side for now.

'For me and Roy, yes.'

'Jesus, Bryant, do I have to pry you open with a crowbar?'

'I went back to see Pippa.'

Kim groaned. 'Alone?'

Bryant nodded.

'Please tell me you didn't go inside.'

'I did.'

'Shit, Bryant, I know you know better than that. What the hell were you thinking? Have you completely lost your senses?'

The woman could level any accusation at him and he wouldn't have a leg to stand on. Having no witness to the conversation between the two of them left him open to all kinds of allegations.

'I just wanted to reassure her that we weren't all bad. Her only image of me was that I was waiting in line to abuse her just like Roy.'

'And you couldn't have given her that reassurance on the

doorstep, or with Stacey as a witness?' Kim asked, trying to keep the anger out of her voice.

'I didn't think.'

'Jeez, Bryant, you've played right into Moss's hands.'

Now Roy's comment about a late night made sense. Obviously, Roy had seen him.

'I know, but she did reveal something. She's clean, and so is everyone else in that house. Eighteen months since she's touched the stuff.'

Kim frowned, recalling her record. 'But she recently did time for...'

'Yeah because she said no to Roy. She found the strength to refuse him, and that night she was hauled in on possession charges. She's bloody terrified, and she warned me to watch out. Pippa reckons he's capable of just about anything.'

'Jesus,' she said, rubbing her forehead. The cesspool through which they were wading was now right up to her knees. 'Even more reason why you should have made sure he had nothing to use against you.'

'It's not even that that's bothering me. I know I've done nothing wrong, and I'll fight that to the death. It's the fact that I feel like I have all the pieces of the puzzle to nail him, and I just can't get them in the right order.'

'Stop beating yourself up about that. From what you've told me, you only have enough to get him suspended on full pay pending an enquiry. That could take months, meaning anyone with the power to speak against him is in danger. He has to believe he's free and clear until we have what we need to bury him properly.'

'And how do you propose we're going to do that?' Bryant asked.

'Let me think on it,' she said as they pulled up outside the house of the Stevens family.

Kim allowed Bryant's question to get in line with the others. She could only deal with so many problems at a time, and right now she had two missing boys who might still be alive.

The door opened to reveal Bobby Stevens, whose expression instantly darkened.

'I thought we made it clear that you're not welcome.'

'I think you'll change your mind when you hear what we have to say.'

'There's nothing you—'

'Let them in,' Kevin said, appearing from nowhere.

Only now, seeing them side by side, did Kim realise how the teenager towered over his stepdad.

Before Bobby could stop him, Kevin had ripped the door from his grip and thrown it open.

Kim strode in and headed straight for the kitchen.

'We have news,' she said, hoping Shirley was going to want to hear what they had to say immediately.

'One minute,' she said, shepherding the last of her young brood across the hall into the lounge.

Kim didn't know if she was genuinely trying to protect young ears or playing for time.

'I'm staying,' Kevin said, taking a seat at the table.

Shirley nodded her agreement as she dried her hands on a tea towel.

'Lewis was definitely abducted,' Kim stated, watching them closely.

They all looked to each other in surprise. Kim was unsure if they were surprised at the news or surprised that she had the news.

'We have the video if you want to see it,' Kim offered.

Shirley shook her head, Bobby looked to the ground and Kevin glowered at both of them.

The truth was staring her in the face.

'You all knew,' Kim said in disbelief.

No one argued with her.

'It'll do him good,' Bobby said, folding his arms. 'Little shit is always fighting anyway – might as well make a bit of money from it. When he comes back—'

'If he comes back,' Kim snapped, unable to believe what she was hearing.

'Wh... what?' Shirley spluttered. 'They said it would be a few months,' she said, looking to Bobby for confirmation.

'Well, give or take,' Bobby said, looking uncomfortable for the first time since Kim had met him.

'Are you lot actually serious? You knew all along that Lewis hadn't run away and you've chosen to deliberately waste police time. What the hell kind of family is this?'

'It's for his own good,' Shirley said, her eyes reddening. 'He'll be back soon, and they said...'

'Who's they?' Kim asked.

'Some guys in the pub,' Bobby answered. 'They train young fighters, like a boot camp. Teach 'em some discipline and get 'em ready for professional fighting.'

'This is what they told you?' Kim asked.

Bobby's nodding motion got more emphatic the longer he did it, making her think she still wasn't getting the whole truth. There was something he was keeping to himself, and Kim had an idea what it might be.

'How long until they bring him back?' she asked.

He coloured. 'Well they didn't really say...'

'You said six months,' Shirley roared. 'You said he'd be looked after and taught how to do it properly. You said that when he came back, he'd be like he was before.'

Bobby shrugged as though he had no more answers to give.

'How much did they give you?' Kim asked, remembering the shopping bags she'd seen from a supermarket this family looked like they couldn't easily afford.

'Five thousand,' Bobby said as though he still couldn't see what he'd done wrong.

'You sold your son for five thousand quid?' Kim growled. No monetary figure made their actions justifiable, but was that really all Lewis had been worth? Had all three of them been so happy to let him go?

Kim turned to Kevin, remembering the footage from the arcade café. 'You tried to stop it?'

He nodded. 'I knew what was going on, and he'd overheard something himself. I tried to get him to ring Mum and apologise, tell her he'd try to do better. I knew she'd call it off if he behaved himself, but he refused. He never would while he was around,' he said, pointing towards Bobby. 'He fucking hated you, and you'd never give him a break. Go on – tell them what you did. Tell them why he was so pissed off. He wasn't acting up. You deliberately got him angry.'

Kevin allowed the hatred he truly felt to show in his eyes. Shirley frowned, unsure what Kevin was talking about.

Kim knew there had been an argument the day Lewis had been abducted, but she didn't know why.

'I was just clearing up,' Bobby said in a voice that dripped of fake innocence.

'He'd been saving those matches up for weeks. His teacher was gonna get the whole class to have a go, and you threw them all in the bin.'

Kim could see the rage building higher and higher in the teenager. If that had been a deliberate act on Bobby's part, she could understand why Lewis had kicked off.

Kevin turned back to her. 'I didn't know it was going to be that night or I'd never have left him.'

Kim nodded that she believed him. The footage she'd seen in the café at the arcade completely matched his story.

She turned back to his parents. 'So, you sold your son for five thousand pounds?'

Bobby guffawed. 'Stop being so dramatic. Once he's back—'

'What was it about these people that made you think they were good guys?' Kim asked. 'Some random men in a pub tell you they're gonna make a man out of your son, teach him a sport, and give you five thousand pounds?'

Bobby looked genuinely befuddled. 'No, it wasn't like that. They knew what they were talking about. They made it sound like an opportunity that—'

'Of course they did. They wanted your co-operation to abduct your son, and you gave it to them. Do you know where he is? Did they give you an address? Can you call him, write to him?'

Bobby was shaking his head, but his pride refused to let go. 'It'll be good for him! You're making it seem—'

'I'm telling you the truth. You sold your son into an illegal, underground fighting ring where young boys turn up dead.'

'No,' Shirley cried out, covering her mouth with her hand.

Kim turned towards her. She might not have had all the facts, but she'd still allowed her twelve-year-old son to be taken by strangers.

'When he comes home, we'll make it right,' Shirley said.

Kim took out her phone and felt no guilt for what she was about to do.

'Another one of the boys abducted by this gang went home yesterday. And this is what he looked like.'

She held up the photo of Josh's bruised and battered body on the mortuary table.

'Nooooo,' Shirley screamed before tears began flowing over her cheeks.

'Four years they had him against his will. Four years he suffered at the hands of these monsters, being held captive, starved, forced to fight—'

'Get out,' Shirley said in a voice that had turned icily cold.

'Mrs Stevens, we—'

'Not you. Him,' she spat across the room.

'Don't be soft, Shirl,' Bobby said. 'He'll be back.'

'Get out of this house or I swear to God, I'll stab you. Police or no police.'

'Shirl.'

The woman launched herself from the chair with murder in her eyes. 'So help me I'll wring your bloody—'

'Easy,' Bryant said, stepping between them.

Shirley's arms flailed around Bryant, trying to make contact with her husband. Bryant held her still while Bobby tried to inch out of her way.

'Just go,' Kevin said, standing. 'No one wants you here.'

Bobby Stevens looked around the room, and nothing but contempt met his gaze.

He grabbed his jacket from the back of the door and slammed his way out of the house.

Bryant didn't need to be told to follow him. They needed to learn everything about the people who had approached him in the pub.

'He is dead, isn't he, that boy?' Shirley asked with a face now devoid of all colour.

Kim put her phone away and nodded. 'Unless we catch them, Lewis won't be coming home,' she said.

The pain ravaged Shirley's face as her tears fell quicker. A low guttural moan came out of her mouth and began to fill the room.

Kevin looked at his mother with compassion if not understanding before heading across the hall to check on his younger siblings.

Kim waited while the woman came to terms with the consequences of her actions. There was no doubting the depth of her regret and pain. Kim was sure she was watching a heart break in two.

Shirley's hand shot out and grabbed her wrist. 'Whether I deserve it or not, you have to bring my son home.'

Kim had every intention of getting Lewis back. She just wasn't sure that home was going to be the right place for him to go.

SIXTY-TWO

Although they were far from home, Stacey derived some comfort from Penn being back. Yes, it was a different office, different surroundings, but there was a familiarity in having Penn opposite her while the boss and Bryant were out on the ground.

The thought of Bryant brought a pang to her heart. The man had looked so miserable at breakfast, which had been due only in part to the boss's absence.

Her surprise arrival had brought some life back to his eyes, but the real cheer stealer was Roy Moss and having to work so closely with him. She could imagine that no amount of hot showers would rid him of the stench.

It was ironic that although he was the oldest member of the team, Bryant was also the most innocent. The man had a built-in optimism, a ray of hope that he used to give even the worst people the benefit of the doubt. He wanted to believe that however deeply buried, the ability to be good existed in everyone. Unfortunately, Roy Moss was battering that belief out of him.

She sighed inwardly, wishing she knew how to help him

back, but she was always at a loss with Bryant, feeling that she had nothing useful to offer a man of his experience. Instead, she kept her head down and trusted that the boss would know how to straighten him out.

'Anything?' Stacey asked her colleague. It felt like his facial expression had been frozen for half an hour.

Penn shook his head, and she didn't envy him one little bit. Spending any kind of time on the dark web was something she avoided. In truth, she was nervous of algorithms bleeding across the line.

She remembered how she'd once idly watched a video on social media of a sheep being rescued. Before she knew it, her timeline had been flooded with footage of animals in distress, each video more graphic than the last. That had been bad enough, but if she was searching for something particularly dark, would the search engine coding transfer over to the clear web? It just wasn't worth the risk.

Her own search to establish a link between Noah and Lewis was proving equally challenging.

Lewis had attended the local comprehensive, while Noah had been schooled privately just outside Lytham St Anne's. Lewis was often in trouble for fighting, but Noah was a straight A student. Lewis played no after-school sports or activities, but Noah played hockey. She couldn't see anywhere the boys would have had anything in common either in or out of school. There were no staff members that had transferred between schools or social events where they'd have been likely to meet.

She'd turned her attention to the parents. Shirley Stevens was a stay-at-home mum. Noah's mum worked part-time at an estate agent's. Bobby Stevens had been in and out of low-skilled jobs for a decade but none that would have brought him into contact with Noah's mum or his dad, who worked between Preston and home as a forensic accountant.

Scouring their social media, Stacey could see no crossover of hobbies or interests and no friends in common. There were no local companies, eateries or events that had been liked or followed by someone from both families.

How these people had found both boys she had no idea.

From Penn's expression, he was having the same trouble as she was.

'Brainstorm?' she asked.

'Yes please,' he said, sitting back in his chair. 'What you got?'

She reeled off all the avenues she'd explored. As she listed them, she could read on his face a new thought that was later discounted as she continued going through what she'd already checked.

'Jesus, that's quite a list, Stace. No contractors or workmen?'

Stacey shook her head.

'Church?'

'Don't think the Stevens family are a God-fearing bunch, and no hint of religion from the Reid family. I just can't find anywhere that both families would have come into contact either with each other or the same person.'

'Are you even sure there is a link?' Penn asked. 'Maybe Lewis was planned but Noah was an opportunistic grab.'

'I might be wrong but my gut tells me that they weren't parked up outside the pier waiting for a boy of the right age to just saunter past alone. I think they had their eye on that family and that the Reids were known to them somehow, but the link is just not coming to me. I need to rest my brain a minute. What're you doing?'

'Trying to find where this illegal fighting ring is hiding.'

'You've tried the obvious searches?' Stacey asked, knowing he wasn't using Google.

'Yep and coming up blank. I suppose if it was that easy, Cybercrime would have found them by now.'

'The search term has gotta be something similar though.

Interested folks have got to be able to find it and know what they're looking for.'

'Dog fighting?' Penn asked.

Stacey thought before shaking her head. 'Not because they're not the kind of despicable creatures who would do that, but it's a contentious issue that would likely get attention.'

'Even from people searching the dark web?' Penn asked, raising an eyebrow.

'Not everyone doing illegal stuff is completely amoral. I'm sure many of them have dogs and would alert the authorities. I might be wrong, but I don't think they'd be that obvious.'

'Okay, Stace, that's given me something to think about... With your problem, it has to be some kind of service that both families have received. Someone must have seen both boys.'

With that, Penn turned his attention back to his screen.

Stacey took a minute to think about all that she knew.

There was only one avenue she hadn't tried.

She logged into the system and did a search on the Reid family address.

'Awww... shit.'

'What?' Penn asked.

'I've found the link. The Reid family also had a break-in recently. Attended by this team. The link between the two families is right here.'

SIXTY-THREE

'Anything of any use about the guys in the pub?' Kim asked as she and Bryant got back into the car.

While Bryant had been chasing down Bobby Stevens, she'd been trying to pry any useful information from Shirley. Sickeningly, all her information had come from her husband. As she'd recounted the course of events in detail, Shirley had seemed bewildered by her own stupidity in what she'd believed was going to happen.

'They're not bringing him back, are they?' she'd asked through the tears.

Kim had shaken her head. That was why they had to be found. These boys were far too dangerous to be left alive once they'd outlived their entertainment value or, like Josh, suffered a complicated injury.

Kim had listened for the next ten minutes as Shirley had recounted how happy they'd been before Bobby had come along. Other than her youngest children, he'd brought nothing positive to the marriage.

From the hatred in her eyes and the venom in her tone, Kim knew Bobby's goose was well and truly cooked. He wouldn't be setting foot in that house again. Kim was slightly unsure if Shirley's threat of killing him was as idle as she hoped it was.

After checking on Kevin and assuring him they would do everything to bring Lewis home, Kim had left the house and met Bryant out on the pavement.

'Nothing,' he answered, putting on his seat belt. 'One phone number to make final arrangements. Text only. Got the number, but the phone is no longer in service.'

Not for the first time Kim wished there was a law against burner phones.

'Any description of them?'

'Yeah, average everything, height, weight, both white, wore jeans, sweatshirts, no distinguishing features, scars or tattoos.'

'Really?'

'Yeah, anyone would think he doesn't want us to track them down. Sure would have loved to slap some cuffs on him.'

'Red's call,' Kim said, trying to remember they were here to assist. But she secretly hoped Red had the bollocks to haul him in.

'Where to now, guv?' Bryant asked, starting the engine.

'Well, I've been thinking about that. Wanna pop by the morgue?'

'For what?' Bryant asked.

'The only thing that could have prompted your man to be arrested so quickly for Jasmine's murder would be some kind of forensic evidence or a full confession. Guessing it's not the latter, so let's go find out what Roy planted on the body.'

'Okay, sounds good to me,' he said, pulling away from the kerb. 'We're literally just a couple of miles away.'

Kim was still unable to imagine that Jasmine Swift was dead. She didn't like the fact that of all the women in Blackpool to turn up murdered, it was one they'd spoken to. And the subject they'd spoken about was inappropriate behaviour of a police officer. Had that police officer somehow found out that they'd spoken? Had Red discovered that Jasmine had shared what he'd done and decided to silence her? She needed a chance to speak to Red alone about Jasmine Swift and hoped she'd know if he was lying.

Bryant had told her about the dressing-down Roy had received from his boss for attending the crime scene, but what if Roy was doing his boss's dirty work and it had all been a very convincing show for the crowd? If Red did have his finger in all these pies, it would explain why he'd blocked her at every turn.

Just the thought that their conversation with Jasmine had somehow contributed to her rape and murder was too awful to contemplate.

Her thoughts and her guilt were interrupted by the ringing of her phone.

'Go ahead, Stace,' Kim said, putting her on speaker.

'Noah's family had a break-in too, boss, just a few weeks ago. Mainly electronics taken from Noah's room and a bit of jewellery. TV was too big to bother with.'

'Shit, so that's the link between the two families. Don't tell me – Red and Roy attended?'

'No, boss. Adil and Dickinson.'

'Okay, thanks, Stace,' Kim said, ending the call.

'Guv, this is turning into a bit of a fish market,' Bryant observed.

'What?'

'The deeper you go, the more it stinks.'

Kim didn't disagree. Red's name was cropping up all over the place. Even if the detective inspector hadn't attended both incidents, he would have known about them as head of department. The focus of the incident report must have been on the boy's belongings, so his name would have come up a lot. Another young boy in the right age range that had floated onto the radar.

With so much new information to make sense of, she remained silent until Bryant pulled up outside the morgue.

'I'll follow your lead,' Kim said. Bryant had already met the pathologist twice.

Her colleague rang the bell, and a woman appeared wearing scrubs and a plastic apron.

Bryant showed his identification and introduced himself. 'Any chance I could have a quick word with Mr Wade?'

She frowned. 'He is rather busy. Would you like to...?'

'Just a minute of his time would be helpful,' he said assertively but maintaining his good manners. A skill that, despite all her time working with Bryant, she still hadn't mastered. Instead, she was fighting the urge to physically remove this woman so Bryant could make a run for it.

The woman huffed but agreed to see if he was free.

They took the opportunity to inch further into the ante-room. Bryant took another step forward in time for the man in the next room to see him. The pathologist hesitated before nodding and removing his mask.

Richard Wade stepped into the room, removing his cap and making no effort to conceal his irritation.

'Would someone like to tell me what's going on over at that station? First, I've got Moss, then I get Crawford and now I get an officer that doesn't even work here.'

'Thanks for sparing me a minute,' Bryant said, immediately taking the wind out of his sails. 'This is my boss, DI Stone.'

The man nodded in her direction before turning his attention back to Bryant.

'I know you're not obliged to tell me, but was there some kind of major discovery during the post-mortem of Jasmine Swift?'

'We did find something that we passed along.'

'May I ask what it was?'

'A hair. One single long blonde hair.'

'And you passed this to?'

'The person I thought was running the case at the time, Roy Moss, who seemed to know who it might belong to. I'm assuming he passed the information straight to Crawford.'

'Okay, thanks for—'

'What's that about?' Kim asked, nodding towards the other room.

Bryant followed her gaze to two photos side by side on the wall. They were crime scene photos of Jasmine Swift and another woman.

From Bryant's sickened expression, she guessed that the other victim had been the subject of the photo in Roy Moss's hall of fame.

'You think they're connected?' Bryant asked.

'There are similarities, not least the positioning.'

From what her colleague had told her about Justin Holmes, the possibility of him murdering two women was growing more and more unlikely.

'Obviously I can say no more,' Wade said, reaching for his hat. It was a clear sign he was done.

Bryant thanked him as her phone rang.

She stepped outside and answered it. It was a short conversation which required very little response from her.

She strode towards the car.

'Where now, guv?' Bryant asked.

'Back to the station. Chief wants to see us. Now.'

SIXTY-FOUR

LEWIS

'Fuck's sake, Lewis, you can do better than that,' Mister shouted at him from the doorway.

After a breakfast of scrambled eggs, toast and bacon, Mister had carried in a pig with a metal ring through its nose and hung it from the steel hook in the wall. The stench of the dead animal filled his pen, and he almost vomited up his breakfast as Mister released him from the chain on the ground before moving to stand in the doorway.

'Pummel it,' Mister instructed.

Three punches to the creamy flesh of the animal and he felt the fatigue enter his bones. Two decent meals had done little to elevate his energy levels. Every muscle in his body felt leaden. Between visits to and from the toilet, he wasn't even allowed to stand. He remembered one time back at home when he'd been kept off school for the flu. He'd thought he was okay until he'd stood up, sneezed and fallen back down again. He had that same sensation now, as if his muscles weren't strong enough to hold him.

'Hit the fucking thing.'

Lewis hit it again, feeling the anger start to build deep in his stomach. Sometimes after the morning tablets he found himself getting angry.

Mister continued to shout instructions.

'Right hook.'

Most times his rage was directed towards his family.

'Left hook.'

He pictured Bobby's face on the head of the pig. He'd over-heard the conversation Bobby had had with his mother. He'd heard how Bobby wanted him taken away and trained to fight. He'd heard him sell the whole plan to his mum: how it would be better for the whole family, about how Lewis couldn't be trusted around the little ones with his temper tantrums. How the house needed a break, some peace and quiet from the fighting and the mood swings.

'Kidney punch.'

He pictured his mum's face on the head of the pig. Her flat refusal to send him away had gradually been worn down by Bobby's arguments. Once her definite no had been eroded to wondering if it really would be the making of him, he'd known he had no one on his side.

'Low blow.'

He pictured Kevin's face on the head of the pig. His brother had tried to persuade him to apologise for all the fighting and the times his mum had been called to the school. He'd asked and then begged him to call his mother and tell her things would be different.

Mister was no longer shouting instructions. Lewis was breathless with exertion, but his fists continued to drive into the animal's flesh because mostly he pictured his own face on the head of the pig.

Why hadn't he listened to his brother? Kevin had tried to protect him. He'd told him what to do, and his own pride and hurt had stopped him from doing what his brother had begged of him.

Despite everything, he loved his mother and Kevin and the little ones. He missed them and would give anything to be back home with them all. And yet, he had the feeling he was never going to see any of them again.

He was pleased he had his back to Mister so the man couldn't see the tears that began to roll down his face.

SIXTY-FIVE

Kim parted ways with Bryant at the bottom of the stairs. He headed back to the squad room while she headed up to see the chief. In hindsight, she should have checked in and updated the DCI on their current progress, but the reporting lines between herself and Red up the chain were a little blurred.

Even though her head was swimming with suspicions and theories, she still didn't have enough to make anything substantial stick against any of the officers, and she was no closer to identifying the member or members of the team who had made a complaint. This was probably going to be a short conversation.

'Come in,' DCI Walker called out when Kim knocked the door.

'Good to have you back,' the chief said as Kim closed the door behind her.

'Yeah, sorry I didn't brief you on my return,' Kim said.

Walker pointed to the seat, indicating Kim should sit. 'It's okay. I assumed that if you had anything of consequence to share with me, you'd have made the time.'

'We're making progress, marm.'

'Care to offer me an update now?'

'We've confirmed that both boys were abducted and very likely by the same group. We also believe—'

'You can skip that part,' Walker said, holding up her hand. 'DI Butler has been keeping me up to date on Noah and Lewis, and it sounds like great work from both teams.'

Kim wasn't sure of the accuracy of that statement, but she wasn't here to offer a performance evaluation on the working practices of the Blackpool team. If so, she could have written a novel.

'And the other area of your secondment?' Walker asked, tipping her head.

'There are issues within the team, marm,' Kim said. They knew that Carly Walsh had used unacceptable force on a suspect. They knew that DI Butler had been inappropriate with a woman who was now dead, and they knew Roy Moss was breaking just about every rule in the book.

She also knew they had no proof to offer that the chief could do anything with.

'Would you like to share your findings with me?'

'Not right now, marm, because I can't give you anything you can use. But I hope to have something soon.'

It looked as though the chief wanted to push further, but she knew that Kim spoke the truth. Accusation and allegations without evidence were like poison darts.

'And the informant?' Walker asked, raising the third reason they'd been asked to assist.

Regretfully, Kim shook her head. 'We haven't identified any obvious source.'

Walker nodded her understanding.

'As a believer of gut reactions, I'm interested in your instinct, Inspector. Do you feel that the complaints came from within the team? Do you feel that any of my officers are in danger?'

Kim thought long and hard before shaking her head. 'I've seen nothing to suggest it.'

'Okay. Thank you for your observations. On that note, I think it's time for your team to take your leave and return to your own case.'

Kim didn't hide her surprise. 'But we're making progress on both the investigation and the internal concerns.'

Walker offered her a smile. 'Unfortunately, I think your presence here is causing a distraction. I still have two missing boys and now a rape–murder case. I need my whole team completely focussed on these active investigations.'

Kim heard what wasn't being said. 'Red wants us gone, doesn't he?'

The chief had the grace to leave the question unanswered, but Kim knew she was right. Red knew they were getting close, and he wanted them gone.

Kim considered divulging everything they knew or suspected about the team.

That their detective inspector had acted inappropriately with the victim of a crime who had been raped and murdered after divulging this information to herself and Bryant. No complainant or witness to substantiate the story.

That one of their detective sergeants had taken sickening photos of female victims at crime scenes and pressured a woman into having sex, not to mention the possibility of planting evidence to frame someone for murder. No complainant or witness to substantiate the story.

That someone within the team was deliberately obstructing the investigation into the missing boys.

Problem was they had absolutely no proof. There was a chance that the chief wouldn't believe her; and even if she did and started an investigation, there was a risk they'd put the tipster in immediate danger. And Kim wouldn't be able to protect them if she had been sent on her way. If only she had a little more time.

'Marm, I'm sure we can continue to assist with trying to find Lewis and—'

'I think your contribution has been substantial. Please don't think I'm not grateful for all you've done to move the investigation forward. I just need my team's focus solely on the cases on their desks.'

Kim understood the decision. She was sure Woody would have done the same in this position, but she really felt that given a little more time, they could have given her evidence about one completely bent copper and maybe even identified the informant.

She wondered if that was something they could continue to investigate remotely.

She owed it one last shot.

'Marm, I really think we—'

'Please understand that your input has been invaluable, and DCI Woodward is lucky to have you, but I need my team free and clear of distraction.'

Kim admired the panache with which she was being told to leave, not once but twice. Regardless of how much she wanted to continue to work the missing boys case, she wouldn't make the chief say it a third time. She resolved to meet with Woody the minute they were back and enlist his help to continue working the cases.

She thanked the woman for her time and headed back to her team, wondering if they were going to be as pissed off as she was.

SIXTY-SIX

Bryant entered the squad room to a wall of silence. The only person present was Roy Moss.

As Red tended to rotate who he left manning the phones, he guessed it was Moss's turn today. Either that or Red still couldn't stand to look at his face.

Moss offered him a salute as a greeting. Bryant acknowledged him and headed into their own war room.

Both Penn and Stacey looked up in surprise.

'Forgot something, Bryant?' Stacey asked, looking around him.

'Guv's with the chief,' he said, taking a seat. 'You two got anything more?'

'Still feeling uncomfortable that both families were victims of burglary in the last few months.'

'Same officers?'

'Nah, Red and Moss attended the Stevens family, and Adil and Dickinson attended the Reid family.'

Bryant could understand the dead end she'd come up against. There had been no hint of impropriety against either of those two officers, but he could understand her discomfort.

'Still feels a bit...'

'Cockfighting,' Penn called out, looking from one to the other.

Stacey began to nod her agreement while Bryant felt one of his eyebrows rise.

'That's what they're masquerading as on the dark web. Vile enough for people to find who know what they're looking for, but not gonna raise as much attention as dog fighting,' he explained before turning his full attention back to the screen.

At a loss as to what to do next, Bryant decided to put the kettle on. The guv would probably appreciate a cuppa before heading off to wherever they were going next.

He grabbed Penn's mug as he headed out the door.

He filled the kettle and stared at it, still trying to make sense of what they'd been told by Richard Wade.

A hair, one single blonde hair, that he was in no doubt would belong to Justin Holmes. If he were to believe the worst of Moss, then everything would make sense: the impromptu visit to the boyfriend, the unnecessary trip back to the morgue. He wouldn't be the first officer to plant evidence to secure an early result, but Bryant sure hoped he'd be the last.

As with everything else, he had no proof. It was circumstantial. Damn that seedy bastard to hell, Bryant thought, throwing Penn's empty mug into the sink.

'Hey, bud, we're up,' Roy called from the doorway. His voice was full of urgency, and his eyes were alight.

'Got a jumper over at the supermarket. He's on the roof, and there's no one else here. Boss said to take you.'

'Okay, let me just tell—'

'I told 'em already. Now come on – we haven't got much time.'

Bryant put down the kettle and followed the man out the door.

SIXTY-SEVEN

Kim acknowledged the deflation she felt as she headed back down to the squad room.

Without intending to, the chief had made her feel as though they'd achieved absolutely nothing, yet her head was full of the information they'd uncovered and put together.

'Okay, folks, pack up,' she said, closing the door behind her.

'What?' Penn said, and Stacey looked equally shocked.

'The chief is standing us down. We're a distraction and—'

'She said that?' Stacey asked.

'Pretty much. She accepts we've been of assistance with the missing boys, but we'll call Red to come in for a handover and then we'll be on our way.'

'We really gonna leave this case?' Penn asked, horrified. An expression mirrored on Stacey's face.

'Not a chance,' Kim said, picturing Josh's body. 'We're not leaving the case; we just can't work it from here.'

'What about Moss?' Stacey asked. 'We just gonna leave him to terrorise the public?'

'Absolutely not, but I need Woody's guidance on how we

handle it from here. I can give him the whole story without compromising him as it's not his team.'

They nodded their understanding.

'Has Bryant gone for the world's longest piss, or has he started heading home without us?' she asked, looking around.

'He went to make coffee,' Penn said, checking his watch. 'A good ten minutes ago actually.'

'I just passed the kitchen and he wasn't there,' Kim said, feeling a pang of unease. None of them knew the station well enough or would be presumptuous enough to just wander around without authorisation.

'Roy was here,' Stacey offered. 'I saw him on the phone, and then he ran out of here. Haven't seen either of them since.'

'Penn, go check the toilets. Stace, check with dispatch to see if they gave him an urgent call.'

They both spurred into action as she took out her mobile phone.

SIXTY-EIGHT

'Sorry to drag you along to this, mate,' Roy said, screeching out of the car park. 'Procedure says at least two people have to attend a possible suicide, and the rest of the team ain't close enough. I'm not taking a woman, and your other guy looks a bit shifty to me.'

Bryant held on to his seat as Roy drove as erratically as though he had a blue light on his roof.

'What's the report?' Bryant asked, wondering if he'd trust Roy to talk to anyone considering suicide.

'A guy in his thirties top of Sainsbury's car park. Called in by a concerned member of the public. Keeps walking close to the edge.'

Bryant knew the supermarket was only a few miles away from the station, but since Roy knew all the shortcuts, the man was in and out of side streets like a boy racer. Bryant was swinging all over the place.

'Sorry about the ride, bud, but you know how it is when you've got the chance to save someone.'

As Roy turned onto Talbot Street, Bryant's phone began to ring.

'No time to take that, pal,' he said, screeching through the car park entrance. 'Imagine if our guy jumped cos you were talking to the missus. Your team knows where you are cos I told them on my way out.'

Bryant realised they were about to go looking for a potential suicide. He couldn't get out of the car already talking on the phone.

Roy pulled the car to a halt at the bottom of the ramp leading up to the roof level.

'Come on – we'll get out here and walk. We don't want to spook him with the noise of the car.'

Bryant shut the passenger door and followed.

The roof of Sainsbury's looked like most other rooftop car parks. A vast open space with a few cars dotted here and there.

There was no sign of any movement.

'Over there,' Roy said, pointing to the plant room buildings. 'That's always a favourite spot.'

He didn't wait before sprinting in that direction.

Bryant followed, having to jump a small fence to get behind the brick building.

He turned the corner to find... nothing. Just Roy, standing there with his arms folded and an unpleasant smirk on his face.

'Ah, fuck. Looks like they must have changed their mind.'

SIXTY-NINE

'Hang on. Slow down,' Red said, holding up his hands.

After Bryant had failed to answer his phone, Kim had called Red, who had luckily been pulling into the car park after receiving a call to return for a final handover.

In the long minutes it had taken for him and Adil to reach the office, Penn and Stacey had been blowing up both Bryant's and Roy's phones to no avail, while Kim had been making a big decision.

Despite the fact that Red's tentacles seemed to have touched every area of their investigation, she was forced to confide in him.

She knew she couldn't find her colleague without him.

Right now, she didn't know if she could trust him, but she had no choice but to trust him with this.

'You're saying that Roy and Bryant have gone out on a call?'

'There was no call,' Kim snapped with exasperation. She really wished he'd catch up without her having to explain it to him.

'There was no call from dispatch,' she said again. 'Roy

pretended there was to get him out of here under false pretences.'

'For what reason?' Red asked in disbelief.

Adil looked far less surprised.

'Red, do you have any idea what kind of man Roy is?' she cried, aware of every passing minute.

He shrugged, still unsure what the conversation was about. 'He can be a bit rough around the—'

'He's bent, Red. I mean, really bent. Not just a little bribe or an occasional blind eye.'

Red began to shake his head, but she detected an imperceptible nod from Adil.

'He's a racist, sexist, disgusting human being. He has photos on his phone from crime scenes. Victims, Red – female rape and murder victims.'

'No, he would never...'

'He's shown them to Bryant. You know what else? He raids the home of a woman named Pippa Jacobs regularly to get sex in return for not shopping her. The first time she refused he planted drugs in her house, and she ended up in prison. She was clean, and he set her up.'

'I was there when she was busted. It was a good arrest.'

'What was your intelligence? How did you know to raid her place? Don't answer because you don't need to. It was Roy, wasn't it?'

He was nodding but only half-heartedly. 'I saw the drugs being—'

'Of course you did. He's pretty clever. But what you didn't see was the visit earlier in the day where Pippa Jacobs refused to give him sex for silence. She dared to say no to him, and look what happened.'

Kim couldn't work out if the look of disgust on the man's face was real or forced... but he was still shaking his head.

'And did he tell you about his impromptu visit to the

morgue yesterday after visiting Justin Holmes? Or that a long blonde hair was coincidentally found on the body of Jasmine Swift after his visit?' Kim stopped herself from asking if he already knew about it.

'You're saying he's framing a man for murder?'

'You gotta agree that it's a little suspicious. He's as bent as they come, Red, and right now he's got one of my officers alone somewhere. If anything happens to him, I swear you'll—'

'What do you want me to do? How the hell would I know where—?'

'I know,' Adil said quietly before turning to his boss. 'He does take photos. He showed me one, and then when he could see how disgusted I was, he warned me to keep my mouth shut. That was at the Sainsbury's car park. He said he could push me over the edge and no one would question a thing. He's probably taken him there.'

'Jesus Christ,' Red said, running his hand through his hair.

'Stay put,' Kim said to her team as she grabbed her jacket.

Red was already heading out the door.

She ran after him and prayed to God that they weren't already too late.

SEVENTY

'What the hell, Roy?' Bryant asked, forcing innocence into his voice. He realised now a part of him had known he was being set up the minute he'd got in the car. Why had he agreed to go anywhere with this man?

'The game's up, pal,' Roy said, positioning himself between Bryant and the only way out. There was one other way, Bryant thought, casting a glance over the edge. He didn't like his odds of surviving that fall.

'You almost had me,' Roy said. 'Almost believed you had something about you and that we played for the same team. Except you couldn't hide that fucking core of weakness—'

'Decency,' Bryant corrected.

'Whatever, it's fucking pathetic. Acting like you accidentally knocked the phone out of my hand when I wasn't hurting anyone. The slag was already dead. And you engineered that phone call at Pippa's, didn't you? You can't even take a free blow job to get you through the day.'

Bryant considered trying to lie about his meeting with Pippa and bluff it out until he wasn't in a precarious situation on the roof of a building with the filthiest copper on the force.

But he could feel that the revulsion was finally showing on his face.

'I wondered if you'd go back to the slag's house. Don't worry, I don't think for a minute you shagged her. You ain't got it in you. Leaves only one reason to go back. What did that bitch tell you about me, and why were you asking?'

'She told me you were a piece of shit who got her sent to jail when she refused to have sex with you.'

Nope, he couldn't pretend any more. The knowledge that was poisoning him from the inside needed to come out.

To his surprise, Roy smiled.

'And here was me thinking she talked shit about me and told you lies.'

'You're pretty calm given what I know about you,' Bryant said.

Roy shrugged, looking over the side of the building.

'You showed me the photos yourself.'

'I did.'

'You took me to Pippa's house and admitted what you did there.'

'Yep.'

'I was with you when you lifted evidence to frame Justin,' Bryant said, expecting some kind of reaction.

Roy shrugged. 'Might have done.'

Bryant tried to understand why Roy wasn't riled or worried.

'Everyone on my team knows all of this,' he clarified.

'Good for them. Ain't nothing there I can't get out of, and you know it.'

'So, why the— Oh shit,' Bryant said as the penny finally dropped.

There was only one end to this scenario, and now he got it.

He'd had the feeling he had all the pieces of the puzzle and he'd been right, but it had taken him until now to put them all together. He was the only person that knew enough, and that was why Roy was unperturbed. He was going to make sure that Bryant could never share what he'd just realised with anyone else. He'd always known that the photo Roy had shown him had significance, and he'd just realised why.

It had been staring him in the face all week, but he hadn't seen it. Now it was the thing that was going to prevent him walking away from the rooftop and making sure Roy faced justice for what he'd done.

'The photo,' he said, meeting Roy's gaze, and knew he was right.

He didn't get the chance to say anything more.

In a flash, Roy had covered the space between them and bulldozed him to the ground.

SEVENTY-ONE

'Were you sent here to spy on us?' Red asked as he pulled out of the car park.

Kim didn't particularly want to chat, but there was little she could do to close the gap between them and her colleague any quicker. Pippa Jacobs had hinted that Roy Moss was capable of anything to cover his own ass, and she believed it. Roy knew that Bryant knew more about him than anyone and that had put him in danger.

'Three names were left in our war room,' she answered, choosing to omit certain information. 'The first one was Jasmine Swift.'

Red swallowed deeply.

She waited, knowing his response to this was important.

'I'm gonna be completely honest here. I fucked up with Jasmine,' he said, shaking his head regretfully. 'After attending her call about the burglary, I became too familiar with her. I misread the signs. She did nothing wrong, and it was my mistake completely. I shouldn't have contacted her.'

His admission was crucial. She hadn't said they'd visited her or what she'd revealed. He hadn't been forced to share that information. He didn't know that she already knew.

'Beyond inappropriate,' Kim said.

'Agreed, and not something I'll ever repeat. I never meant to make her feel uncomfortable.'

Kim could see the look of disgust on his face and it was obvious that his own shame would ensure he never made that mistake again. There was nothing more she could do to get justice for Jasmine, but there would be no others. 'Let's talk about Carly. Our second name claimed she got a bit rough during an arrest.'

'You talking about Dean Jackson?'

Kim nodded. 'Refused to make a complaint. Too scared.'

He laughed but not with humour. 'I've got the video on that one, which I'm happy to share with you any time.'

'Did she kick him in the nuts?'

'Oh yeah. He was high as a kite. Had his hands on her throat from behind. Impressive back sweep into his nuts and he soon let go.'

'He said he asked for a solicitor three times and was denied.'

'In his head, maybe, but the guy couldn't string a sentence together. Trust me, we did nothing wrong, and I'd defend our actions to anyone.'

She wasn't totally surprised. Carly Walsh hadn't given the impression of being bent, and Kim's instincts hadn't detected it.

'And the third name was Pippa Jacobs?' Red asked.

'Yeah, and you already know the reason for that one.'

'Who left the names?'

'I dunno, Red, but even if I believe you about those names, you're never gonna convince me that you didn't fuck up the Lewis investigation. You messed up by assuming he was a runaway. You should have gone deeper, and I think you know it. Stop me if I'm wrong, but it just looks lazy and bloody incompetent.'

A muscle twitched in his jawline, but she didn't care. He deserved the truth.

'I don't disagree, but everyone thought he'd done a runner. Even the chief was convinced by the family's insistence,' he defended himself.

Kim shook her head as they pulled onto the car park ramp. Her thoughts were no longer about any of the names that had been left for them. Her only concern was that her colleague was in danger.

She wondered if Adil had been correct or if they were in completely the wrong place. Then Red pulled to a screeching halt beside a Toyota.

'That's Roy's car.'

Kim felt both jubilation and trepidation. They were in the right place, but had they made it in time?

Historic events meant she didn't like her team members in high places.

She shuddered at the memory as she got out of the car. Any second now, she could hear a sickening thud as a body fell to the ground.

She followed Red up the ramp wondering what the hell they were going to find.

SEVENTY-TWO

Bryant blinked away the blood seeping into his right eye long enough to see the drop over the railing to the ground.

When Roy had rushed him, he'd been thrown against the corner of the brick plant room. The pain had momentarily frozen him, which had given Roy all the time he'd needed to haul him towards the barrier that was the only thing separating him from certain death.

Roy was grunting and cursing while trying to lift him high enough so that gravity would take over.

'S... sorry, b... buddy, but you g... gotta go, cos I know you know,' he said, panting with the effort.

Bryant was flattening his body against the barrier and holding on to the thin wire.

'Know what?' he gasped, playing for time.

Pain shot through his calf as Roy kicked him in the back of the knee.

'Everything. I can't have you ruining my life.'

Every second was like torture, but he wasn't going to reveal what he'd pieced together. His only chance was to pretend he didn't know exactly what the bastard had been up to.

Roy bent down behind him and tried to pull up his injured, weakened leg.

Bryant cried out, knowing he couldn't turn around. If he loosened his grip on the metal, there was a chance Roy could bundle him over. His only chance was to hang on for as long as he could and pray that someone was on their way.

'Doesn't matter what I know,' he protested. 'Pippa will never testify—'

'Fuck Pippa. I ain't losing sleep over that slag.'

He cried out as Roy's foot hit the back of his other leg. His knees were trembling and begging for him to fold to the ground, but that would mean letting go of the metal, the only thing keeping him from going over.

'What then? I've got no proof you planted the evidence on Jasmine to frame her ex. Even my boss thinks I'm clutching—'

'Your boss is a fucking bitch who needs a good—'

'Fuck,' he cried as Roy landed a blow to the small of his back. The pain shot through his whole body, white-hot pain that brought nausea and dizziness.

'You're still not getting it, you stupid twat, even if you haven't put it together, you will eventually. That's why I can't let you live. I should never have shown you...' His words trailed away as he landed another punch between Bryant's shoulder blades.

Bryant knew he was going to pass out, and when he did, he'd let go of the railings and Roy would be able to...

'Over my dead fucking body,' he heard before the weight was pulled away from him.

He fought the nausea down as his legs gave way and he crumpled to the ground. He didn't know how, but his boss was holding a writhing Roy to the ground with the help of Detective Inspector Butler.

The guv looked at him and saw the state of his face.

'You're a fucking bastard,' she spat down at Roy. 'And I'm gonna make sure you never hurt anyone again.'

'Fuck off, bitch,' he said, trying to roll onto his left side. He had no chance of getting up, but he was trying it anyway.

'Get his phone,' Bryant croaked.

'Bryant, just rest for a—'

'Get his phone – out of his pocket,' Bryant insisted. Suddenly he knew exactly what the man was trying to do.

Noting his urgency, Red reached around and took the phone from Roy's pocket. He handed it to the guv while he put a knee in Roy's back and took a pair of cuffs from his back pocket.

'Fuck off, Red. You don't have to do this. It was a misunderstanding, an argument that went too far. Brummie bastards coming up here and trying to tell us how—'

'Shut up, Roy,' Red said, moving the man to the wall of the plant room and forcing him to sit. 'If even half of what I've been told is true, you're never going to get to use that badge again.'

Bryant could see that the screen of Roy's phone was cracked from the rolling around but hopefully that was the extent of the damage because Roy had pretty much given him the evidence he'd been seeking.

'Password?' the guv asked.

Red took the phone and lit up the screen. 'It's his birthday, like every other one he uses.'

'Give me my fucking phone,' Roy raged as colour flooded his face.

'Photos,' Bryant called out.

His boss frowned at the urgency. They already knew he'd taken inappropriate pictures at crime scenes.

Bryant could tell when Red reached the photo in question by the disgust that formed on his face.

The guv leaned over and frowned immediately. She already knew what was coming. They'd both seen the actual crime scene photos at the morgue earlier, when Wade had been comparing photos of Jasmine and the earlier victim.

'The first victim's hair is dry,' Bryant explained.

Red frowned. 'But it was raining when I arrived at the scene.'

'The crime scene photos show her with wet hair too,' Bryant said.

Red's mouth fell open as he realised the significance. The photo on Roy's phone had been taken long before the body had been discovered.

Red turned to face his former colleague as sirens sounded in the distance.

'Roy Moss, I am arresting you for the murder...'

Bryant tuned out as he expelled a breath that he felt he'd been holding since Monday.

The guv stepped towards him. She helped him to his feet, but his left leg buckled, so she placed his left arm around her shoulders and supported his weight.

'Come on, buddy – lean on me,' she said, and for once he did as he was told.

SEVENTY-THREE

It was almost five when Bryant re-entered the squad room at Blackpool police station.

Due to the severity of the charges against DS Roy Moss, he'd been transported directly to Preston station. Red had gone along for the handover process, and the chief's door was tightly closed as she took direction from her superiors.

Red's team had gathered in their own squad room, and Red had assured them a full explanation on his return. Kim had been tempted to answer their questioning glances, but it was Red's team and his responsibility to ensure their welfare after he gave them the details. She suspected it would come as more of a shock to some than others. They knew that Jasmine's ex-boyfriend had been released without charge, and that Roy had been placed under arrest. Red was already on his way back to help them connect the dots.

'All right, Bryant, stop milking it now,' she said, glancing down at his left leg, which seemed to have suffered more than the rest of him.

He'd refused to go to hospital and had instead gone downstairs to make a full statement, after Stacey had worked wonders on his face with wet kitchen towel and a first aid kit.

In the meantime, Stacey had been busy preparing a written handover statement to leave behind for Red.

'Finished,' she said, glancing over at the printer in the squad room.

'Thank God,' Bryant said as Red walked in the door.

Red looked like a man who had aged twenty years in one afternoon. For once, he wasn't looking quite as sharp as he had when his shift started.

'Reckon we should leave them to it?' Bryant asked, making no secret of the fact he wanted to be on the road as soon as possible. She didn't really blame him.

'One sec,' Penn said, holding up his hand. It was the first time he'd spoken since they'd got back.

Bryant plonked himself down in the chair as Stacey started to gather her belongings.

Kim watched as Red removed his jacket and motioned for his team to come in closer. What he had to share about their colleague was going to be hard to hear. Whether they liked the man or not, their team would never look the same, and they would all have to be prepared for closer scrutiny. Red wouldn't be the only person being asked some difficult questions.

'Boss, listen, I think I've got something,' Penn said excitedly.

She nodded for him to continue, ignoring the look of despair that crossed Bryant's features.

'I've been trawling cockfighting pages on the dark web all afternoon, looking for something that stands out, something that's different to the other sites.'

'Okay,' Kim said, already able to see why that would be a good cover.

'And throughout there are terms that have been consistent. Gaffs and guineas and references to giros – a type of fighting rooster known for its white feathers. They use the same terminology throughout, and there's always the same number of fights. Except this one site where there's only three fixtures.'

'Go on,' she urged, feeling the excitement grow in her stomach. Even Bryant's attention was focussed.

'No cockfighting venue lists only three bouts. You're normally talking at least twenty, which take place over a couple of days. It's taken a lot of decoding to get deeper into the details, but...'

'What exactly do you have?' Kim asked, sitting forward.

'I know where the venue is, and I know the first fight is at seven o'clock.'

Kim sprang up from her chair. 'Jeez, Penn, why didn't you say that in the first place?'

She strode out into the main squad room and approached the huddle surrounding Red.

'Sorry to break this up, folks, but I think we're going to need your help.'

SEVENTY-FOUR

Followed by her team, Kim strode out of Blackpool police station right into the path of Steve Ashworth.

'Oh, for fuck's sake,' she cursed. The man could not have worse timing.

'Inspector, fancy seeing you again.'

'Thrilling,' Kim answered as her team shored up behind her. Bryant and Penn knew full well who he was, but Stacey had never met him.

'Care to give me a comment before we find out the country's opinions on your actions?'

'The only opinions I care about are right here,' she said, folding her arms.

He cast a glance over the three people standing behind her. 'And they know all about Amber Rose?'

'Why would they? We weren't a team then.'

'So, they don't know you killed an innocent man?' he asked.

To her team's credit, not one of them reacted to his words.

'Tell them then,' she said, realising she'd been waiting for this moment, and she just hoped he'd make it quick. They had a long drive ahead.

'You were a detective sergeant, weren't you, when the call came in from fourteen-year-old Amber Rose?'

She said nothing, but he was correct.

'She claimed that her foster dad had been abusing her. You had her taken into care and then proceeded to destroy that man. You badgered him, harassed him, followed him, pretty much stalked him to make him confess.'

Still, she said nothing because he wasn't wrong.

'He lost his job, his wife, his friends and his reputation because you wouldn't let it go.'

'Those are all statements. Do you have an actual question for me?' she asked, pushing out her chin.

'Just one. Was it before or after he took his own life that you found out Amber Rose was lying?'

'After,' she said simply and waited for his next shot.

He'd told no lies; he'd embellished nothing, and she had done exactly what he'd said. It had been her darkest time in the force, and she had never stopped trying to atone for it. She had believed every word that had come out of the mouth of the four-teen-year-old girl. She had seen herself and her own time in foster care reflected in every sentence. She had listened too closely to the words she'd uttered instead of using her skills to build a fuller picture. If she had, she would have seen a girl who had made allegations against members of staff at every care facility she'd been housed in. There were many things she should have done. And many lessons had been learned.

Again, her team offered no reaction to his words, but she was sure they were all eager for an answer.

'You want the truth, I'll give it to you – all of it,' she said, and she didn't just mean Ashworth. 'I fucked up. I saw myself in that kid, and I believed every word that came out of her mouth. I believed that the man had gone to her room almost every night and forced her to do unspeakable things. I fell for the fear and terror I saw in her eyes. I recoiled in horror at the things she described and believed every tear that fell from her reddened eyes. I knew the only way to stop him from doing it to other kids was to get him to confess, so I made his life hell. I badgered him and I harassed him until he couldn't take it any more. And there's nothing I wouldn't give to go back and change what I did. Not one day goes by that I don't think about Amber Rose. When her story began to change after his death, I knew I'd been deceived in the worst possible way and that I, not Amber, was responsible for that man's death.'

She paused. No one said a word, which was good because she wasn't finished yet.

'And because I can't take it back and undo it, I remember it, I relive it. I use it to question everything. I use it to make sure I'm the best copper I can be. If you think I'll ever forgive myself for my actions, you haven't learned a damn thing about me. If you go public with it, I'll say exactly what I've just said. I won't hide and I won't lie, but most likely I will be forced to resign. So you should know that you're not ridding the force of a bent copper, but removing someone who made a mistake once and who works doubly hard to make up for it now.'

'It's true,' Bryant offered.

'She does,' Penn said.

'Bang on,' Stacey added.

Ashworth looked over all four of them. He held up his hands. 'Erm. I wasn't expecting...'

'Now, I've got a question for you, Steve,' Kim continued. 'You think you're any good at this reporting shit?'

'Of course. I just keep—'

'Only you've had two months, and this is the best you've got, which means you're either a shit investigator or I've got nothing more to hide. Which is it? Because both things can't be true.' She paused. 'Thing is, Steve, I've done my research too, and I don't think you're just a nuisance. You've done some good stuff. You've done some shit stuff too, but I know you honestly felt I was a corrupt copper.'

'I did,' he answered.

'Then crack on, my man, cos you will find nothing else,' she said and meant it. 'If, however, you are actually interested in digging into a story that could save lives, feel free to follow us again right now, one more time. Your call on whether you want the opportunity to make a difference.'

She strode towards the car with no idea what the man was going to do.

SEVENTY-FIVE

By the time they were nearing Burnley, Red had called to say they were right behind and there was a car between them.

She enlightened him about the reporter, and he told her that he'd been unable to get anywhere near the chief. She was working hard to delay the announcement about Roy and getting prepared for when the news broke.

Right now, there was no formal operation and the eight of them were on their own.

Kim felt her excitement start to grow as the satnav said they were only a couple of miles away from the postcode Penn had tracked down.

Most of the forty-mile journey to Burnley had been spent in silence as Bryant had focussed on the driving. Motorways had taken them around both Preston and Blackburn, and they were now on the other side of Burnley, driving in the dark.

The roads had become narrower, with hedges on both sides, giving Bryant no visibility. Both Stacey and Penn were operating Google Maps, giving them daytime views of the area.

'Just approaching the postcode area now,' Penn offered.

'Stace?' Kim asked.

'Nothing yet.'

Kim knew that postcodes covered around twelve properties, but out here that could stretch for miles. It had been almost a mile since they'd passed any kind of building.

'Slow it,' Stacey said. 'There's something coming up on the left.'

Bryant slowed to ten miles per hour.

'Nope, it's just a farmhouse,' Stacey said. 'Keep going.'

Bryant picked up speed but not by much.

There was a feeling in the car that they were getting close.

'Slow again,' Stacey said. 'This time on the right. Half a mile ahead. Single building at the end of a dirt track.'

There was silence in the car until Bryant pulled to a stop at the next break in the hedge.

Kim got out of the car as Red pulled up behind. A third car pulled up behind him.

Steve Ashworth had managed to stick with them.

Kim was met with a locked field gate. The dirt road was a good half mile long but straight, and appeared to lead to a single building like a cowshed or a barn.

'You see that?' Kim asked Red, who had appeared beside her.

'Lights and cars, lots of them.'

'Why?' Kim asked.

'Exactly,' he agreed.

Kim felt in her bones that they were in the right place.

'We need a closer look,' she said, putting her foot in the first rung of the field gate.

Bryant tried to follow suit.

'Yeah, not you,' she said. With the limp he was still sporting, he'd never make it over the gate, never mind the half-mile walk to the building.

Red took her cue and began to climb the gate.

Kim couldn't help but think that his nice suit wasn't going to like following her around.

'Bryant, explain to Steve what's going on and then don't let him out of your sight. Everyone else focus on getting these cars hidden before anyone attempts to leave.'

She stepped away from the gate and moved to the left of the dirt track, using the cover of the trees in case anyone was watching from up ahead.

'I didn't know, all right,' Red said, moving quietly behind her.

Instantly, Kim knew he was talking about Roy.

'Don't get me wrong, I knew he was a bastard, but I didn't think he was capable of murder.'

'I don't think any of us thought that,' she said honestly. But a part of her still couldn't believe he hadn't seen some signs of the man's corruption, given how closely they'd worked together.

As Roy's superior officer, Red was going to have to answer some difficult questions and justify himself to someone far higher up the food chain than her... but right now she needed him and his team on her side.

As they neared the building, Kim could see there was no one standing guard. They obviously felt that secrecy and a padlocked gate was enough security.

A few metres closer and it was clear that the light being cast was coming from inside the building. A gentle hum told her that a portable generator was powering that lighting, some of which was leaking out of slatted boards to illuminate the vehicles.

Closest to the building were two vans, the nearest being the one they'd seen on CCTV.

Her pulse quickened as she realised they were definitely in the right place. Lewis might be in that building, possibly even Noah too.

'Let's look around the side,' Red whispered.

She followed as he led the way. If someone came out right now, they'd be caught.

Bramble and brush had been allowed to grow up the side of the building, and Red's suit took another hit as he stamped a path through.

Being this close to the building, they could now hear the sounds from within. There were oohs, aahs, cheers and boos, but what struck Kim most was the sound of excitement. The sheer exhilaration of what they were witnessing.

She swallowed her disgust as she joined Red at a narrow clearing along the west side of the building.

The lower half of the structure was formed of breeze blocks that were now covered in green moss. The upper half was made up of wooden panels, plank width, with half-inch gaps in between allowing thin lines of light out into the darkness. There was an inch-wide ledge where the wood sat on top of the blocks.

'Okay, go on,' Red said, lowering himself to his hands and knees so she could stand on him.

She now knew the only place that suit was going was in the bin.

She stepped up onto his back, and to his credit he didn't even groan.

Even though she'd switched her phone to silent, she felt it vibrate the receipt of a text message.

Hell no, Frost, Kim seethed. *Now really ain't the fucking time.*

She reached for the ledge to steady herself before putting one eye to a gap in the wood.

The scene that met her gaze was even worse than she'd imagined.

From her vantage point, she could see that the focal point was a make-do boxing ring formed of cheap metal fencing, the kind normally used to line the streets for crowd control. There were no niceties like referees or stools or judges, just two kids beating the shit out of each other in their underpants.

Kim had to hold in a cry as one of the fighters staggered backwards and fell to the ground.

His opponent danced around him, waiting for him to get up while the crowd jeered and booed. Kim waited for someone to approach him, to check on him, see if he was unconscious – or worse.

No one moved towards the boy lying on the ground.

After what seemed like hours, the boy staggered back to his feet. He swayed once before seeming to find a burst of energy. He swung and caught his opponent on the chin. The other boy took a second to refocus, and as he lifted his head, she saw that it was Lewis, the boy who had been missing for over ten days, the boy that had been in her head since Monday. Only this Lewis looked even younger than his twelve years, and he was a thinner, frailer version of the boy she'd seen on the CCTV. His blonde hair had been shaved crudely, and although it wasn't on a par with Josh, his body was mottled with cuts and bruises.

She took a second to glance around the space beyond the four spotlights aimed at the ring.

Against the far wall sat another four boys with adults either side of them. Kim guessed they were the rest of the fighters for the night.

All of them stared at the ground. They looked defeated and scared already.

The rage was building within her.

Every one of these boys had been stolen from their lives and their families for the sick entertainment of monsters. She pulled her gaze away. Red couldn't support her weight for much longer.

A brief head count told her there were fifty plus spectators to this horrific event.

She wanted to barge in there right now and close it down.

'You ready?' Red asked as she stepped down off his back.

She knew he intended to burst in there and make some arrests.

'We can't do it, Red,' she said with a heavy heart. 'If we just barge in there, we'll never find the others. We'll never find Noah.'

'We can't just let—'

'Give me a minute,' she said, leaning against the wall.

Suddenly, a huge cheer erupted, and Kim guessed that was the end of fight one. She didn't need to get on Red's back again to know that the end of the fight probably meant one of the boys had been knocked unconscious.

'Running out of time,' Red urged.

Kim thought about the tools she had at her disposal.

'Okay, Red, I've got an idea, but I'm gonna need your help.'

SEVENTY-SIX

LEWIS

Lewis tried to stand after the blow to the side of his head, but his legs turned to jelly and he crumpled to the ground. He'd been blinking the blood from the cut above his other eye for minutes, and now he was too exhausted to raise his swollen lid.

Mister pulled him out of the ring and sat him against the wall next to the others, then grabbed the next boy in line.

Lewis allowed his head to loll against the wall as his body tingled and ached all over. In particular, his hands and wrists throbbed from punching the pig earlier in the day and then fighting his opponent.

His breathing started to regulate and slow in his chest. The assault on his body was luring him towards sleep.

Mister returned to stand beside him. His face looked like thunder.

Missus turned to Mister and hissed loud enough for Lewis to hear, 'He's done and he's making us look bad. Cost us a fucking fortune. Take the loser out of here.'

Lewis felt himself being dragged along the ground behind the large group of men already focussed on the next fight. He knew that it was time for him to return to his pig pen and his chain on the floor, and that Mister and Missus wouldn't feed him again for a couple of days. He was being returned to silence and seclusion and what felt like a fate worse than death.

The rough concrete floor ripped at the skin on the back of his legs as he was dragged along.

Right now, he didn't care how it happened, but he prayed for this nightmare to end.

SEVENTY-SEVEN

'What do you mean she's in the fucking van?' Bryant asked when Red returned.

Even in the semi-darkness, he knew his profanity had startled Penn and Stacey, but he hadn't expected Red to return alone. In his absence, they had gained access to an empty field opposite the locked gate and hidden the cars behind the dense hedge. After hearing footsteps, they'd used a good old-fashioned whistle to get Red's attention, but he hadn't expected the guv not to be with him.

True to his word, Bryant hadn't taken his eyes off Steve Ashworth, who had been surprisingly helpful.

Everyone was huddled using their phones for illumination and awaiting an explanation.

After everything they'd learned this week, he still wasn't convinced that they could totally trust Red. For all he knew, the guv was lying back there in God knows what—

His thoughts were interrupted by the receipt of a text message.

As though she'd read his mind, the message was from the guv. He smiled briefly before holding up his phone.

'She's fine. She says to follow Red's instructions.'

With his mind pacified slightly, he turned his attention back to his boss. Okay, she was safe for now, but she was in the back of a van that belonged to people with no regard for human life. He'd seen the photos of Josh Lucas's body. If they could do that to a kid, they'd have no issue doing it to an adult.

'I know what you're thinking,' Red said, 'but it's a risk she was determined to take, and she's not wrong. I don't know what she saw in there, but even I know some kid was getting the shit kicked out of him.'

'Lewis?' Stacey asked.

Red nodded. 'But no Noah.'

Bryant could immediately see why his boss had changed her thinking.

The plan had always been to come here, break it up, get the boys and make as many arrests as possible.

'If we go in now, we get six boys, a wall of silence from the organisers and other boys being stranded somewhere, possibly left to die. In addition, we can't contain fifty or more spectators with this small a team quickly enough to stop phone calls and text messages being fired off. If the rest of the network gets that kind of advance warning, we'll never track down all the others, and God knows what'll happen to the other boys then. We don't know how widespread this thing is.'

Bryant already understood the problem. He just didn't like the fact it wasn't his boss sharing the update.

Red looked at his watch. 'We haven't got a lot of time. There are two vans up there – the grey one we know about and a white transit.' He nodded towards Bryant. 'You follow the grey one with your boss in it; we'll be following the other one,' he said, indicating Walsh and Dickinson.

'Adil, Wood and reporter guy are to stay here.'

Bryant frowned. 'We need to go and get our vehicles at the end of the road so we can pick up the vans when they leave.

There are going to be another thirty or more vehicles leaving at the same time. We need the registration numbers of every one of them.'

'Got it,' Stacey said.

Adil and Ashworth nodded their understanding.

'Two more things, directly from DI Stone. You,' Red said, pointing at the reporter. 'None of this gets shared with anyone. Got it?'

He nodded his understanding. Bryant was pleased to see that the man appeared to have grasped the importance of what he was now a part of.

'Last thing,' Red said, turning his way, 'your boss is going to try and communicate with you from the back of the van, but if there's any chance you're going to look suspicious, you have to back off.'

Bryant's instinct was to argue with the instruction, but he knew that the guv's priority was to find the other boys. If the people in the van suspected they were being followed, there was every chance they'd divert, and then they'd be lost forever.

'Got it,' Bryant said grudgingly.

'Okay, folks, we really haven't got much time. Everyone get into position.'

Bryant headed for his car with Penn in tow.

The plan was a good one, but one that would worry him less if they were part of a task force that included an additional twenty officers.

Only then would he be happy with the risk the guv had taken.

SEVENTY-EIGHT

Kim wasn't sure how much longer she could tolerate the stench.

Red had helped her gain access to the back of the van, where she'd found a musty dark blanket she could cover herself with. She had pushed herself to the furthest point away from the doors to avoid being detected once they were opened.

Once positioned, she'd realised how her absence would appear to her team, so she'd fired off a quick message to her colleague to assure him all was well. She didn't need Bryant doing something rash that could jeopardise the only plan she'd been able to come up with.

After sending the message, she lay perfectly still beneath a blanket that was suffocating her. The smell of body odour, blood and urine was making her feel nauseous, but she couldn't chance peeping her head out.

The silence surrounding the van was interrupted by the sound of footsteps on gravel and something being dragged.

Suddenly the doors were thrown open.

'You can wait in here until we're done,' said a female voice.

Kim dared not breathe as someone was shoved into the van before the door was slammed shut again.

She kept perfectly still for a minute, having learned one important detail. The small amount of light escaping from the venue wasn't enough to reach all the way inside to where she was lying. It would give her a fighting chance.

The boy who'd been thrown inside had moved to the right-hand side of the van. She could feel his closeness. If he edged any more to the right, he'd be touching her feet. She heard what sounded like snuffling, as though the boy had a cold. It took her a moment to realise it wasn't a cold. He was trying to choke back tears.

She held her breath, trying to decide the best thing to do. If she remained silent, he could discover her at any time. Not good if the kidnappers were back when that happened.

She had no choice but to take a chance.

'Lewis?' she whispered.

He cried out in fright and pushed himself back against the metal of the van as she removed the blanket.

She'd called it right. Huddled against the back doors was the boy who had been on her mind all week. He looked absolutely petrified.

'It's okay, Lewis. I've been looking for you,' she said, moving towards him slowly.

She shone her phone at herself, praying he could tell that she was one of the good guys.

'We're gonna get you out of here,' she whispered.

Fear shone from his eyes as he pulled up his knees in front of him and pushed himself further into the corner. Kim was reminded of a beaten and broken dog in an animal shelter.

She moved towards him slowly, using the phone to light her way.

She didn't care how big and tough he'd once been. He was now a terrified twelve-year-old boy who would be slow to trust any stranger.

She reached out and touched his arm.

He let out a little cry of fear.

'I swear, Lewis. I'm a police officer, and I'm going to get you home.'

He shook his head. 'Th... they... don't... want...'

'Bobby is gone, sweetheart. Your mum and Kevin love you very much and want you back.'

He stopped shivering as a single tear rolled over his cheek.

Instinctively, Kim reached out and pulled him closer. His frail and beaten body was wracked with sobs as he rested his head against her shoulder. She would have stayed in that position for as long as he needed, but the kidnappers could return at any time.

'Lewis, I need your help. Is there anything you can tell me about where they keep you?'

He pulled his head away and wiped at his eyes with his hands. 'It's a stable. We're chained up, and they bring us out to go to the toilet and for training.'

Kim pushed the picture of Josh out of her mind.

'Do you know how long it took to get here?'

'Thirty, forty minutes,' he said, shrugging.

In the back of this dark van, there would be little concept of time.

'Were there any noises you can remember hearing?'

'A train, slowing down and then speeding up.'

A station, Kim realised, probably within a mile.

There was no way he'd know the times. He probably only knew night and day.

'How many times each day?'

'A few. Maybe ten.'

'And the place—'

'They're coming,' he said as the sound of footsteps on gravel met her ears. This time there were more. Other voices shouting, cars starting.

She scrabbled to her position at the back of the van and

pulled the blanket over her. She prayed that nothing was showing to give her away.

As the door handle was pulled down, Lewis slid into position in front of her. She silently thanked him as his back nestled against her stomach.

If they looked deep into the van, the main thing they would see was Lewis.

'Get in,' she heard the woman say. 'You're all fucking useless.'

The van rocked from side to side as the other two boys got in.

She sensed that each had gone to either side of the vehicle, while Lewis stayed in front of her, shielding her from their view. She considered speaking to the other boys but couldn't risk their reactions giving her away.

Under the cover of both her coat and the blanket, she took out her phone. The screen illuminated. She sent a text to Bryant telling him they were off and then held the phone tightly as two people got into the cab of the van.

'Well, that was a fucking shitshow,' said the female voice as the engine started. 'The boss ain't gonna be pleased.'

'There was forty grand on Lewis,' the male voice replied.

'Three losses in one night. We are in the shit,' she said.

Kim listened keenly as the van reversed.

The woman sighed heavily. 'Lewis is done. Hang him up when we get back.'

Kim's stomach turned, knowing exactly what that meant. The little boy who had cried in her arms was going to be turned into a punching bag.

She closed her eyes and prayed that everyone had followed instructions and were already in place.

She pictured what she knew of the journey and felt the van turn left at the end of the dirt track. A half mile later, it turned right and headed towards the main road where Bryant should be waiting. Occasional moans and groans sounded from the boys as the vehicle swung around corners or drove over potholes.

The people in the cab fell into silence, and Kim focussed on trying to keep still and hidden behind Lewis, her phone clutched in her hand.

She guessed they'd been travelling ten to twelve minutes when the male voice spoke again.

'Hey, see that car behind. It's been...'

Kim needed nothing further. She lit up her phone and typed two words to her colleague.

The text was simple. It read:

Back off.

SEVENTY-NINE

'Shit,' Bryant said, taking a left turn and letting the grey van drive away, out of sight.

The guv's instructions had been clear. They were to do nothing that would jeopardise her getting to the location where the boys were being held.

'Now what?' Penn asked, still holding Bryant's phone.

He pulled over to the side of the road. 'All we have is possibly a thirty-to-forty-minute drive and maybe close to a train station,' Bryant said, referring to the clues the boss had sent.

Penn took out his own phone, but Bryant knew they were too far away to start narrowing down locations. They were only a quarter of an hour into the possible thirty to forty minutes.

'Shit, too many,' Penn said, looking at a map of the area.

'How the hell are we going to—?'

He stopped speaking as his phone lit up. It was a text message from the guv.

One word.

Left

He smiled as they pulled away. There was now space between them, and the guv was dropping them breadcrumbs as to her direction of travel. He backtracked onto the road they'd left and continued forward. Just out of sight was a left turn. He took it.

'Left again,' Penn said.

Bryant didn't take the next left. That would have taken them around in a circle. He had to try and gauge the time between messages to figure out which turning she might mean.

He took the following left turn and kept to the prescribed speed limits, feeling sure the van would be doing the same. They couldn't afford any attention.

'Nothing else yet,' Penn said, both phones in his lap.

'Must mean just keep going,' Bryant said, assuming the guv would only text when there was something he could use.

'This road lasts for a good seven miles and takes us through a small town called Mereclough.'

'Train stations?' Bryant asked, taking care not to exceed the speed limit. The last thing he wanted was to catch them up. He also didn't want them getting too far ahead.

Penn shook his head.

They drove in silence for the next few miles. Bryant calculated the time on the road to be approaching twenty-five minutes.

'Right,' Penn said as the phone lit up.

Bryant tried to estimate the time ahead and ignored the next right turn.

His next option to turn right was at a set of traffic lights in the centre of the town of Todmorden.

He took it.

Penn continued to keep track on his own phone. 'This road leads to a village called Walsden.'

'Train station?' Bryant asked, repeating his earlier question.

'Yes, just on the other side of the village.'

Bryant hoped they were on the right track.

'What's beyond?' he asked.

'Stopped,' Penn called out.

He had no idea if that meant they'd reached the destination or whether they were stopping for fuel or some other reason.

'Beyond is another village with a train station.'

'They can't be too near to the villages,' Bryant said. 'Folks in small villages know each other and each other's business.'

'The stretch between the two villages is four miles long,' Penn said.

Four miles of countryside, having to search properties on both sides of the road.

He prayed that the guv would manage to drop one more crumb before she was completely on her own.

EIGHTY

Initially, Kim had had no clue why the van had stopped moving. She didn't know if they were at lights or a give-way sign or a crossing. She'd sent the text to Bryant anyway.

The engine had continued running and someone had got out. Were they getting something from a shop? It would most likely have to be a service station at this late hour, but she couldn't detect the giveaway smell of petrol.

A few seconds later, the van had moved forward and then stopped again, and the person got back into the front of the van. Not long enough for anyone to buy anything.

Opening and closing a gate, she realised now.

They were here, but not knowing how far the gate was away from the building, she couldn't chance another text. She put her phone back in her pocket and felt Lewis lean against her. *Not long, buddy*, she thought, laying a hand against his back for reassurance.

The van door opened, and Lewis scooted forward slowly, letting the other two boys get out first.

'Shut it,' the woman called back to Lewis, who pushed the door closed but not locked.

Thank God she'd let Lewis know she was there. Both his quick thinking about moving in front of her and not locking the door of the van had given her a fighting chance.

She pushed the blanket aside and took a moment to breathe in slightly cleaner air.

Then she moved slowly towards the van doors, ensuring she did nothing to move the vehicle. She waited and listened so she didn't push the door open too soon.

Within a couple of minutes, there was silence.

She had no idea what was outside this van. The rush of cold air told her it was parked somewhere in the open air, not in a garage. But was it in a position where she'd be spotted the second she opened the door?

She nudged it open just an inch and saw the building. Its last coat of white paint was peeling, and a drainpipe ran down the side of the wall.

Part of her hoped she'd given enough detail to Bryant and wondered if she should sit tight and wait. With a better signal she would have sent her colleague a Google Maps pin, but she knew if she tried, it wouldn't reach him and she'd just be wasting time she didn't have. The other part of her pictured Lewis being tied up like a piece of meat.

The visual spurred her into action.

She pushed the door a little at a time until there was enough of a gap to squeeze herself through, then she dropped out of the vehicle and lowered her body into the shadows.

The van was parked at the side of a two-storey farmhouse. There was just a single small window on the upper level, which she guessed was probably on the stairs landing. She inched around the front of the house, taking care to step lightly on the gravel. The front windows were dirty, and the double glazing had failed, giving a misted effect to the glass.

She crawled beneath the windows to the other side of the property.

On the west side of the house was a barn with metal doors. Seeing no other buildings, she quickly crossed the thirty-foot space that separated it from the house. Once at the doors, she stopped for a moment and listened. Although lights were on in the farmhouse and she could see movement, the only sounds to meet her ears came from the inside of the barn.

She could hear a soft, muffled cry and then a shouty whisper telling the crier to shut up.

She took another brief look at the farmhouse windows and saw two figures moving around the kitchen. As long as there were only two captors, she was safe to enter the barn.

Kim cracked the door open to see that the lights were on. That probably meant they weren't yet finished with the boys, so she had very little time to form a plan.

She pulled the door open, praying there would be no creaking to give her away.

She stepped inside and quietly pulled the door closed.

There were no windows in the building, and the stench hit her immediately. The space reminded her of an old stable block. The entire area was divided into pens. Four on each side with a walkway down the middle. The first pen on her left held food supplies, tins and cereals. The pen on her right held tools, wood, rope, offcuts of stumps and spare plyboard.

She took a few steps forward, and a voice cried out in terror. The boy hadn't even seen her, but he was afraid because there was someone coming. What had those bastards done to these boys? she wondered, pushing down her rage until she needed it.

Two more steps forward and she was between the next two pens.

Both boys were huddled in the far corners of their straw-filled pens.

'It's okay,' she whispered. 'I'm here to help. I'm a police officer.'

One of the boys had turned his face into the wall, but the other looked at her doubtfully.

She continued moving forward to the next two pens.

Like the ones before, they were filled with straw. She saw two boys there too. Again, she was overcome by the stench of urine and faeces.

She put her fingers to her lips as she passed by. Kim realised they should have been making more noise. Clearly it had been drilled into them to remain silent.

Her insides started to vibrate with anger. They were like dogs in a pound, terrified, broken... but even the dogs in the pound were allowed to fucking bark.

She moved forward to the last two stalls.

On her left, she was relieved to see Noah, who had come as far forward as his chain would allow.

'It's okay, Noah,' she murmured, again holding her finger to her lips.

On her right in the last pen, already strung up with his feet dangling two feet above the ground, was Lewis.

The carcass of a dead pig lay at his feet.

Emotion numbed her throat as she threw open the gate into his enclosure. She stepped over the decomposing flesh of the animal and reached above Lewis's head to the knot that bound his wrists.

It wasn't complex, but he would never have been able to reach it.

'I've got you,' she said, easing him down to the ground.

'They've never done that to me before.'

And she knew exactly why. They'd decided Lewis couldn't win fights and make them money. His only useful purpose now was to replace the pig.

'It's okay, Lewis. I swear they'll never hurt you again, but I need you to help me, okay?'

He nodded eagerly. She wanted so badly to comfort this

battered kid who was still willing to offer his trust to a stranger, but they had to get out of there.

'Is it just the two of them?'

'I think so. We call them Mister and Missus, and I haven't seen anyone else.'

'Will they come back out here tonight?'

He nodded. 'Mister will come soon with supper. Cold toast and jam.'

That wasn't going to take long to prepare, so now she knew she couldn't just wait. She'd be discovered and wouldn't have a chance against them.

She couldn't take them both on in the house, and she couldn't risk them getting away.

She had to get them out on her terms.

'Okay, I'm waiting for my friends to come, but I've got to do some stuff first. There are bolt cutters in the top pen. Are you up to freeing the other boys and getting them to the door?'

Despite the beating he'd had in the ring earlier and his many injuries, he nodded energetically. She just wanted to hug the life out of him, but she didn't have the time.

'Okay, do it,' she said before heading back to the top of the barn.

There were two of them and one of her. She had to think quick if she planned on getting out of this alive.

EIGHTY-ONE

She opened the gate to the storage pen and stepped inside.

She grabbed some of the things she could use and headed back out the door, taking care to crouch down into the darkness as she headed towards the van. Starting on the side furthest away from the building, she hammered a nail into every tyre and then paused.

No one was getting away in this vehicle.

There was no sound from the front of the house, so she tied a piece of rope to the drainpipe nearest the van and then crawled in front of the windows and front door. She raised the rope one foot up from the ground and tied it to the drainpipe on the west side of the house.

She looked along the line of rope. Perfect.

Then she rushed back to the barn and opened the door.

'Ready?' she asked, walking into the group of boys, all dressed only in underpants. Every boy except Lewis still had a metal ring attached to their wrists. Lewis had had the sense to cut at the thinnest point of the chain for speed.

Six pairs of eyes looked to her as they all stood shivering in the cold air. Their gazes shone with a mixture of fear and hope.

She wanted to wrap them all up in blankets, but the priority was to get them to safety.

'Lewis, I need you to get them away from here. Get away from the barn and hide. You don't come out until I call you or you hear sirens – can you do that?'

Lewis nodded emphatically and led the other boys out of the barn.

She looked over to the farmhouse. The activity was still obvious through the windows, and both the man and woman had put their jackets back on. Their return to the barn was imminent, but it had to be on her terms if she was to have any chance at all. She had to put them at a disadvantage and retain the element of surprise and confusion.

She grabbed the can of fuel and the firelighters she'd seen and poured the fuel into the first two stalls.

She would have liked to douse every pen that had held a boy captive. Yes, she'd be destroying evidence, but she'd seen their conditions with her own eyes.

After lighting both pens on fire, she sprinted out of the barn, careful to leave the door open slightly.

She crouched down at the west side of the barn and waited.

Within seconds, the smell of smoke started to permeate the air.

What had looked to be an airtight structure was nothing of the sort, she realised as smoke began billowing out of gaps in the roof.

She could feel her heart beating in her chest as she waited, grasping the hammer in her hand firmly.

Five seconds later, she heard the front door being thrown open and urgent exclamations.

Just as she'd hoped, they both fell to the ground, having run into the taut rope. An old trick but effective nevertheless.

'Fuck,' the man cried out. 'What the...? Go... go... go!' he shouted, thinking that their meal tickets were still in the burning building.

The woman sprang to her feet and ran past Kim in the shadows, totally focussed on the flames coming out of the barn door.

Kim darted around the corner and barged into the man, who was trying to get to his feet.

He fell back down and landed on his side. Kim was immune to his cries as she focussed on what she needed to do. She swung the hammer down onto his right ankle and heard the bones crack beneath the blow. She raised the hammer again, thought about the six boys in the barn, then brought it down on his left kneecap, leaving both legs incapacitated.

He screamed out in pain and reached down, trying to locate both of his injuries. Every movement elicited a howl of agony. Kim was satisfied he was going nowhere.

'Wh... wh... who... the... fuck...?'

'Your worst fucking nightmare,' she hissed, reaching into his jacket pocket. Empty. She tried the other one. Bingo. She grabbed his phone and put it in her own pocket. Now he couldn't escape or call anyone for help.

One down. One to go.

Kim turned and retreated as his accomplice returned from the barn.

'Tom, the boys aren't—' The woman's words trailed away as she saw her partner writhing and screaming on the ground.

Kim stepped out of the shadows.

A quick appraisal told her the woman was in her early to mid-thirties with short straw-blonde hair. She looked familiar somehow. Kim felt she'd seen her before.

Shaking the thought away, Kim moved towards her at speed with the hammer still clutched in her hand, but the woman was quick and dived to the ground out of reach of the weapon. She rolled against Kim's legs, sending her crashing to the ground. The hammer fell from her grasp as she hit the dirt.

The woman hesitated before reaching for the weapon, giving Kim the opportunity to try and get herself upright. But the hammer was just out of reach, and the woman thought better of it, choosing instead to push Kim back down to the ground. Kim felt the wind being knocked out of her body as the woman punched her in the stomach – hard.

She writhed and bucked, but the woman had her knees clamped into Kim's ribs. Kim punched and kicked out but couldn't make contact with any flesh.

Another blow landed in her sternum, causing her head to spin.

She tried once more to lift the woman's weight from her body and topple her, but the knees just dug in harder. The woman leaned down and placed both hands around her neck. Kim thrashed and moved her head from side to side, but the fingers had a vice-like grip right at the top of her throat.

'D... do... it. F... finish her,' Mister called out as he tried to crawl along the ground.

Kim felt the hands tighten around her throat. She tried to gulp air into her body, but it couldn't get past the chokehold.

Come on, Bryant, she silently prayed. *If you ever wanted to be a hero, now's your time.*

The woman's face swam before her eyes as she heard the sound of footsteps on gravel. Lots of them.

'Get her!' Lewis shouted from the darkness.

Suddenly, hands and feet appeared from nowhere: grabbing, punching, kicking.

The pressure released from around her neck, and she began to cough.

The woman was on her back, her hands over her face as she rolled around, trying in vain to avoid the blows being rained down on her from six angry boys who had miraculously found the spirit to fight back.

Kim opened her mouth to stop them when she saw headlights coming up the drive. A siren in the distance told her she was safe, but the boys instinctively gathered around her, leaving the woman to lie groaning on the ground.

'It's okay,' she reassured the boys, seeing the familiar number plate. 'They're with me.'

Bryant stopped the car and jumped out, sprinting towards her despite his earlier injuries.

'Did you stop for coffee on the way?' she asked.

He pointed to the smoke billowing from the barn. 'Took a wrong turn somewhere, but that seemed to have your name all over it.'

She nodded her understanding.

'You okay?' he asked, also taking a look at the boys.

'We're all fine,' she said, squeezing Lewis's arm.

Penn approached, and both men started removing jackets and jumpers to give to the boys. Most of them took the clothing, but Lewis just leaned further into her.

'It's okay, buddy,' she said, patting his shoulder. 'You can trust these men. They'll take care of you.'

He moved towards Bryant, who was fetching a high-vis jacket from the boot of the car.

A movement to the right caught Kim's attention.

The woman was reaching into her back pocket.

Kim swatted her hand away and took the phone.

As she did so, the screen came to life with an incoming call.

Kim stared at the ringing phone for long seconds before raising her gaze to her waiting colleague. The last pieces of the puzzle fell into place. She finally had the proof she'd been after.

'Bryant, I'm taking the car. Text Red immediately. This is what I want you to say.'

EIGHTY-TWO

Stacey was just gathering up everyone's coffee mugs as Iris entered the squad room, pulling her vacuum cleaner behind her.

'Late tonight, Iris,' Stacey said, passing her on the way to the kitchen.

'It's my anniversary, so I changed my shift,' she said, switching on the vacuum cleaner and preventing Stacey from striking up any further conversation.

She washed out the mugs, her mind playing over the events of the night. Once the fight venue had emptied, there had been nothing more for her and Steve Ashworth to do.

The reporter had been helpful, and between the two of them and Adil, they'd managed to record the registration number of every vehicle leaving the venue. They had been surprised at the number of luxury car models they'd seen, indicating that this was a lucrative sport that attracted many wealthy spectators. Ashworth had offered to drive her and Adil back to Blackpool station, and with no further instructions she had accepted.

She'd expected the drive back to be uncomfortable, given

that he'd been trying to destroy her boss's reputation. In truth, he'd been a pleasant travelling companion, who, after admitting he'd been wrong about her boss, had regaled her with funny stories about some of the minor celebrities he'd dealt with over the years.

She realised that he hadn't been the only one to have made a mistake.

He'd dropped them at the station after giving his assurances that he wouldn't divulge any details of the unofficial operation. He would now focus on assisting the police to uncover and expose the rest of the fighting ring and return every other boy to his family. She had believed him.

Adil had headed home to await instructions from Red, and she had mounted the stairs back into the office. At that point, she'd received a call from Penn, giving her a full update. Six young boys were now safe and would never be forced to fight again. No calls had yet been made, but Stacey felt a rush of pleasure that six families were about to get an early Christmas present. She'd also been told that the boss had rushed off somewhere, leaving Bryant and Penn at the scene.

She had no doubt that someone would collect her once they could safely head for home.

In the meantime, she'd finish off her statement and call Devon.

When she returned to the squad room, Iris had stopped vacuuming and was now flicking her trusty duster around the desks.

The woman was humming, a smile on her face.

'It was you,' Stacey said, moving towards her.

'What's that now?' Iris asked. Her forehead should have been more furrowed if Stacey was going to buy her confusion.

'You left the list of names under my keyboard.'

Iris shrugged. 'Don't know what—'

'You're invisible, Iris,' Stacey said, sitting on the edge of

Roy's desk. 'You hear things, you see things, but no one notices you.' Stacey paused as the full picture came to her. 'The tip-offs were you too. You called the anonymous line to complain about inappropriate behaviour, didn't you?'

Iris shook her head and carried on dusting.

'You know what went on here today?' Stacey asked, tapping the desk she was sitting on.

'I've heard rumours.'

'Then you should understand that we'd never have known what a truly despicable character Roy Moss is without those names, and we'd never have been brought in at all if it wasn't for those anonymous calls.'

Stacey paused again. Iris stopped dusting.

'You should also know that Roy Moss will never get the chance to hurt anyone again.'

'Thank God,' Iris said under her breath. For the first time, she met Stacey's gaze properly. 'I could lose my job. I've signed stuff, and if anyone ever thought—'

'The thing about theories is that without any proof it's best just left in your head,' Stacey said, having already decided she'd keep this information to herself. Even the rest of her team didn't need to know. Roy Moss was safely behind bars and would never taste freedom again.

Before placing the knowledge in a sealed vault in her mind, there was just one more thing she wanted to say.

'Iris, thank you for trusting us to do the right thing.'

The woman smiled and continued to go about her business.

EIGHTY-THREE

To be fair, the chief looked as tired as Kim felt, which wasn't surprising given the day she'd had. But Kim had information that needed to be shared straight away.

'Take a seat,' the chief said, and for once Kim did as asked.

The woman offered her a weary smile. 'So, you didn't leave when I told you to.'

'Almost,' Kim admitted, 'but then Roy Moss abducted one of my officers.' She opened her hands to indicate there was little else she could have done.

'The quick thinking on your part and the assistance of my team ensured that no one else got hurt, and for that I thank you.' Walker shook her head with disbelief. 'I'm a few hours into this and I still can't believe we had a double murderer on our team.'

'That's not all he is, marm, but Red has more information on that. He now knows exactly what Roy Moss has been up to.'

'And the rest of the team?' the chief asked.

'Nothing else untoward. With Roy out of the picture, I think Red has a great team.'

'Did you uncover the source of the complaints?'

Kim shook her head. 'Unfortunately not, and I don't think we'll ever know unless they choose to reveal it themselves.'

The chief nodded her understanding. 'Well, on behalf of everyone here, I'd like to thank you and your team for helping to uncover a clever and dangerous man. We owe—'

'That's not really why I'm here, marm. I've got a serious update on another matter.'

The knock at the door couldn't have come at a better time, Kim thought as she stood to open it.

Red entered and offered a nod of greeting to his boss.

The chief frowned. 'This all looks rather serious, Inspector.'

'It is, marm,' Kim replied. 'Earlier this evening, DI Butler and I became aware of an illegal fighting ring that appears to be operating nationwide. Both Lewis Stevens and Noah Reid were abducted for the purpose of being forced to fight. We tried to brief you, but you obviously had your hands full already.'

The chief looked to them both In horror.

Kim kept her voice calm. They had her full attention, and they were nowhere near the good bit yet.

She continued. 'We formed a joint operation and attended the venue of an illegal fight meeting. Through our efforts, and by means which will be detailed in the reports, we have secured two crime scenes and rescued thirteen missing boys.'

Red had texted confirmation of his team's success in following the second van, minutes before she'd entered the station.

The chief's mouth was still open. Now they were getting to the good bit.

'Two people were apprehended at the site in Lancashire, one of whom was your sister.'

Kim paused to let that information sink in. Everything had fallen into place when the woman's phone had illuminated with a call. The contact was saved as *sister* and the chief's photo was attached. She had been certain someone in authority was involved. Her suspicion had initially fallen on Red, but the strings had been pulled from someone above his head. The chief had been the one blocking them.

Walker began to shake her head as Kim took the phones from her pocket.

'There has to be some kind of—'

'There's no mistake, marm, as you well know,' Kim said. 'In fact, the only surprise you have is that they've been caught.'

Walker's face turned thunderous as she continued to protest.

'I knew there had to be a link here somewhere,' Kim said. 'The families of both boys had been visited by Red's team following a burglary. I did wonder who on the team was involved, but different officers attended each scene. Only someone more senior would have access to all the reports and be able to point the kidnappers to families with boys of the right age. You passed on the details of the boys to your cronies, and they did the rest. Lewis was an absolute godsend, wasn't he? You already knew the kid could pack a punch. You knew how to target that family, what weaknesses to hit and what lies to tell. But you knew that wouldn't work on the Reid family. I'm guessing your sister simply followed them until there was an opportunity to grab Noah.'

'Detective Inspector, you are coming dangerously close to—'

'I hope I'm better than dangerously close. I mean, it's big business,' Kim said, interrupting the idle threat that was about to come. 'Forty grand on one fight, I heard your sister say. Oh, by the way, he lost.'

Walker stood. 'This is the most ridiculous thing—'

'Prove it,' Kim said simply. 'Take out the second phone you have and show us all the messages between you and your sister. That's all you have to do.' She pointed to Red. 'Only us three know about this conversation, so if I'm wrong, you can send me back down to the Midlands with a serious disciplinary to face, and you and Red can go about your business. Simples.'

Walker reached into her drawer and took out a phone.

Kim's heart stopped for a minute. If Walker handed her that phone, she'd called it wrong, and her career was over.

Walker hesitated before launching the phone across the room, where it hit the far wall.

Red was quick to retrieve the phone. The disappointment in his face confirmed that all his questions had been answered.

He stood tall. 'Marm, I apologise in advance, but I'm going to place you under arrest once Inspector Stone is done.'

Kim stood and stared her down. 'I will wash my mouth out with soap for every time I called you chief. I am sickened by the level of respect I afforded you given your background and achievements. You are a foul, evil, disgraceful excuse for a police officer, who has used her authority and position to cultivate a network of illegal fights and cause untold suffering and death.'

Hatred shone from Walker's eyes, but Kim wasn't finished yet.

'It all makes sense now. You knew that the top brass was going to insist that you get help, given the short time frame between the disappearance of Lewis and Noah. You got greedy, but you thought you could still control it. You pre-empted the instruction from above and called in the team that had just been made to look like national fools. You thought we would add nothing to the missing boys case and that your network would remain safe. You probably thought you could blame the failure to solve the case on our incompetence, leaving your own team untouched. You brought us here to fail. But what you did want was for us to find whoever had made the anonymous complaints, and the detail of those complaints, in case any of them led back to you. You kept pushing us in that direction. You made it a priority but not so you could protect the informant. If we'd offered you a name, I have no doubt that the person would have somehow met an untimely end.'

The rage deepened on the woman's face, and Kim knew she was right.

'Thing is, you arrogant, despicable excuse for an officer, you forgot one important point about the Jester case. Yes, he had us running round in circles chasing his clues around the Black Country. Yes, we were forced to dance to his tune, making us look inefficient and incompetent. But ultimately, through hard work and determination, we got him. We saved the lives of a gifted heart surgeon and an eight-year-old girl. We put the Jester behind bars for the rest of his life because we refused to give up. An important point it would have served you well to remember.'

Walker regarded her with pure hatred, which bothered Kim not one bit. Detective chief inspector or not, she was just another piece of shit who was going to be removed from the streets.

Kim sat back in her chair and let out a long, deep sigh.

Only one question now remained in her mind.

She turned towards Detective Inspector Butler. 'Now, for the love of God, can I finally go home?'

EIGHTY-FOUR

Kim stared at the coffee on the other side of the table, dreading the conversation she was about to have.

After arriving back home in the early hours of Friday morning, she'd spent the day tying up loose ends from the mammoth events of the previous few days.

Her first visit had been to Woody to fill in the details of the text message she'd sent on the way back from Blackpool. His disbelief had given way to rage and disgust and eventually acceptance. He'd congratulated her on an excellent job, even though part of the result was his former friend behind bars.

Red Butler sure had some sorting out to do. His later text message to thank her and the whole team only confirmed her opinion that she'd been wrong about him in the first place.

Although he hadn't gone into detail, he had confirmed that the evidence found on Walker's phone had been damning and would likely result in a plea deal. He had taken no pleasure in arresting his boss. He'd held a great deal of respect for her and had somewhat relieved when he'd been able to hand her over to the custody officers. News of her arrest hadn't yet made

the news, but it wouldn't be long until both her name and reputation were ruined for good.

Kim had believed Red when he'd admitted he'd made a
mistake with Jasmine. He had misread her gratitude for
personal interest, and it wasn't a mistake he was likely to make
again.

Lewis and Noah had been returned to their families after
making detailed statements. Although it couldn't be proven at
this point, they were all sure that the pills mentioned by both
boys had been steroids. Whether they'd been meant to induce a
higher level of aggression she wasn't sure, but thankfully the
short time they'd been subjected to the drugs wouldn't cause
any long-term health problems.

Once Lewis's statement was complete, Kim had insisted on
being the one to take him home. Dressed in clothes much too
big for him, he'd sat in the back of Bryant's car, Kim next to him
with a reassuring hand on his arm. She'd felt his growing
tension as they'd neared the house and understood it. However
desperate he was to see his family, a small part of him knew that
they had been complicit in his abduction. When he'd last been
in this house, he'd been public enemy number one, a burden
that no one wanted to carry. Even though she'd assured him that
Bobby was gone, she'd still sensed the anxiety running through
him. He was twelve years old, and he had a lot of big feelings to
deal with.

'They've missed you,' she'd said, squeezing his arm.

She'd felt his hesitation as Bryant had pulled up, and yet
once he'd seen Shirley throw open the front door, he'd fumbled
the door handle in his haste to get out of the car.

Kim had watched them run towards each other and collide
into a fierce embrace, both of them crying as Lewis buried his
head deep into his mother's shoulder. Kevin had stood in the
doorway, holding back his younger siblings, all eager to greet
their brother, and Kim's earlier doubt as to whether home was

the right place for the boy had evaporated. Despite what had happened, there was a lot of love in this family.

Though she'd enjoyed every second of the reunion, Kim hadn't been able to stop herself thinking about Josh's fate, and she just thanked God Lewis and Noah had been found in time.

'Oi, come here, yer little shit,' Kevin had called when Lewis came up for air.

Lewis had done as he was told, and his older brother had grabbed him hard, Shirley sobbing openly as she'd watched them.

Kim had stood beside her as Lewis bent down to hug the little ones.

'He's happy and relieved right now,' Kim had advised. 'But tomorrow or the next day he's gonna be angry, hurt and disappointed. You've got to earn his trust back.'

Shirley had nodded. 'I'll do whatever it takes,' she'd said, touching her arm. 'I have him back thanks to you.'

'Just look after him,' Kim had replied. 'And for God's sake, get the kid some matches.'

Shirley had smiled as Kim had taken one last look at them all before heading back towards the car.

Her hand had been on the door handle when she'd felt a tap on her back.

She'd turned as Lewis had thrust his arms around her waist and hugged her hard.

'Thank you,' he'd whispered against her shoulder.

Kim had swallowed down the emotion constricting her throat. 'And thank you too,' she'd said, kissing the top of his head.

She was pleased to learn that Kevin and his mum had already packed up all Bobby's belongings. Their family looked different now, but she had no doubt that they'd manage somehow.

Bobby Stevens had already been arrested for obstruction,

and Kim knew that Red was talking to CPS with a view to applying child trafficking charges to ensure a prison term. In addition, he was having his team look closer at the burglary which had brought the family to their attention in the first place. They all felt Bobby had arranged it, and Red was determined to make the man pay for his crimes. Red's intention with regard to Shirley remained unclear and was between him and the Crown Prosecution Service, but Kim hoped they'd feel that she'd suffered enough. She knew the woman would spend the rest of her life making things right with Lewis.

Red had informed her that Noah's mother had refused to let her son out of her embrace for a good twenty minutes.

The parents of the other four boys she'd rescued had been traced to other police territories, one as far away as Dumfries. All of the boys recovered were now safely back home, and a task force had been assembled to track down the rest of the operation.

It gnawed at her heart that there were still boys out there not yet discovered, but she trusted that every effort would be made to bring each one of them home safely.

By far her hardest conversation of the day had been with Josh's mum, who had just collected her wife from the hospital.

No one had uttered a word as she'd explained what had happened to their son in the years since they'd lost him. She'd tried to keep the graphic details out of her account, but she couldn't be responsible for the horrors their own imaginations would insert. They weren't going to heal overnight, but the process could now begin.

And after she'd shared all the horrific details, the family had thanked her. They had fucking thanked her. She had left their home fighting a wave of emotion.

Her most recent update from Red had been to inform her that after obtaining a search warrant for Roderick Skidmore's property, they'd broken into the basement the cleaner had told them about. They'd discovered a dedicated computer room where they'd found links to the website for the fighting league and more than forty thousand indecent images. Red also had a lead on the paedophile's property in Thailand, and with luck it wouldn't be too long before the man was back behind bars.

She was pleased to see that Red was proving himself to be one of the good guys. When they'd arrived in Blackpool at the beginning of the week, none of them had known what they were going to find with the home team. At different points, it had appeared that every one of them was corrupt. She'd even suspected her fellow detective inspector of murder and collusion, to find that in reality, he'd become complacent and lazy. His energy and motivation had now been reignited and was trickling down to his officers. They seemed to have been electrified into action as she'd bid them goodbye.

She felt that Red now knew he had to cultivate a deeper feeling of trust within his team. Adil had held valuable information on Roy but hadn't trusted his boss enough to share it. Who knew what might have been prevented if he had? But she'd been pleased to hear Red addressing the young officer by his first name instead of his nickname as she'd headed out the door.

The sour taste had still not left her mouth at the thought of Miranda Walker. She had respected, even admired the woman who'd headed up the north-east part of the illegal fight network. She'd identified with the woman's past: her childhood in and out of the care system; her struggle to survive and even excel in the police force; her determination to succeed despite the system's unspoken bias. She had overcome it all, and for no other reason than to feather her own nest. Walker was hiding behind her solicitor, so there were no further details on how long she'd been a part of the fighting ring or how it had been established, but Kim hoped that both the criminal investigation and the internal review would eventually give them all the answers they needed.

She was sure this case would leave a mark on all of them, not least her friend Bryant.

She'd never tell him so, but she'd never met a more decent man in her life. He wasn't unaware about corruption in the police force or naïve about life in general, and he hadn't baulked at the task of befriending one of the most despicable and cruel men they'd ever had the misfortune to meet. She wasn't sure anyone would ever understand the enormity of that achievement when all he'd wanted to do was beat the man to a pulp.

But Bryant was aware that without that pretence at friendship, without that time spent together, it was possible that they'd never have joined the dots between the photo on Moss's phone and the photos taken by the forensic team. Bryant's sacrifice would ensure the man remained behind bars for the rest of his life.

And for that Kim had granted him one last wish before they'd left Blackpool.

With her watching from the car, he'd knocked on Pippa Jacobs's door and assured her that she no longer had anything to fear. The woman had all but collapsed with relief before thanking him profusely.

The look of satisfaction on Bryant's face had accompanied him all the way home, and to a long weekend with Jenny.

Roy Moss's continued silence while hiding behind his lawyer meant they might never know how or why he'd chosen Jasmine Swift as his second victim, but she hoped they'd receive an update from Red sometime in the future.

That left only her own unfinished business. This conversation was long overdue. It was a tough one, but she could avoid it no longer, she thought as the door to the café opened.

Frost offered a wide smile and a wave as she approached. Kim's heart sank. Clearly her full memories hadn't returned while Kim had been away.

'Hey, buddy,' Frost said, leaning in for a hug.

Hell no, Kim thought, turning sideways to indicate that a cuppa was awaiting her.

Frost sat and placed her handbag on the spare seat.

'How've you been, pardner?' Frost asked in an awful cowboy voice.

Damn, she'd rehearsed this so many times in her head, but now the words had deserted her. She resolved that she wasn't leaving this table until Frost knew the truth.

'Hey, I'm glad you called, Kim,' Frost said, filling the silence. 'There's a new eatery opened in Sedgley. I'd love to try it. Wanna go?'

Even her first name sounded weird coming out of the woman's mouth.

'Listen, Frost, we need to talk.'

'What's with the surname?' she asked, frowning. 'Since when was I not Tracy?'

Kim groaned inside. How the hell was she supposed to do this to a woman whose brain had not yet recovered?

She was given another minute's reprieve as the reporter continued to talk.

'You know something, Kim, I don't think I've ever properly explained to you how it felt having you beside me when I came out of that coma. I felt safe. I really thought I was going to die, but I remember hearing your voice and it was like I was being pulled back from the edge. I knew my friend needed me, and I had to come back, for your sake.'

Kim's leg began to twitch beneath the table. She felt like the worst person on earth for what she was about to do, but surely it was crueller to let her believe they were best friends?

Frost continued. 'Every day I'm so grateful that you were there for me, holding my hand, reaching into the darkness to pull me out. That's the sign of a true—'

'Frost, we're not friends,' Kim blurted out.

'Wh... what?'

'I'm sorry, but I have to tell you the truth. We can barely tolerate each other. Your brain isn't fully recovered yet, but we've never been for a drink, swapped recipes or exchanged memes. I'm glad you're on the road to recovery, but you have to know that we're not best buddies, and we never were.'

Kim waited to see the hurt on Frost's face, the confusion at the tricks of her memory, the embarrassment at her assumption.

She saw none of those things. Instead, what appeared was a genuine, honest smile filled with unashamed amusement.

'Bloody hell, Stone. You took your fecking time.'

Kim's mouth fell open at the level of subterfuge employed by the reporter. But as she joined in the laughter, she had to admit that, on this occasion, Frost had got her pretty damn good.

EPILOGUE

At 6 a.m. exactly, Kim and her team were staring down at the screen of her phone. No one spoke as they watched the conversation unfold between the studio anchor and the roving reporter.

From the anchor: *Good morning, Steve. We hear you have a big story to share with our viewers this morning.*

Ashworth: *I do indeed, Jessica. I'm currently standing outside the headquarters of Kent police in Maidstone.*

Oooh, lovely area. Are you taking a holiday?

Probably soon, Jessica, but I'm here to report on a case I've been following for a few weeks.

Kim moved away from the desk to face the window. She didn't need to see the reporter standing windswept in front of the police building. She only needed to hear what the man was going to say.

The anchor: *Tell us more, Steve.*

Ashworth: *I can finally report that just an hour ago, the final branch of a nationwide illegal boxing ring has been uncovered and arrests have been made.*

'Yes,' Stacey shouted, punching the air. Kim heard Penn and Bryant high five each other across the desk.

The anchor: *Illegal boxing?*

Ashworth: *Bare-knuckle fights involving children aged eleven to fifteen. All of the boys were abducted from their homes and families.*

'Bastards,' Bryant said.

The anchor: *How many children are we talking, Steve?*

Ashworth: *With the five boys rescued this morning, the total is thirty-one boys, all now reunited with their families.*

'Thirty-one families made whole again,' Penn said with wonder.

Ashworth: *Operation Joshua was a high-security undertaking, involving almost every police force in the country. Great effort has been made to keep the whole operation secret so that the country's combined forces could target the infrastructure of the underground ring while ensuring the safety of the victims.*

The anchor: *Goodness, Steve, this is an unbelievable story. Do you know how many arrests have been made?*

'Yeah, how many, Steve?' Stacey called out.

Ashworth: *To my knowledge, twenty-two people have been arrested on kidnapping charges and a further seventeen on accessory charges. The police will now be turning their attention to the spectators at the events, and more details will be coming out shortly.*

There's a lot to unpack here, Steve. Can you tell us how this all got started?

'We can tell you,' Penn offered.

Ashworth: *The underground boxing ring was uncovered a few weeks ago by Detective Inspector Kim Stone from the West Midlands police force. She...*

Kim heard no more as she left the phone on the desk and headed into the Bowl. She didn't need the details. She'd been there for all of it. She'd heard what she wanted to hear. The boys were safe, and that was all she truly cared about.

Her team was enjoying the triumph, and they thoroughly deserved it.

Bryant appeared in her doorway and leaned against the frame with his hands in his pockets, while Penn and Stacey continued to heckle Ashworth's report.

The viewers didn't know this had only been half of the case they'd worked. The other half, the one that had seen them investigating fellow officers, had affected them all but no one more than the man standing before her. A man who had been distant and preoccupied since their return from up north.

'You okay?' she asked.

For the first time in weeks, she saw an open, honest and genuine smile form on his face as he nodded back to where the report was still playing on her phone.

'I am now, guv. I am now.'

A LETTER FROM ANGELA

First of all, I want to say a huge thank you for choosing to read *Little Children*, the twenty-second instalment of the Kim Stone series, and to many of you for sticking with Kim Stone and her team since the very beginning.

I know this book is being published later than expected, and I am truly sorry for the wait. Unfortunately, health problems have hampered my writing time, but I hope to be back on the old schedule next year. Unexpected issues can appear from nowhere and hinder all aspects of life, but I truly appreciate your support and patience.

Onto the book and my reasons for writing it. Many books ago, I challenged Kim by removing her from the team and giving her a new team to work with (in *Dead Souls*), and I've always wondered about taking the whole team out of their comfort zone to assist another team with an emotional and intense investigation.

In addition, I wanted to explore the subject of police corruption and the levels of abuse of power within the police force.

I should add here that any corruption in relation to the Blackpool police team is totally fictional and that I am a great fan of Blackpool and have visited regularly for many years.

I thoroughly enjoyed writing *Little Children*, and if you enjoyed it, I would be forever grateful if you'd write a review. I'd love to hear what you think, and it can also help other readers discover one of my books for the first time. Or maybe you can recommend it to your friends and family...

I'd love to hear from you too – so please get in touch on my Facebook or Goodreads page, X or through my website.

And if you'd like to keep up to date with all my latest releases, just sign up at the website link below. Your email address will never be shared, and you can unsubscribe at any time.

www.bookouture.com/angela-marsons

Thank you so much for your support – it is hugely appreciated.

Angela Marsons

www.angelamarsons-books.com

facebook.com/angelamarsonsauthor
x.com/@WriteAngie

ACKNOWLEDGEMENTS

Where to even start with this one? My first thanks, as ever, go to my partner in crime, Julie. This book has been one of the hardest books to write due to health issues encountered over recent months, during which Julie has had to hold my hand on so many levels. Not only has she had to talk me through periods of anxiety and fear, but she's also had the unenviable task of trying to keep my mind focussed on the other love of my life – writing. She knows that regardless of life's missiles, the best place for me to be is at my desk, and she always succeeds in getting me there. For that I am eternally grateful.

Although no longer with us, my eternal thanks goes to my mum, who would tirelessly spread the book news to anyone who would listen.

Thank you to my dad and to my sister Lyn, her husband Clive and my nephews Matthew and Christopher for their support too.

Thank you to Amanda and Steve Nicol, who support us in so many ways, and to Kyle Nicol for book spotting my books everywhere he goes.

I would like to thank the awesome team at Bookouture for their continued enthusiasm for Kim Stone and her stories.

Special thanks to my editor, Ruth Tross, who has no idea how important she is to the production of every book. There have been recent challenges and obstacles to the writing process, and not once have I felt that this lady had anything other than my best interests at heart, offering only encouragement and understanding on both a professional and personal level with support that has gone beyond our working relationship.

To Kim Nash (Mama Bear), who is so much more than a publicist for the Kim Stone books. She is a personal friend who has been an incredible shoulder and has offered guidance with the gentlest of hands.

To Noelle Holten, who has limitless enthusiasm and passion for our work, and to Sarah Hardy and Jess Readett, who also champion our books at every opportunity.

A special thanks must go to Janette Currie, who has copyedited the Kim Stone books from the very beginning. Her knowledge of the stories has ensured a continuity for which I'm extremely grateful.

Thank you to the fantastic Kim Slater, who has been my writing buddy and an incredible support to me for many years now. Our friendship formed before either of us were published, and our writing journeys have been travelled together. Massive thanks to Catherine Thomson; also to the fabulous Renita D'Silva and Caroline Mitchell, all writers that I follow and read voraciously and without whom this journey would be impossible. Huge thanks to the growing family of Bookouture authors who continue to amuse, encourage and inspire me on a daily basis.

My eternal gratitude goes to all the wonderful bloggers and reviewers who have taken the time to get to know Kim Stone and follow her story. These wonderful people shout loudly and share generously not because it is their job, but because it is their passion. I will never tire of thanking this community for their support of both myself and my books. Thank you all so much.

Massive thanks to all my fabulous readers, especially the ones that have taken time out of their busy day to visit me on my website, Facebook page, Goodreads or X.

PUBLISHING TEAM

Turning a manuscript into a book requires the efforts of many people. The publishing team at Bookouture would like to acknowledge everyone who contributed to this publication.

Audio
Alba Proko
Melissa Tran
Sinead O'Connor

Commercial
Lauren Morrissette
Hannah Richmond
Imogen Allport

Data and analysis
Mark Alder
Mohamed Bussuri

Editorial
Ruth Tross
Sinead O'Connor

Copyeditor
Janette Currie

RAISING READERS
Books Build Bright Futures

Dear Reader,

We'd love your attention for one more page to tell you about the crisis in children's reading, and what we can all do.

Studies have shown that reading for fun is the **single biggest predictor of a child's future life chances** – more than family circumstance, parents' educational background or income. It improves academic results, mental health, wealth, communication skills, ambition and happiness.

The number of children reading for fun is in rapid decline. Young people have a lot of competition for their time, and a worryingly high number do not have a single book at home.

Hachette works extensively with schools, libraries and literacy charities, but here are some ways we can all raise more readers:

- Reading to children for just 10 minutes a day makes a difference
- Don't give up if children aren't regular readers – there will be books for them!

- Visit bookshops and libraries to get recommendations
- Encourage them to listen to audiobooks
- Support school libraries
- Give books as gifts

There's a lot more information about how to encourage children to read on our websites: **www.RaisingReaders.co.uk** and **www.JoinRaisingReaders.com**.

Thank you for reading.

Made in the USA
Las Vegas, NV
16 August 2025